I0691929

CRYSTAL SHARDS

Book One of Kiril's Chronicles

Cil Gregoire
Alaska Sci-Fi Queen

PUBLICATION
CONSULTANTS
We Believe In The Power Of Authors

PO Box 221974 Anchorage, Alaska 99522-1974
books@publicationconsultants.com, www.publicationconsultants.com

ISBN Number: 978-1-63747-118-0
eBook ISBN Number: 978-1-63747-119-7

Libruary of Congress Number:

The events, people, and incidents in this story are the sole product
of the author's imagination. The story is fictional; any semblance to
individuals living or dead is purely coincidental.

Manufactured in the United States of America

Dedication

For Herman Thompson and
Becky Smith.

I miss you greatly.

Books by Cil Gregoire
Oracle of Light

CRYSTALLINE AURA

ELEMENTAL FORCES

ANTHYA'S WORLD

INTERSTELLAR RUSE

Kiril's Chronicles
Crystal Shards

Acknowledgments

Completing a novel is exhilarating. I want to thank the whole world around me. Narrowing it down a bit, I would like to thank Dawn Rinehart and Tim Buechle for reading a rougher draft of the manuscript and offering so much encouragement.

Thanks to my husband Joe for putting up with so many hours of writing and for reading the manuscript.

Thanks to Evan Swensen, publisher at Publication Consultants, for making the continuing saga possible.

Thanks to the authors at Author Masterminds for their constant encouragement and support. It is an honor to be part of such a prestigious group of great authors.

And a very special thanks to all of you who continue to believe in the worlds I create.

Books by Cil Gregoire

Oracle of Light series:

Crystalline Aura
Book One of the Oracle of Light

Anthya's World
Book Two of the Oracle of Light

Elemental Forces
Book Three of the Oracle of Light

Interstellar Ruse
Book Four of the Oracle of Light

Table of Contents

Children Born in the Valley

Birth Rank (In Earth Years)	Name	Estimated Age	Sex	Parents
1st born	Halren	13	M	Wessid and Zaloka
2nd born	Aurora	12	F	Kiril and Ilene
3rd born	Selyzar	11	M	Ollen and Caleeza
4th born	Theon	10	M	Kiril and Ilene
5th born	Setas	9	F	Rojaire and Kaylya
6th born	Alaia	6	F	Ollen and Caleeza
7th born	Jack	7	M	Rojaire and Kaylya
8th born	Caponya	6	F	Ollen and Caleeza
9th born	Little Sarus	4	M	Ollen and Caleeza

Prologue

An angry mob has taken to the streets demanding my arrest. I can hear it approaching ever closer. They have been convinced their princess has been kidnaped. Nothing could be further from the truth. As Aaia's Mentor to Twaka it is my responsibility to maintain peaceful relations between our two worlds.

I jump, startled by someone pounding on my door. "Open up! The throne demands an audience with you."

I could easily escape by teleporting to another location, but it would not resolve the issue. I open the door. Six armed guards of the throne enter and surround me.

"Mentor Kaydra of Aaia, you are under arrest for the kidnaping of Princess Thayla of Twaka. You will have to come with us."

The guards don't look me directly in the eye. I know them, they know me, but they are showing no friendly recognition at the moment. Their missing princess is my best friend. I should never have invited her to my world taking responsibility for her safe return. I wish Thayla had returned with me.

"I will go with you, peacefully."

Without laying a hand on me, they lead me down the ponderous granite roadway, parting the angry crowd on our way to the palace gates. I tune out their shouts. They are simply part of the pageantry organized by Princess Xanthe. I detect no real malice. The outer gates to the palace grounds are heavily guarded. We are expected. The gates readily open giving us access to the fountained courtyard. My escort leads me across the courtyard to the palace entrance. Two guards open the massive ornate doors allowing us to pass through. Across the long reception hall more guards stand at rigid attention in front of the doors to the throne room.

Twaka is a matriarchal society. The queen sits regally on her throne in a crimson gown embroidered in gold. The gown nearly matches the drapery adorning the cold granite walls. Princess Xanthe, Thayla's older sister, stands at the foot of her mother's throne. Her brother Prince Lozar stands guard off to the side.

"Mentor Kaydra of Aaia, you are under arrest for the kidnapping of Princess Thayla of Twaka." It was Princess Xanthe who spoke. The queen remains silent.

"So I've heard," I said in response.

"Another snide remark from you and I will charge you with the murder of my sister," Princess Xanthe hissed.

"You know I haven't kidnapped or murdered Princess Thayla. She joined a colony on the devastated island continent Lynnara on my world. You can find her there." I don't like Princess Xanthe and I know what is going on here. The queen is in decline and Xanthe wants to secure her secession to the throne. By Twakan law the princess warrior who defeats her rivals becomes the next queen. Xanthe cannot defeat Thayla if she can't find her.

"I don't think you understand the seriousness of these charges, Mentor Kaydra," Princess Xanthe said.

"I think I do," I said demurely with the slightest bow.

"You will be held prisoner until the High Council of the Crystal Table returns Princess Thayla to Twaka. Take her away," she ordered the guards.

I offer no resistance. It is my duty not to resist except to preserve my life and well-being. I have pleaded my case time and time again to no avail. This is now an interplanetary incident in the jurisdiction of the Worlds' League.

CHAPTER 1

Ilene

"I think we will have plenty enough bread for everyone to soak up Tassyn's kurper stew," Caleeza said pulling two more round loaves of leavened bread from the community outdoor oven. A damp strand of red-orange hair clings to her creamy white skin. Caleeza's violet eyes and blazing hair match the valley's colorful rocks and foliage while my own mossy brown hair and dark gray eyes more closely resemble the grays and browns of rocks back on Earth.

"This is the last batch," I agreed putting two more loaves in the oven. The aroma of the simmering stew along with an array of other prepared dishes staying warm on top of the oven has my stomach growling.

"I should check on the children," Caleeza said gazing in the direction of the loudest shrieks and laughter where her heart mate Ollen is officiating a vigorous game of tag ball. As the mother of four, Caleeza has become the village mother hen. Two of Ollen and Caleeza's children are the youngest in the community. "Ollen would probably appreciate some help by now."

"You go ahead. I can finish up here. Check on mine too," I added distractedly. Theon and Aurora don't really need checking on, they should be watching over the younger ones. I want to be alone with my thoughts. Sadly the festive mood has evaded me.

"I'll do a general head count. Are you alright?" Caleeza asked. "You seem a little distant, not your usual vibrant self. Is there something on your mind?" Caleeza asked.

Caleeza is always so receptive to my moods. "I was just reflecting."

"We've come a long way, haven't we?" she said. "But there's something else bothering you, isn't there?"

"I guess I'm just a little homesick for Earth."

Caleeza didn't know what to say. Instead she placed an understanding arm around my shoulder. After all, it is unlikely any of us will ever leave the valley. The blue-violet formidable Crescent Mountains close off our valley like fortress walls. The underground passage that led us here has long since been shut off by seismic activity. I watched forlornly as Caleeza left to check on the children.

It was around Seaa Rising that most of us arrived in the valley, barely escaping with our lives. I have been here for six cycles of seasons on Aaia, equivalent to fifteen years on Earth. Fifteen years is a long time. I joined the rogue colony to be with my Aaian father Theon at the end of his longevity. Our time together proved short. He died before Aurora was born. Do I regret my decision? No, of course not. I cannot imagine life without Kiril and the children. Still I can't help but wonder. Is my mother still alive? What would she think of being a grandmother? Unfortunately she will probably never know her grandchildren.

Depositing the already baked loaves on the food tables, I head down the short trail to my father's grave for a quick visit while the rest of the bread bakes. Tinsel trees line the rocky pathway, their curled green and violet leaves twill in the breeze. I named the tinsel trees, no one here is familiar with tinsel. Two callelas, their small furry bodies nearly hidden by an abundance of circular, lacy pinkish-gray translucent wings, flutter by on their way to the top of the plateau across the river where thousands roost on the sun-warmed rocks during the long Aaian night.

Blue-violet stones mark two graves. Captain Setas lies beside Father. "I miss you, Father. I miss you too, Captain Setas. The colony would never have been possible without you." Whenever I need a quiet moment to myself, I come here. Chatter from the community circle of people arriving for the celebration and squeals of laughter from the children playing tag ball in the giant nut tree grove drift in through the tinsel trees.

I need to hurry back to the ovens to take out the last batch of bread. The enticing aroma of baking bread greets me as I rush to the ovens. The bread is ready. Grabbing a hot pad, I pull them out.

Soon it will be dark. I've gotten used to the Aaian day, 144 Earth-hours, equivalent to 6 Earth days. That's 3 Earth-days of daylight and 3 Earth-days of darkness. But darkness on Aaia is rarely inky black. There are so many stars in the sky, the planet seems to be smack in the middle of a dense arm of the Milky Way. And when Seaa rises, barring cloud cover, it never gets darker than early dusk.

The community circle buzzes with activity as people arrive in a festive mood with dishes of food and cheerful greetings. Edty and Tassyn bring in more wood for the fire ring and dump it on the refueling stack for later. Edty, aged and grizzled but childlike in demeanor, follows Tassyn, a pillar of strength, like a shadow. Edty works hard and he especially loves the children, spending all his free time making things for them including the tag balls they use for their games.

The fire ring marks the center of the village circle and the village circle marks the heart of the community. Eight roughly hewed benches, large enough to seat two or three people each, form an octagon around the fire ring. Beyond the benches, three outdoor tables provide space for a feast.

Tassyn walks over to check on his kurper stew while Edty heads off to catch the end of the tag ball game. "How is it going?" Tassyn asked hanging his dark bushy eyebrows and straggly orange-brown hair over the simmering pot to sniff.

"Everything is ready. Your stew smells delicious," I assured him. He probably can hear my stomach growling.

"You are one of the few to really appreciate it," Tassyn said gratefully.

Many in the community had never eaten meat before arriving in the valley. Some still don't. But hailing from Alaska, I have always been a meat eater. When Aaia was nearly destroyed, few people survived and even fewer animals. Only the fish of the sea made a come-back over time. Our valley, so recently rediscovered, a mere sliver of an opening in the expansive Crescent Mountains, is an exception.

I spot my heart mate approaching through the trees as the community starts gathering around the fire ring. The tables are laden with the valley's bounty.

Kiril looks nervous. As chronicler for the village he will address the community before the feast. Kiril is the youngest adult male in the community. He was still a student at the Academy when he joined Rojaire's colonists against the High Council's directives.

"How do I look?" he asked anxiously when he reached me.

I stifled a giggle. His thick tan curly hair tousled about wildly as always. "You look totally endearing," I assured him and kiss him affectionately on the cheek.

Kiril wasn't quite sure of the English word "endearing," but the kiss conveyed a lot of meaning. "Crystal shards, Ilene, I'm serious."

"What are you so nervous about? You see these people every day. They know you as well as you know yourself. It's not like you are speaking before the High Councilors of the Crystal Table. Get a grip on yourself!"

Aurora and Theon come running up. "I'm hungry; when do we eat?" Theon asked. Named after my father, Theon has Kiril's thick tan hair and golden eyes. I figure he is about 10 in Earth-years. With a half breed mother and an Aaian father, my children are more Aaian than Earthen. Earth is a world they know only from stories.

"Dad, you should have seen how Theon beat Halren at Tag Ball and Theon is fourth born," Aurora gloated. With straight white gold hair and blue gold-specked eyes, Aurora doesn't look like either of us, but she definitely looks Aaian.

"Sounds like it was a great game. I'm sorry I missed it," Kiril said.

"Why do you children do that?" I admonished. "The order of your birth in the community isn't important."

"Yes it is," Theon and Aurora chirped in agreement, disagreeing with me.

Wessid and Zaloka's son Halren, Kiril's little brother, was the first child born in the valley. Kiril was shocked, even embarrassed, when his chosen mother and chosen father produced a second child. The concept of siblings is unheard of on Aaia. Now he has two children of his own.

Mainland, under the ironclad rule of the High Council comprises eighty percent of the planet's landmass. Across the Golden Sea, the remaining twenty percent comprises the island continent Lynnara, our home. Except for our village, the rest of the continent is uninhabited.

Blaming people for the world's destruction, the High council controls every aspect of everyone's lives, including reproduction. By

Edict from the High Council, a community can raise only one child at any given time, produced by the gene pool of their choosing. From birth, a child is designated a new person until molded by the Academy and the High Council into an Accepted One.

Aurora was the second baby born in the valley, about 12 Earth-years ago. Selyzar, Ollen and Caleeza's oldest, was the third and our son Theon the fourth. I'm not fond of the children's self-imposed ranking system, but I let it go for now.

"There's Halren and Selyzar, come on, Theon," Aurora urged.

"We will be eating shortly," I tell them as they rush off to the edge of the clearing to join the others. The four of them, always conspiring together, comprise the older group of offspring.

Kiril put his arm around me tenderly. "Thinking of Earth and home again?" he asked. I nodded. Kiril also reads me well. "You know, you are the love of my heart."

"I know. I love you too."

That was all it took. I may never see my world again, but I have a family and friends right here. The reminder of all I have is what I need to dispel my gloom. I take a deep breath, melt into Kiril's waiting arms and let him lead me to join the group ready to celebrate.

CHAPTER 2

Rojaire

I watch the love of my heart dress for the celebration. She is still the most beautiful woman ever. Her auburn hair, golden eyes and smooth chestnut skin glow, even in the fading light. Kaylya and I spent many cycles of seasons together exploring the devastated island continent together when it was forbidden. Captain Setas had been posted on Alaia Island to guard the portal. But Captain Setas could be bribed. Kaylya and I made it to the center of the continent and then she vanished in the Crystalline Landscape. Our love endured many cycles of seasons before she was found on Earth and brought back to Aaia.

"I would like to suggest to the community tonight that we put together another expedition to find a route out the valley." I spoke softly, but earnestly, gazing into Kaylya's eyes. How I wish I could take her with me. But, of course, with two young children that would no longer be possible, for now.

"How long will you be gone? What about the schoolhouse we were planning on building?"

"I'm putting you in charge of the schoolhouse project. Meanwhile, First Shelter can be used both as a meeting hall and a classroom."

"How many do you plan to take with you?" Kaylya asked. "The adults barely outnumber the children now."

"No more than two. I don't want to greatly diminish the work force here. Speaking of children, where are Jack and Setas?"

"Playing tag ball. What makes you think anyone will want to leave the valley even if you do find a way out ... including me? We have worked so hard and achieved so much. Everything we need is here."

She is right, everything we need is here. When we first arrived with what we could carry on our backs, everyone not handicapped by age or injured in the ground shake worked extraordinarily hard to build shelters, forage for food, and aid the sick and injured. We have not only survived, but thrived. For six cycles of seasons we have built not only shelters, but families and a community. But I feel there are other things to consider.

"I'm responsible for these people. I brought them here. I want them to thrive."

"You saved these people and they are thriving. You gave them something very important – personal freedom."

"There are worlds out there. Our children have only seen the 23 people living in this valley, including themselves. They are young now, but one day they will want to broaden their perspective." I can see Kaylya would prefer not to have to listen to it all again, but I can't help myself.

"We have yet to explore the far reaches of our own valley. Unless we find a way out, we are prisoners. We can't even explore this great continent."

There have been many shorter exploratory endeavors in search of an exit. As a result, we have discovered many edible and medicinal plants and other natural resources, but the valley extends far longer than we once thought and the mountain walls remain impenetrable.

"Fine, Rojaire." She didn't sound angry, just resigned. "There is a dessert dish on the table. Grab it on your way out. I need to go and help Caleeza round up the young crowd. Our children are running wild just as the High Council once predicted." And with that she left, leaving me to take the sweet dish she prepared for the gathering.

I think I understand Kaylya's reluctance to find a way out the valley. As a community we have worked hard together to achieve a remarkable level of comfort and security and unlimited freedom. But we have to think of the future. I pick up the dish and step out the door.

Our home, like the other structures in the community, is constructed of wood, stone, and clay, the materials of the valley. Rooms were added on as the family expanded. Standing in front of our shelter, I can hear the nearby waterfall stream through the trees north of us flowing merrily on its way to the river. The pathway leading south toward the village circle passes between the giant nut tree grove, now quiet with the tag ball game over, and Wessid and Zaloka's shelter, also silent.

Upon reaching the village circle it looks like I'm the last to arrive. The small clearing is teeming with activity and buzzing with chatter. The younger children are gathered around the playground structures Drak had designed and constructed with Edty's help. Setas and Jack come running up to me. "Theon won," they announced. I know they are referring to the tag ball game.

"Well, that's great!"

I can't find anywhere to place Kaylya's dish on the overloaded tables. "Good, you're here," Ilene said coming to my rescue and by some sleight of hand creates a spot.

"Was there any doubt I would make it?"

"Kiril has been anxiously waiting for you." We share a knowing smile and I join Kaylya, Ollen and Caleeza on the benches. Kiril paces around waiting for everyone to settle down.

Thayla, who rarely sits, stands guard as usual, a tall, muscular bronze statue, like she is expecting an invasion. Thayla's discovery of metallic ores and her knowledge as a blade smith has led to the production of many useful tools for the community. Making tools instead of weaponry was a hard transition for the warrior princess from Twaka to make.

I wasn't the last to arrive after all. Inventor Sulyan, the image of the mad professor, his silver-streaked bright red hair sticking out in all directions, enters the clearing carrying a pack. Strange how we still think of him that way after all this time, like "Inventor" is part of his name. Sulyan places the pack carefully away from everything then sits where he can watch that no one disturbs it. Curiosity gets the best of me. I walk over to join him.

"What do you have in the pack, Sulyan?" I asked.

"Oh..., Rojaire ...well, it's a surprise...for later," Sulyan stammered.

Having taken a mental count to assure everyone is present, Kiril picks up one of Thayla's metallic platters and beats on it with a utensil to gain everyone's attention. The chatter fades off and Kiril jumps in.

"Greetings, exalted citizens of this great valley. We gather to celebrate Seaa Rising, the start of a new year. For six cycles of seasons we have survived all odds and we have thrived. I usually announce the new arrivals at this time, but for the first time in four cycles of seasons there has not been a new person born to the community."

"It's about time the breeders take a break!" Drak shouted out boisterously. Everyone laughs as he intended.

"Fortunately, we haven't lost anyone either, so our population remains at 23," Kiril announced. "We have proven we are powerful, we are warriors, and we are all Accepted Ones. We are not rogues as the High Council has branded us, but free men and women, capable of choosing to follow our own talents, pursue our own pathways to happiness, and determine our own destiny."

There is a roar of approval. "I say we have a drink to that!" Drak shouted and reaches for the nearest jug of his special brew. Another roar of approval.

Drak is the community's chief furniture maker and distiller of fine liquor. Judging by his disheveled long silvery hair and glowing weathered face, I would guess he tested the drink for tonight's celebration. It was Drak's great grandfather Vestan who mapped this valley and another unknown valley long ago. How Vestan accessed the valley no one knows.

Hands gripping tumblers reach out to be filled. Kiril has lost his audience. Knowing Kiril, I'm certain he had more speech prepared, but Drak's brew supersedes him. In his defense, our chronicler graciously concedes and accepts a tumbler of the iridescent blue liquor. Kiril throws back a gulp and then shouts, "Bring on the feast!"

I can't help but notice Ilene giving him a warning glance reminding him of the potency of Drak's brew.

By the time everyone has eaten their fill, the period of darkness has descended on the valley. Zillions of stars twinkle above signaling the arrival of their distant light. With appetites sated, a quieter anticipation hangs over the colonists as they wait for Seaa's appearance marking the beginning of another cycle of seasons.

I feel the time to present my proposition has arrived. Following Kiril's example, I tap a utensil against a metallic platter.

CHAPTER 3

Aurora

It just isn't fair. Halren is the tallest, most handsome of the boys and first born. Since I'm second born Halren should rightfully be mine. I don't mean actually own him, of course. Mother says no one can own another person, not even as heart mates. But that could never be because Dad and Halren are brothers. Mother says that makes Halren my uncle. How strange is that?

"I'm ready for dessert," Theon said still gnawing on a kurper leg. My little brother eats like a bear beast.

"I'm stuffed," Selyzar said burying his face in a fruity dessert.

"Then quit eating," I advised.

"Aurora's right," Halren agreed. "You have to know when to quit."

I hate my name. "Aurora," what kind of name is that? Mother is from Earth, some place called Alaska. I wish I had an Aaian name like the others. Mother says the Aurora Borealis is a beautiful light show in the sky. At least she didn't name me Borealis.

Everyone else in the valley is Aaian, except for Thayla. She's Twakan.

Kaylya, Rojaire and Caleeza have been to Earth, so all of us children and many of the adults speak both English and Aaian. Thayla has made attempts to teach us Twakan, with less success. But everyone knows two Twakan words, "pviek" and "rofk." We believe they mean "yes" and "no," but they may have some added hidden meaning. Mother says our traditions are a blend of three worlds, Aaia, Earth and Twaka, combined with new ideas, and our family units more closely resemble Earth and Twaka culture than that of Aaia.

My grandfather Theon lived most of his longevity on Earth, much of that time in Alaska. There are legendary stories about Grandfather Theon. Grandfather Theon was a follower of Droclum when the evil sorcerer nearly destroyed Aaia. Later he turned to the good and searched for the Dark Orb containing Droclum's evil essence, to destroy it. A headstone marks Grandfather Theon's grave at the burial grounds. Captain Setas lies next to him. There are a lot of stories about her too. As chronicler, Father has been writing these legends down. He often tells us stories when we gather around the fire ring.

There aren't any great stories about Grandmother Elaine on Earth, but she may still be alive. I know Mother wishes she could visit her. Anyway, that makes me and my brother Theon three-quarters Aaian and one-quarter Earthen. Our Aaian grandparents live here. Theon and I are the only children in the valley with grandparents. Grandmother Zaloka and Grandfather Wessid say they are everyone's grandparents so no one feels left out.

"I wish Seaa would hurry up and rise so Kiril would light the fire ring. It's no fun sitting around a fire ring with no fire," Selyzar complained.

"Father says ceremony and tradition are very important. The traditions we establish as a community define us and bring us together," Halren said. He is definitely the most studious of the four of us.

Rojaire is banging on a platter for attention. "What do you think that's about?" I asked the others. When Rojaire speaks it's usually important. Mom and Dad say we have no leader, but everyone knows Rojaire is our leader. Rojaire is the most handsome man in the valley by far; tall, lean, muscular, long dark wavy hair, blue-green eyes streaked with gold. Kaylya is so lucky to have him as her heart mate.

"Maybe there's going to be another expedition," Halren said. We move in closer to the action so we can listen.

"As we await Seaa's light, I would like to make a proposal," Rojaire began. "We have yet to reach the end of our valley. Now that we are strong and sheltered and our immediate needs are met, we should consider further exploration. Our attempt to follow an underground lead failed, but there must be a route to the sea, a pass through the mountains perhaps. We just have to find it."

"Told you," Halren said softly.

"Why?" Ollen shouted out when Rojaire takes a breath. Ollen was badly hurt during the great ground shake that closed off the valley. Though recovered, his crushed body never completely regained its full strength. Unable to do any heavy lifting he turned to weaving to make himself useful. Now he is our master weaver.

"I wish I could go on an expedition. Adults get to have all the fun," Theon moaned.

"A colony of 14 adults and 9 children cannot survive long term, we cannot sustain longevity," Rojaire continued. "Sure there are mating possibilities for our children now, but in a generation or two there would be a lot of inbreeding. Do you really want to limit our children's future to this valley?" There are murmurs of discussion among the listeners.

"If you are looking for volunteers, count me in," Traevus said speaking up.

"Me, too," Thayla volunteered. "You will need my protection."

Traevus is quite handsome too in a softer more delicate way. Golden highlights streak his dark brown hair and green eyes. He is thin and lithe and super energetic. Thayla is the love of his heart, but Thayla is a warrior princess from Twaka and refuses to make a commitment.

Thayla is super fascinating. She is an actual princess, although she doesn't act like one. She's taller than everyone else in the community and muscular too. Her hair is more green than gold and she has vermillion eyes. Her golden complexion, Mother says it's bronze, and the permanent scar on her left cheek give her an exotic appearance. Not that I would want a scar on my cheek.

"Good," Rojaire said. "Traevus, Thayla and I will make the journey. We will leave during the next period of light, giving us some time to plan."

"Our community will seem small indeed with all of you gone," Ollen observed. Ollen was a member of some lost expedition team sent by the High Council that disappeared on Lynnara long ago, so were Traevus and Caleeza. According to Dad, the High Council believes only Traevus has been found. Ollen and Caleeza have never returned to Mainland.

Then Mother spoke.

"I think Kaylya should make the journey with you. Kiril and I will be glad to keep Jack and Setas while you are gone."

My jaw dropped and I saw Dad do a double take. What was Mother thinking? Setas and Jack are 5th and 7th born!

Then Dad must have been struck by a duty-to-the-community hammer for he quickly agreed!

Everyone else volunteered to help too.

"Should I?" Kaylya asked Rojaire not sure what decision she should make.

"Yes, of course," Rojaire said. "The children will be cared for by the community."

I can't believe it; Rojaire, Kaylya, Thayla and Traevus may be leaving for a long time. It makes me feel sad inside. I think everyone else is feeling a little sad too. As things settle back down, the sky begins to noticeably lighten. In the east, Seaa, the closest star to Aaia's solar system has begun to rise. Seaa occupies a space so close to our own sun it shines dimly like a distant sun for half the Aaian year. As Seaa rises higher in the sky she dispels some of the darkness, dimming the surrounding stars.

With ceremonial awe Kiril lights the bonfire to celebrate Seaa's rising. As the flames leap higher, everyone cheers. Then Drak, the brew master, begins pouring another round.

"And now for my surprise," Inventor Sulyan announced jumping up to put it into action. This is likely to be good. Inventor Sulyan comes up with some amazing things. We watch intently as Sulyan picks up his pack and moves away from the crowd. Opening the pack, he pulls out four tubular objects mounted on sticks. Theon, Halren and Selyzar close in. I skirt around them to get a better look.

"I give you fireworks!" Sulyan proclaimed.

"Fireworks!" I shouted in disbelief.

Mom and Kaylya often tell stories of fireworks used to celebrate New Year's on Earth. Inventor Sulyan has questioned them repeatedly on their construction. It turns out, Thayla knows a little about explosives from her own world and began working with him on the project.

Sulyan inserts the sticks into the ground a pace apart, then taking a lit candle from one of the tables, he is ready.

"Now stand back everyone. Let's hope this works." Not all of Sulyan's "inventions" work as intended. Rojaire steps up to move curious onlookers, we are included, a safe distance away.

Then Sulyan lights the first wick and steps back. A tiny flame runs up the wick and vanishes inside the cylinder. The rocket whistles as it shoots up in the air and explodes into a starburst of color. A shout of awe fills the village circle. Sulyan fires the second rocket, following up with the third to reverberating cheer. But the fourth rocket has a mind of its own. The flaming missile spirals around hissing and spitting, sending parents grabbing for screaming children and everyone running for their lives before exploding amidst the celebration.

Wow! Sulyan was a great success!

CHAPTER 4

Anthya

"**I** wish I could join Ilene and the colonists on the devastated continent...I mean Lynnara," Melinda said wistfully as we gaze out at the sunlight sparkling on the Golden Sea from the Academy balcony.

Six cycles of seasons have passed since I brought Melinda here from Earth. By then, the colonists had already left Mainland. She has lived in the Community of the High Council ever since.

It was Melinda's choice to come to Aaia. She has been psychically damaged by an unspeakable evil that originated on Aaia and attacked her on Earth. I have been able to offer her healing. Still I worry about Melinda. She has worked hard to learn our language. And she has met all the High Council and the Academy's demands on her. But she makes no efforts socially to make friends, staying to herself.

"I wish I could take you there," I admitted honestly. I didn't know at the time, I may soon be fulfilling her wish.

It is then, Councilor Renna, Representative to the Worlds League, telepaths me a message. *Councilor Anthya, meet me at the garden portal!* Strangely, the telepathed message held a sense of unease. I've never known the councilor's fortitude to be ruffled.

"I have to go," I informed Melinda. "Councilor Renna has summoned me and it sounds urgent."

"I hope it's nothing too serious," Melinda said. Her straight black hair, almond shaped dark eyes and warm brown skin shine in the Aaian sunrise. On Earth she is a native Indian from Southeast Alaska. On Aaia she is an Earthen.

I quickly teleport to the garden portal. Intoxicating scents emitted from the brilliant tapestry of blooming foliage assails my senses. Quaylyn, his golden blond hair tousled, has already arrived. Extensive gardens, arbors and pathways surround us. Before I can ask why we had been summoned, Renna fills us in.

"Councilor Kaydra is arriving with a contingent of Twakans. From the wording of her message, I believe she is being held for some kind of ransom."

Before she can elaborate, the space before us shimmers into a group of four armed warriors and two dignitaries with unhappy faces. Their weapons, though deadly, are primitive. The Twakan people have not developed the ability to draw on the natural available energy from the elemental forces that freely flow around us.

I recognize Princess Xanthe. The gentleman with her may be her brother. I'm certain the warriors accompanying them are highly skilled, but I feel equally as certain any one of us could stop them from committing any violence. Whether the Twakans realize it or not, the three of us present a formidable force. Councilor Kaydra, Mentor to Twaka, is not among them.

Apparently, Renna recognizes them too. "Greetings, Princess Xanthe and Prince Lozar. I am Councilor Renna representing High Councilor Clova of the Runes of the Crystal Table. How may I serve?" she asked with authoritative calm.

The princess is first to speak.

"Spare us your pathetic greetings." Princess Xanthe is a slightly smaller, but more intense version of Thayla, without the facial scar. She is known for her belligerence. "You have failed to serve for a long time."

I notice Quaylyn struggles not to retort. A tiny spark of rage flashes in his deep blue eyes, replacing the usual cheerful twinkle.

Renna takes charge, "Where is Councilor Kaydra, Mentor to Twaka? She is not among you."

Prince Lozar speaks up. "We have come to demand the return of our sister, Princess Thayla. She has not been heard in eight Twakan years. We believe you hold her prisoner. Councilor Kaydra is being held on Twaka until the High Council has met our demand."

Prince Lozar is quite handsome in a bronze statue sort of way. Tall and muscular, his scant clothing, loose breeches fastened below the knees and a sleeveless brown open vest over his bare chest, exposes the same bronzy gold complexion as his sisters. It is noticeably unmarred by any imperfections.

Princess Xanthe, dressed much the same as her brother except for a top covering only the breasts, threateningly steps forward to speak, her hand resting on the hilt of a blade. "You will get Mentor Kaydra back when you return our sister," she snarled.

"I will need assurances Kaydra is safe and unharmed before we can begin a dialogue," Renna said.

"I thought you people could read minds," the prince countered. "If true, you should already know she is unharmed."

Prince Lozar has assumed correctly. I believe he is smarter than his sister. I have already scanned the Twakans' thoughts to confirm Kaydra is safe and I'm certain the others have too. I even know where she is being held.

Renna does not respond to the prince's snarky remark. "We will convene the High Council of the Crystal Table. You will be summoned when the chamber is ready. Meanwhile Councilor Quaylyn and Councilor Anthya will show you around."

I can't help wonder what this whole episode is really about, but I suspect it has something to do with secession to the throne on Twaka. My interactions with Princess Thayla before she joined the rogue colonists had been brief, but she struck me as a princess who didn't want to be a princess or a queen.

"It will be a pleasure to show the prince and princess the grounds," Quaylyn said, speaking calmly. I readily agree although I'm certain it will not be a pleasure at all.

"Till then," Councilor Renna said and vanishes leaving Quaylyn and I to entertain our unpleasant guests. For a moment we stand speechless in the beautiful, fragrant garden. Princess Xanthe and Prince Lozar stare at us questioningly, defiantly waiting for our next move.

"Shall we stroll through the gardens?" Quaylyn suggested. "There are some shady arbors where we can sit and rest. Aaia is quite a bit warmer than Twaka."

"One of the most beautiful flowers in the garden comes from Twaka," I quickly added. "Would you like to see it, Princess Xanthe?" I asked in an attempt to soften the sharp-edged princess' disposition.

"I am not interested in flowers. Where is my sister?"

"You know your sister joined a group of colonists..."

"The details of Princess Thayla's disappearance will be unveiled at the Crystal Table," Quaylyn gently interrupted.

"We will see the flower," Prince Lozar announced unexpectedly. Then to his sister, "Be patient," he admonished.

It quickly becomes apparent the gardens will not hold their interest for long, no matter how many exotics we present.

"I want to see your armory," Princess Xanthe demanded.

"Perhaps we should pay a visit to Councilor Jarlon, Master of Sorcery and Defense at the Academy," Quaylyn suggested and leads the way.

Quaylyn has a complex history. He is the son of the evil Sorcerer Droclum and the great Sorceress Anthya, my name sake, who sacrificed herself to destroy Droclum. Quaylyn didn't learn of his heritage until later in life and has struggled with the knowledge ever since.

Quaylyn guides us out the garden through a lavender and rose stone arch to a wide, cool crystal-domed avenue. "This pathway is called The Way," I said as we pause to appreciate the cooler air, the mosaic art work on the walls and the fractured patterns of light thrown by the crystal dome. More stone arches open up all along The Way. "At one end of The Way sits the High Council Chambers, at the other end is the Academy."

"This way," Quaylyn said bowing toward the Academy. The Academy, built as a monument to the survival of humanity, looms ahead. Crimson and orange creeping vines choke the massive lavender stone structure. The Way leads directly into the Academy's enormous octagon central hall. Along the walls, glow globes light displays of relics from an age destroyed. Quaylyn leads us across the stone floor and down a corridor to the gymnasium.

Arriving at the gymnasium we find Councilor Jarlon on the mat with a student. To my surprise it is Melinda. Although Melinda is in her mid-thirties in Earth-years, the Academy still considers her a new person.

"What are they doing?" Princess Xanthe asked after watching for a moment.

"They are sparring," Quaylyn said.

"Sparring? Where are their weapons?"

"They are practicing a weaponless martial art called yizi. A master of yizi doesn't need a weapon." I detected a hint of a challenge in Quaylyn speech.

Melinda is first to break her concentration, forfeiting the match. Councilor Jarlon heads over to greet us.

Princess Xanthe turns to me. "Are you a master?" she asked.

"I'm skilled." Our skills are constantly honed. I don't know anything about the princess's training or skills, but without her sword I deem her harmless.

"Greetings, Councilor Anthya, Councilor Quaylyn and friends," Jarlon said indicating the six Twakans with us. "How may I serve?"

"I believe the princess here has challenged me to a match."

"Is that so? Then be my guest." Jarlon gives me a nod and Xanthe and I step out onto the arena. Jarlon quickly intercepts Xanthe. "No weapons are allowed."

Xanthe gives him a cold look, but she turns back, hands her weapons to her warriors and steps back out onto the court. Jarlon and Melinda join the rest of the spectators on the sideline and Princess Xanthe and I face off.

CHAPTER 5

Quaylyn

I don't trust these Twakans. I watch intently as Anthya and Princess Xanthe face off, ready to detect any trickery the princess may try to pull off. I can't imagine Xanthe having the calm calculating patience paramount in the practice of yizi. Calm calculating patience defines Anthya. Anthya looks frail and vulnerable compared to Xanthe's muscular frame, but yizi isn't about brute force.

As expected Xanthe makes the first move, leaping for Anthya's throat. Anthya's counter move is so quick, smooth and subtle, it leaves Xanthe grasping air as she stumbles forward, fighting to regain her balance.

"Only a coward evades a fight," Xanthe hissed with bruised dignity.

Anthya remains silent and focused. A yizi master never reacts to a taunt. Angered, Xanthe launches another attack.

This time Anthya makes contact, dipping, rising and twirling with the grace of a dancer, sending Xanthe spinning sprawled out on the gymnasium floor.

"Enough!" Prince Lozar commanded stepping forward.

"The High Councilor is ready," I announced, receiving Renna's summons in time to defuse the situation.

"We go," Prince Lozar said.

"This is not over," Princess Xanthe snarled picking herself up off the floor. "I will deal with you later." I fear Anthya has made an enemy.

It is a relief to finally be summoned to the High Council chamber, the timing couldn't have been better. Princess Xanthe, more obnoxious than civil, is barely kept in check by Prince Lozar while their armed warriors stand threateningly by. Still I'm not looking forward to this session. I probably know more about Thayla's disappearance than anyone and the Runes of the Crystal Table will force me to reveal all.

Anthya and I lead our charges down The Way toward the High Council Hall. Along the wide stone avenue sheltered under the crystal dome, more lavender and rose stone archways invitingly open vistas of the surrounding orchards and gardens. The Way ends at two massive doors set in a stone wall guarded by two unarmed warriors of our own, barring the entrance.

"Only Prince Lozar, Princess Xanthe, Councilor Anthya and Councilor Quaylyn are allowed entrance," one guard said. "The others must stay."

One does not have to be a councilor to sit at the Crystal Table. There are eight seats, not counting that of the High Councilor, and all seats must be filled, but no more than eight individuals are ever allowed in the chamber. Lozar and Xanthe's warriors will have to remain outside the High Council Hall.

"I say they can come with us," Xanthe protested. But Lozar is catching on and orders the four warriors to stay.

Xanthe and Lozar are obviously awed upon entering the chamber despite their efforts not to show it. The massive oval crystal table of legend dominates the vast airy space. The eight runes of great power; Sun, Air, Crystal, Soil, Fire, Water, Moon and Void, etched into the table's surface glow softly under the light of the high crystal dome overhead. Before each rune sits a massive crystal chair softened with silver seat and arm rest cushions embroidered with silver thread. A ninth chair sits on a raised dais overlooking it all.

Long ago, three great wizards pooling their powers wrought a great oval table from the purest crystal. With their combined strength, they drew in the wisdom and power of the elemental runes and worked together on a spell to aid anyone who sits at the Crystal Table in making wise, impartial decisions for the greater good of all the people. With the power of the runes of the elemental forces, they etched into the table the runic symbols for crystal, water, fire, sun, soil, air, moon, and void.

Several of the councilors called to fill the seats have already arrived. Anthya and I direct Lozar and Xanthe to choose places to sit. Lozar readily sits in front of Fire, although I doubt he can read the runes. Xanthe hesitates, wary of unknown magic. With great hesitancy she slips into the chair for Void. I decide to take the seat next to her in front of the Sun Rune. Anthya walks over to Moon and sits next to Lozar. The other seats quickly fill and High Councilor Clova enters the hall. The doors to the chamber close behind her with a soft swoosh. I wonder what would happen if someone were to try and leave once the chamber is in session.

With lithe grace High Councilor Clova mounts the steps to the dais and addresses the assembled. Her dark velvety skin and long jet black hair restrained in jeweled ribbons glistens in the refracted light. High Councilor Clova is as mysterious as she is alluring. I've never seen her out in the public and I've never been summoned to her private chambers. I hope I never will.

"Welcome councilors, friends and visitors. I am Clova, High Councilor of the Crystal Table. You have been summoned here before the eight Runes of Power: Crystal, Water, Fire, Air, Soil, Sun, Moon and Void to find solutions to an interplanetary dispute. The Crystal Table will help us make wise decisions. Together we seek purpose and direction for the greater good of all. Here are the rules.

"When the Rune in front of you moves above the center of the table, it is your turn to speak; the Rune wants us to hear what you have to say. While your Rune is in place, no one else, besides me, is allowed to speak. You must speak truthfully. A spoken falsehood would be instantly recognized. The Rune will not release you until the truth has been revealed. Not all present may be called on to speak. If you are ready, this meeting will begin."

The High Councilor graciously takes her seat and as the great hall darkens, the glow of the Runes of Power intensify. Princess Xanthe stiffens with unease, but she doesn't make a sound in the quiet chamber. Everyone watches intently as the glowing Crystal Rune in front of Councilor Renna, Representative to the World League, rises and moves above the center of the table.

"Councilor Renna, you have been chosen by the wisdom of the Runes to speak first."

Councilor Renna stands in response to the summons, and introduces herself by protocol, but there is little need. The Twakans know her well. As Representative to the World League, she has worked closely with Twaka's dignitaries.

"Well, let me begin by outlining the basic known facts. Six cycles of seasons, eight Twakan years ago, Princess Thayla visited our planet with Kaydra, our Mentor to Twaka as a welcomed guest. Here she met a group planning to start a colony on Lynnara, the island continent destroyed and transformed during the Dark Devastation long ago. The leader of the group was Explorer Rojaire. He appealed to the High Council for permission to colonize. The High Council opposed colonizing Lynnara, but offered Rojaire the award of a charter if he could find twenty colonists to sign up in a given span of time." Renna's wild reddish-brown hair and golden eyes gleam in the Crystal Rune's light.

"Since the Crystalline Landscape in the center of the island continent blocks the drawing of energy from the elemental forces, life in the colony would be hard. Rojaire failed to recruit the required number of colonists, but a small group of followers defied the High Council. With the aid of Captain Setas, guardian of the portal on Alaia Island and ferry access to Lynnara, they fled Mainland. Princess Thayla, of her own free will, decided to join this group leaving Mentor Kaydra to inform her family of her decision."

Renna is leaving out some minor facts, but basically that's what happened. Xanthe nearly jumps out of her seat in protest. Perhaps she didn't understand the rules or she assumed the rules didn't apply to her. I don't know, but in a flash, Lozar grabs her wrist, pulling her back into her seat, and stares her down hard to quell any outburst. Complying reluctantly, she yanks her arm free from Lozar's grasp and settles down quietly.

The Crystal Rune remains in place so Renna continues. "Twaka is demanding the return of their princess, accusing the High Council of holding her prisoner. We have negotiated with Twaka in good faith. We don't have access to Princess Thayla. We can't return her. We cannot access the portal on Alaia Island and neither the colonists nor Captain Setas have been heard from since a major seismic event that occurred not long after the colonists left."

I can see Renna's relief when the Crystal Rune returns to its place. There is no mention of Kaydra being held by the Twakans. In fact, Kaydra has already been rescued from her prison, but Lozar and Xanthe don't have this information. All the attendees hold a collected breath in the pause wondering who will be next. Then the Water Rune in front of Councilor Kreeze rises to take its place in the center of the table. Kreeze stands in response to the summons. Kreeze's thin graying hair indicates advancing longevity. Kreeze is kind, studious and judicious, but he has been steadily resistant to change.

"I'm Councilor Kreeze, Proctor of the Northern Communities. I have the dubious reputation of having four members of my own community, Zaloka, Wessid, Drak and Kiril, join the colonist group. Now Drak has always been a bit eccentric, but Zaloka and Wessid were a total surprise. Kiril was still a new person and had been forbidden by the Academy to join the colonists. Rojaire, Kaylya, Traevus, Kiril and Princess Thayla even visited our village looking for people to join the colony. It gave us a chance to get to know the princess. Nice girl, forceful, but nice."

Kreeze hesitates. "I guess we didn't realize how serious these would-be colonists were. At the time I opposed the idea of colonizing the Devastated Continent, but I must say, after a few cycles of seasons thinking on it, well, now I'm not so sure why I opposed the colony in the first place. I do find it interesting though that Zaloka happens to be Kiril's chosen mother and Wessid his chosen father." Still the Water Rune remains in place. For a moment, Kreeze doesn't seem to know what to say.

"My greater concern comes from the extreme seismic activity that later occurred in that region, sending a small tsunami wave even to our distant shore. I hope nothing bad happened to them."

Kreeze brings up an important point. Perhaps the reason Captain Setas can't be reached is because the portal no longer exists. This must be the information the runes are seeking because the Water Rune flows back into place allowing Kreeze to take his seat.

My time to speak arrives. The Sun Rune, blazing brightly, rises before me taking the Water Rune's place in the center of the table. I stand in response to the summons. How should I begin? I took a deep breath.

"I am Councilor Quaylyn. I share Councilor Kreeze's concern for the whereabouts and safety of the colonists. Many of the colonists were also personal friends. I can assure you Princess Thayla's decision was her own." I take a deep breath. "I knew Rojaire and his group were leaving and I did nothing." I stare around at startled faces while I take another steadying breath.

"Why you may ask? Why didn't you say something? We could have stopped them. I'm not sure why, other than a part of me wanted to go with them." I'm glad no one else is allowed to speak. The ensuing quiet gives me time to collect my thoughts.

"Among the ten colonists that departed Mainland was a young woman from Earth, Ilene daughter of Theon. As part of her Aaian heritage she discovered an ability to heal. She desired to learn more and was brought to The Academy to study. I knew she also wanted to rejoin her father who had stayed behind on Lynnara with two others, Tassyn and Edty are their names. Ilene and I have an established friendship from my time spent on Earth. Although she is a promising healer, she lacks ability in shielding her thoughts. I suspected Rojaire would attempt to leave with his followers against the High Council's will. It has been long suspected that Rojaire had influence on Captain Setas. So I met with Ilene and verifying Rojaire's plans warned her of the possible consequences of joining the colonists. But Ilene's desire to see her father again overrode the possibility of never returning to Earth. Admittedly, I did nothing to stop them."

I confessed my guilt for which I have little remorse, unless by not stopping them I let them go to their deaths. Having cleansed my soul, I feel certain the Sun Rune will let me go to face punishment later. Yet it remains in place. Are the Runes seeking an apology? I don't think so, the Runes seek facts; they do not cast moral judgment.

"I believe we need to find out what happened to not only Princess Thayla, but all the colonists. I am including Captain Setas in there. Surely Rojaire would have convinced her to go with them to protect her from the High Council and to inconvenience anyone trying to follow since her ferryboat is the only means of reaching Lynnara. At least I hope that is what happened. For I fear our inability to access Alaia Island is because the little portal island no longer exits." The Sun Rune wants more. All I can do at this point is volunteer.

"I feel certain a search for the colonists should be undertaken and being a part of it, I offer my service, if you will have it, to launch an expedition to find the missing colonists."

That does it. To my relief, the Sun Rune finally returns to its place on the table and I gratefully sit down.

The Fire Rune rises from in front of Lozar and moves to the center of the table. Lozar is going to have his chance to speak. Xanthe can barely contain herself any longer. Surely she feels she should be the one asked to speak instead of Lozar. Only vicious stare-downs from her brother keeps her in check.

Lozar stands to address the High Council.

CHAPTER 6

Lozar

Finally the light in front of me activates. It's about time either Xanthe or I have a say. I stand to speak my mind with my blood raging. The backwards stupidity of these people! Following the others example, I introduce myself.

"I am Prince Lozar of Twaka. I've come to rescue my sister. I cannot believe you people! A princess of Twaka goes missing in a desolate land and no one goes to investigate? And what is your excuse? Well, we can't reach the portal," Lozar said mockingly. "Send a ship! Send a fleet of ships! Oh, that's right, you don't have ships, you teleport."

The chamber is quiet, too quiet. I'm expecting angry voices shouting back in self-defense, but there is only silence. No one else is allowed to speak because of that light thing above the middle of the table. How primitive for such an advanced world! What can I tell these people to educate them?

"I would think you would have some concern for your own missing people. Are there no family members concerned for their love ones? Princess Thayla and I are both worthy sea captains. Are there no ships that can navigate the Golden Sea? If you can't build ships, we can. We demand a search for these colonists."

I have lots more to say, but that darn light thing comes back to the edge of the table before I can finish. Now I am expected to shut up and sit down? I'm tempted to continue, but I suppose defiance will only make things worse. For Thayla's sake I'll sit, for now.

As soon as I sit down, another light thing moves to the center of the table and another councilor rises to speak. Her thin white hair and aging brown skin indicates she is even more ancient than the other one, Councilor Kreeze. Her voice rattles in her throat.

"I am Councilor Zilka, Proctor for the Southern Communities. I have always been opposed to the colonization of the Devastated Continent and I still think it is a bad idea. But this is not about me. Since I had no contact with Princess Thayla I assume what I have to offer is resources. Contrary to what Prince Lozar may believe, we do have sea-faring, deep water fishing vessels in the southern provinces. It is possible we could provide a couple of vessels that could be outfitted for a mission to Lynnara. There I said it...Lynnara. I invite anyone planning on undertaking such a mission to visit my home village Twala and take a look at the possibilities."

That's more like it. I want to take a look at these boats. I am hoping she will say more, but the light for the proctor leaves the center of the table. How do they ever expect to get anything down this way? The light rises in front of the woman councilor sitting next to me who took us on our tour and humiliated Xanthe at the gymnasium. I can't remember her name, but I'll get it again when she introduces herself. She is all pale yellow and white from her long light blonde hair to her creamy white, almost translucent skin, more closely resembling a spectral spirit than flesh and blood. Even her eyes are the lightest shade of bluish gray.

"I am Councilor Anthya."

That's it, "Anthya."

"I have listened carefully to both the facts and our concerns. Prince Lozar has some very valid points. I feel this would be a perfect opportunity for cooperation between our two worlds on an important endeavor. Let's find out what has happened to the colonists and the land across the Golden Sea. I would be willing to help facilitate that venture in any way I can."

Well, at least someone around here has some sense. Good, maybe she can help me find some answers. The other one, Councilor Quaylyn, by his own admission could have stopped Thayla from leaving on this crazy adventure in the first place.

"If I may, I would like to bring up something else." Apparently the Runes don't object, since the light remains in place. "Earthen Melinda is a hero, a warrior who actually faced Droclum on Earth. She has been living in our community for some time where I've been mentoring her. It has long been her desire to join Colonist Ilene on Lynnara. I believe reuniting her with a friend from Earth would be good for her. Our world owes her that much."

These Runes must agree with her for suddenly the proceedings are over.

The crystal dome becomes transparent again and daylight floods the great hall. The High Councilor rises from her seat on the crystal dais. I've been told she has the power of final decree. What will she decide?

"The Runes of Power have guided us to make an informed decision," High Councilor Clova announced. "Prince Lozar, Princess Xanthe, Councilor Anthya, Councilor Quaylyn, Mentor Kaydra, and Earthen Melinda will work as a team to make the journey across the Golden Sea to Lynnara to search for Princess Thayla and the rest of the colonists."

This is what we asked for. I glance at Xanthe. She too looks satisfied for the moment.

"The Runes of Power have enlightened us to make another decision. If found, the colonists will be granted a legal charter and Princess Thayla will be free to stay or leave by her own choosing. This is the wisdom of the Power of the Ruins of the Crystal Table."

And that's it. Without another word, the dark lady steps off the dais and walks out the room. The other councilors rise and exit just as quietly, leaving the four of us to assess our alliance.

"I will captain my own ship," Xanthe proclaimed, finally allowed to speak. No one argues with her. When we exit the chamber, Arpen, Rabiam, Yanzic and Glisa are gone.

"Where are they?"

"They have been provided meals and accommodations for a period of rest," a guard explained. "If you will follow us, we will show you to your quarters."

The councilors release us into the care of the guards and walk away, no doubt grateful to be rid of us. Xanthe and I follow the guards without protest.

CHAPTER 7

Ilene

Kiril sits bent over his writing, lit by one of the solar charged lamps once used to navigate the underground passage that brought us here. The lamps still work after all this time, which is a good thing, since we have yet to come up with anything better to replace them than rendered bear beast fat candles.

I don't hear any sound coming from Aurora and Theon's rooms. I'm guessing they are sleeping by now. They should be exhausted. I know I am. The Seaa Rising celebration went on far longer than expected. Yet here I am sitting up with Kiril while he meticulously chronicles the details of the celebration in the community journal while they are fresh in his mind. Oftentimes he consults my recall of events to verify his own.

The celebration had been long and joyous, but also subdued by the explorers' imminent departure. There had been much discussion on how our lives and the lives of our children might change if a route to the sea was discovered. Fear and concern carefully balanced out the hopeful aspirations expressed.

Suddenly Kiril pauses in his work and looks up as though suddenly remembering something very important. "Two more children under our roof? Younger ones at that! Crystal shards, Ilene. Taking care of children is a serious responsibility. And there is always the possibility Rojaire and Kaylya may never return," he said seriously.

"Why do you say that?"

"Anything can happen. We almost didn't make it here six cycles of seasons ago. The ground shake nearly collapsed the underground passage on top of us. We barely escaped with our lives."

"It's not certain. Kaylya may decide not to go. Plus the whole community will help. Besides, you love having children around. Just think, you will always have a captive audience to tell your stories to." That steers him toward his favorite topic.

Kiril put down his stylus. "It is imperative that the children know their history; the story of how their parents arrived in the valley and why they came here in the first place. Eventually we will be only stories of legend like your father and Captain Setas."

I love his dedication to chronicling our lives. And I'm thankful he didn't jump up to volunteer to go on the expedition. I stand behind him, placing my arms around him, possessively keeping him safely close to me. "It will be lonely around here without Rojaire, Traevus, Thayla and Kaylya, if she decides to go."

"What if the expedition does find a way out of the valley? Will you try to return to Earth?" Kiril asked with a bit of insecurity.

"Not without you," I said blowing softly in his ear and kissing his warm neck. "I can't return to Earth without the High Council's help and now I'm as much a fugitive as you are." Kiril doesn't respond, instead he resumes writing.

It is unlikely I will ever see Earth again, but I can't help but think with sadness of Mother constantly waiting for my unlikely return. Theon certainly didn't expect to see me when I arrived in the valley. Tears moisten my eyes remembering our joyful reunion. I joined the colonists just for the chance of seeing him again. Father barely lived another season after my arrival before dying of advanced old age.

Theon and Kiril had a special bond before I arrived on Aaia. Kiril became Theon's youthful admirer and sidekick, enthralled by his knowledge of Earth and the Devastated Continent long before I came on the scene. And then when I arrived, Kiril became fascinated over me.

I smiled remembering Kiril's shocked surprise over meeting Theon's daughter from Earth at the Community of the High Council and chuckled over his early infatuation. He was even more blown away when I joined the rogue colonists.

"What are you laughing about?"

"Nothing," I said affectionately running my fingers through his thick curly tan hair. Weariness overtakes me. "I'm off to bed."

"I'll sleep when I finish here," Kiril said. He doesn't look up.

I barely shut my eyes when I hear a banging on the door followed by Kiril rising to answer. It is Ollen.

"Selyzar is sick. He's delirious with a high fever."

Detecting the worry in his voice, I jump out of bed and rush to the front room. "What's wrong?"

"It's his arm; it's red and swollen and he's hot. I hate to bother you like this. Caleeza and I...."

I didn't hear the rest. Grabbing the pouch containing the star stone hanging by the door, I take off running down the pathways to Ollen and Caleeza's sprawling cottage. Seaa lights the night, washing out the surrounding stars. Upon arriving, I rush in without knocking and find Caleeza by Selyzar's bed applying a cold compress to her son's forehead.

"Oh, Ilene, my gratitude is boundless...."

"You're welcome," I cut in avoiding the Aaian propensity for long statements of gratitude. "What happened?"

"Remember the scrapes on Selyzar's arm I told you about? It looks like they have become infected. I've given him some herbal tea to bring down the fever and help him sleep. Look at this." Caleeza pulls back a poultice wrap from Selyzar's upper arm to reveal angry red pussy sores.

Caleeza reigns as our expert in herbal medicine, her herbal garden a beauty to behold. Many of the herbal remedies she uses are from the seeds brought in by Captain Setas. Horticulture was the ferry captain's passion and her tiny island home featured cultures from around the galaxy. The valley presents Caleeza new opportunities for herbal research. Shut off from the rest of the world, our great valley offers flora and fauna never seen before. Through careful tasting and testing she has found many plants possessing medicinal properties as well as culinary delights, and some plants to be avoided.

"Tell me again how Selyzar scratched up his arm," I said.

"Selyzar said he was climbing a yicil tree trying to catch a pykee for Aurora. When he slid back down the tree trunk his arm caught on the jagged end of a broken branch."

"Sounds like something Aurora would put him up to. I will have a talk with my daughter later."

Pykees are fast moving little long-haired purple creatures that live well camouflaged in the thick purple canopies of the tall bluish brown yicil trees. The children have long wanted to catch a pykee for a pet, but the pykees will have nothing to do with them, and they move like lightning making them impossible to catch. I have a different concern. The yicil trees grow far south of the village, further than the children are allowed to roam without adult supervision.

"It's not Aurora's fault; children will climb trees."

"They shouldn't have been there in the first place."

"That's true; the older children are becoming increasingly independent."

I turn my attention to the problem at hand. "Chances are there may have been some remnant of pykee feces on the tree that contaminated the wound, causing the infection." I feel Selyzar's forehead; it is hot with fever. Fear gnaws at the pit of my stomach. We have never lost a child in the valley, please don't let it happen now. I pull the star stone from its pouch.

I first discovered I had inherited the Aaian talent of drawing healing energy from the elemental forces out of desperation when I tried to help my father back on Earth. But on Lynnara energy from the elemental forces cannot be readily drawn as elsewhere. Lynnara was ground zero for the Dark Devastation that nearly killed all life on the planet; it totally destroyed the island continent. The center of the continent, dominated by Mt. Vatre, crystallized into a vast landscape of crystals. The dangerous Crystalline Landscape is a mine field of time/space warps and emits an energy field that interferes with the drawing of energy from the elemental forces. A star stone counteracts that disruption within a limited radius, allowing me to draw some healing energy from the elemental forces around us.

I touch Selyzar's swollen arm. Even in sleep he flinches from the touch. Drawing energy freed by the star stone, I connect with Selyzar's feverish mind, then seek out the infection. I can sense his body's fight, but the infection seems to be winning. Drawing healing energy from within, I strengthen his resistance to the infection. I strengthen his ability to fight for his life. Ollen must have spread the word throughout the village. I note only vaguely the arrival of Kaylya and Zaloka.

"How is he doing?" I heard Kaylya ask. I don't hear anyone answer. I go into a trance, aware only of the fight on a molecular level. I don't know how much time passes, but eventually I must have collapsed from exhaustion. I feel gentle hands lifting me from my position on Selyzar's bed and guiding me to a chair.

"I'll take over for a while," Caleeza said. "My ability isn't as great as yours, but you can't go on without a rest." I hand her the star stone without argument.

Zaloka places a cup in my hands and urges me to drink. "This will help restore your strength." I take a sip and screw up my face. It tastes awful.

"Drink it," Caleeza ordered noting my resistance. Obeying orders, I drank it down in one gulp.

"Good girl," Zaloka said taking the cup.

I don't know what was in the drink, but I do start to feel better.

"Are you hungry?"

"No."

"I've made my decision," Kaylya said into the ensuing silence. "I will not be joining the expedition. I need to be here." We understand without further explanation.

Eventually I take Caleeza's place again. It is a long fight. Throughout the rest of the long Aaian night we take turns sitting by Selyzar's side, sharing our strength. Eventually the fever begins to recede. It isn't until I am certain Selyzar is out of danger, I allow Kaylya and Zaloka to walk me home. By then Seaa has long set, the sky to the east promising sunrise.

CHAPTER 8

Rojaire

Kaylya has decided not to join us on the expedition after all. I can't say that I blame her. To everyone's relief, Selyzar's fever has finally broken. It is a stark reminder how important our lives are to each other. Accordingly our departure is postponed. Outside a cloudy mist blankets the valley after a heavy rain. The postponement of our venture spared us from the discomforts of the storm. Now with Selyzar out of danger, plans are being resumed. I am looking forward to the adventure, but dreading the departure. Kaylya and I are making the most of our extended time together. It will be the first time Kaylya and I have been apart since I lost her in the Crystalline Landscape so many cycles of seasons ago.

With two items on the agenda and inclement weather outdoors Kiril has called a community meeting in the first permanent shelter we built. First Shelter is the oldest building in the village. Once it sheltered all of us, now it serves as a multipurpose community building. Until it was built, we sheltered in stick lean-tos or in the entrance of the collapsed cave by the waterfall.

Everyone is here except for Caleeza, Selyzar and the younger children. We dropped off Jack and Setas, by Caleeza's invitation, to play with Alaia, Caponya and Little Sarus. First Shelter's single room is only large enough for a table and a dozen chairs. Halren, Aurora and Theon sit on the floor against the wall. Friendly chatter fills the rest of the space.

Kiril claps twice to collect everyone's attention. "We will begin with Ollen giving us an update on Selyzar."

"Yes, well, Selyzar is improving, sitting up and eating ravenously now. That boy can put away some food. His arm is looking better too. We are grateful and blessed," Ollen said solemnly. "Selyzar wanted to be here today, but of course Caleeza objected to that." Chuckles and nods wave through the group.

"It will be next Seaa Rising before she lets that boy out again," Drak said causing everyone to laugh. We all know how protective Caleeza can be.

"Alright, first thing on the agenda, the new schoolhouse," Kiril said, taking back control of the meeting. "The topic is open for discussion."

I give Kaylya a nudge of encouragement. The school building project means a lot to her. Kaylya touches my arm in acknowledgement and speaks up. "Since I've decided not to go on the expedition, I would like to focus my efforts on building the schoolhouse. After all, I will need something to keep me busy while Rojaire is away."

"Maybe we need a new community building instead," Tassyn said glancing around the crowded room.

"The schoolhouse will serve as a community building as well," Kaylya said.

"Where are you planning on building it?" Ollen asked. Ollen participates as much as he can in all affairs of the community. His body, crushed in a land slide during the great ground shake, has never fully regained its strength. Although he can no longer do heavy, strenuous work, he has become our master weaver and is a pillar of supportive strength for the community.

Ollen unrolls the woven map of the village he created and smooths it out on the table. Existing structures are embroidered onto the fabric. Besides the locations of the buildings, the map's details include the village circle, complete with fire ring, trails, the waterfall and its run-off stream, the stone pavilion and cave, and the river. Even the plateau across the river is represented.

The location for the schoolhouse has been under debate for quite some time. I know Kaylya has given the question a lot of thought. "There is a large area of ground along the waterfall stream between our place and Traevus' shelter on the river I think would be the perfect location. It would be close to a water source and the homes of the children."

"Why not put the school on the other side of the waterfall stream?" Thayla asked.

"No, it's too far away," Ilene protested.

"I'm sure Caleeza would agree with you," Ollen said.

Even though a footbridge now spans the little stream, no one has settled on its opposite bank. Across the stream the forest quickly thins into grassland, the range of kurpers. The grassland extends a day's hike before the land and flora changes again.

"I think we need to choose someone to head the project," Kiril suggested.

"I would like to appoint Kaylya leader of the schoolhouse/ community center building project," Tassyn said. "I'll do all I can to help," he added.

"I agree," I said speaking up for the first time.

"Is there anyone else interested in heading the project?" Kiril asked. There is no response. "Then everyone in favor of Kaylya leading the project raise your hand." It is unanimous. "Although naturally everyone will give a hand with the work, Kaylya will need a committee to assist her in decision making. Those of you who would like to work with Kaylya on the building committee please raise your hand."

Wessid, Zaloka, Ollen, Tassyn, Edty and Drak raise their hand to volunteer. Kaylya writes down their names.

"I want to be on the committee," Halren said standing up. "Can I be on the committee too?" he asked.

"Yes, of course," Kaylya said and adds his name to the list.

It's a pleasure to see a student volunteer. Halren is quickly becoming a young man. The other two are looking at the floor, dodging being noticed. Theon is still young, but I'm surprised Aurora isn't volunteering too.

"Any more discussion on building the schoolhouse?" Kiril asked. No one speaks. "I need not remind you, Kaylya, the whole village is your labor force when you need us."

"Which we will be short of without Rojaire, Thayla and Traevus," Drak said lamentably.

"I regret I won't be here to help you," I said apologetically.

"I'm just ribbing you, Rojaire. We wish you a safe journey and a quick return."

"We will help you finish the project when we get back," Traevus promised.

"They'll be finished by then," Thayla predicted.

"So that brings us to the second item on the agenda, the expedition," Kiril said. "Rojaire, I believe that's your project."

Ollen rolls up the village map and I spread out the crystal floss map of the valley on the table in its place. This map was made by Drak's great grandfather Vestan, before the Dark Devastation. Ollen's woven village map is based on Vestan's crystal floss map of the valley. In all honesty, Ollen's map is far more accurate in scale than Vestan's map which greatly distorts distance. The woven crystal floss map has survived the ages since crystal floss is nearly indestructible. Where Vestan found crystal floss is unknown. It is a rare substance.

No one knew an immense valley lay lodged deeply in the formidable Crescent Mountains, the same mountain range that offered the valley some limited protection during that catastrophic event. The Crescent Mountains rise straight up from the valley floor, tall, sharp dark purple monoliths, stacked closely behind one another, surrounding the valley like an impenetrable fortress. Our village is located in the southwest sector of the valley.

After much exploring, we have learned the meaning of most of the map's mysterious symbols, but not all. Overlapping loops like links to a chain denote caves. Lines off the mountains are waterfalls. There are three waterfalls according to the map. The river flows from north to south through the center of the valley starting at the waterfall at the far north end of the valley and ending in a hole in the mountain at the southern end. Another waterfall comes out of the mountains from the northeast (according to the map). The closest waterfall cascades down the mountains not far from the village and serves as our water source. All the waterfall runoff streams empty into the river.

"We have yet to explore the northeast corner of the valley," I pointed out. Since the great ground shake of six cycles of seasons ago, we can assume any underground passage that may have existed at one time has since caved in. I propose we follow the river across the grasslands then head northeast. Eventually we should reach the stream coming out of the east. This textured area here may indicate hills."

The biggest mystery remaining is a complex rendering of squiggly lines with cross hatches marking the side of the mountains in the northeast corner of the valley. "It's time we find out what all this stands for." Everyone leans over the table to better see the symbol I point to. "I believe the northeast end of the valley may extend into the coastal mountains close to the edge of the continent and the Golden Sea."

"So you are looking for a path through the mountains?" Zaloka asked, her gold flecked eyes sparkling with intensity. Her unruly gold highlighted auburn hair adds to the sparkle in her eyes. Zaloka has volunteered as expediter for the mission; her input is highly valued. Mother of two generations, she reigns first in longevity among the women.

"Either we go through the mountains, or over them. We may be doing some mountain climbing. Thayla has forged for us some rock hammers and hooks and we have plenty of rope. I don't know how high we will have to climb or how cold it may get. If you are afraid of height, this may not be the trip for you," I added looking at my team. Neither Traevus nor Thayla offers objection.

"You may have to find several mountain passes the way these mountains are stacked, but I believe Rojaire is right. Based on what we know about Lynnara's coastline and the valley's extension toward the northeast, the distance to the Golden Sea may be shorter than we think," Ollen said.

"How much food do you plan on carrying?" Zaloka asked focusing on practical matters.

"We'll take as much dried food as we can carry for the mountain passes. Hopefully the valley will provide nourishment till we reach the mountains."

"When are you planning on leaving?" Kaylya asked meeting my gaze. My heart does a little jolt, but I meet her gaze with loving strength.

"When we are packed and ready...and when the rain stops," I added.

CHAPTER 9

Aurora

Selyzar gets hurt and I get blamed. Where is the justice in that? Mother really believes it's my fault that Selyzar scraped his arm and it became infected. She really believes that! It's true I've always wanted to catch a pykee, they are so small and cute. Selyzar climbed up the tree to try to catch one, but really he just wanted to impress me. What am I supposed to do, forbid him from climbing trees? I'm not his mother. We're nearly the same age!

I stomp off blind with anger. I don't care where I'm going. I just want to get away from here. Avoiding the village circle I take to the pathways. Halren is outdoors, sees me and tries to wave me down. I speed up, pretending not to see him. As soon as I am out of his line of sight I take off running heading south along the river trail leaving the village.

And then Mother gets on my case about not volunteering for the school building committee like Halren did. I don't want to be kept prisoner in a schoolhouse. What's wrong with doing lessons in different places?

The rain has stopped and the clouds are breaking apart, but the trees and foliage along the pathway are still dripping from the rain. Rays of sunlight break through the clouds turning water drops into diamonds. I've already gone farther than I am supposed to go alone, but I keep going.

I reach the log bridge that crosses the river to the yicil grove on the other side and rush over. Am I the guilty returning to the scene of the crime? No, I am not guilty. I didn't force Selyzar to do anything. I pause to catch my breath and check my sobs. Life is so unfair.

The big bluish brown trees tower overhead, their trunks too big for me to put my arms around them. The interlocking canopies of the trees block out the sky allowing little light to reach the forest floor. I can hear scuffling sounds in the high branches above, but the thick foliage prevents me from seeing the source of the noise.

Immersed as I am in self-pity, it takes me some time to notice a tiny sound close by on the ground. The little long haired creature, the same dark lavender color as the soil, is hard to see at first. Searching the ground, I finally spot it. A pykee! It could just as easily be a clump of moss except it is moving.

A pykee is so small it can fit inside a drinking cup with room to roam around. It was Thayla who gave the pykee and the yicil trees their names, naming them after similar life forms on her native world. A tiny little head and four tiny little feet with claws scratch, nibble and tumble around with something golden bright. The shiny object holds the pykee's attention. It wrestles with the little stone probably trying to pick it up. Maybe I can sneak up on it and catch it while it's not looking.

A pykee can dash up a yicil tree and out of sight faster than the speed of light. Well, maybe not that fast, but almost. Probably the only reason it hasn't bolted yet is its involvement with the stone.

I stealthily take a step forward and pause. Very good. It's still here, still struggling with the stone. As quietly and slowly as I can, I attempt another step. I barely move and make no sound, but instantly the pykee is gone. All that remains is the stone.

I stomp my feet grumbling with disappointment. "Come back here," I shout up into the tree. "I'm not going to hurt you." Frustrated I reach for the little golden stone on the ground to throw at it. Not that I'm likely to hit it. But I stop. There is something familiar about the look and feel of the stone. I examine it closely. The stone is as round and golden as the star Seaa.

"Why, this is a star stone," I gasp in disbelief. Rubbing the smooth, golden stone between my fingers, I marvel over such a find. I have a star stone!

For the longest, all I can do is stare at it. Dad says in Mainland people have varying abilities and talents for mentally drawing energy from the elemental forces and they don't even need a star stone to do it. But on Lynnara the land of crystals prevents us from being able to do it here without a star stone.

How can I test the star stone to see if it works? Do I have any talents or abilities? Mother uses her star stone for healing. Should I cut myself and see if I can heal the wound. No, I don't think so.

Maybe I can teleport from one place to another. I better start small. I'll try to teleport to that tree. It's only a couple of arm lengths away. Now how do I do that?

I stare hard at the spot where I want to be, squeezing the star stone in my hand. *Take me there, take me there,* I whisper over and over in my head.

Nothing happens.

I try it again, this time with my eyes shut, picturing the spot where I want to be in my mind. I concentrate hard, willing myself there, but when I open my eyes I am still standing on the same spot.

Maybe it isn't a star stone after all. What a disappointment! Anyway, I stash the stone in my tunic pocket just in case and reluctantly head back. I need to get back before anyone notices I'm gone. There is no point adding trouble upon trouble.

With some relief I once again reach the edge of the village. The sun, having burned through the mist, is out in full force again. When I reach Halren's house, he and Theon are outdoors playing ball.

"Mother is looking for you," Theon announced as I approach. "Where have you been?"

"Out walking."

I CAN READ HIS THOUGHTS! I really can.

He relishes the idea of me being in trouble for running out without doing my chores. Other than that, there isn't a serious thought in his head. Halren is thinking about his plans for building a model of the new schoolhouse.

I CAN READ THEIR THOUGHTS!

"Are you sure you're alright?" Halren asked. "You look like you just saw the dead walking."

I need to learn to better control my reactions. I can read Halren's genuine concern for me. Cousins are much better than brothers.

"Yes, I'm great," I reassured them, erasing the astonishment off my face. "Well, I better go and see what Mother wants." I need to be alone for a moment to think about this. I can tell what people are thinking.

I feel stronger, more confident in myself as I approach the house. The ability to read minds gives me a sense of power. Arriving home, I find Zaloka and Mother working together in the kitchen. "Hi, Aurora," Zaloka greeted. "Want to help?"

"Sure."

"Wash your hands first," Mother said. I don't detect any lingering anger from Mother, just contentment and enjoyable comradery. All seems to be forgiven. That's good. It's strange though, I can't pick up anything from Zaloka. I would love to ask questions about star stones and drawing from the elemental forces, but of course I don't dare.

After washing and drying my hands I join Zaloka and Mother in mixing the ground nuts, nut oil, toasted grains and dried fruit used to make the nutrition bars for the expedition. Then we roll out the mix and cut it into bars before carrying them to the village ovens to bake.

While I work, I think about the star stone, keeping a blank expression on my face. I don't need Mother asking me what I'm grinning about. Yet, I can't resist from time to time feeling the stone through the fabric of my tunic pocket, to reassure myself it is still there.

CHAPTER 10

Anthya

Relieved from the duty of taking care of the Twakans, Quaylyn and I plan for the whole team to meet after a period of rest before teleporting to Twala. There is much to do before we can leave, but first I need to bring Melinda into the group. Sending out a mental search, I locate her signature waiting for me on the Academy balcony overlooking the Golden Sea.

"That was pretty good fighting," Melinda said referring to my battle with the princess earlier at the gymnasium.

"Thank you. I didn't make the princess very happy." Melinda smiles at that. I relate all that transpired at the High Council meeting, except the part about her being part of the adventure.

"What do you think of the High Council's decision to grant Rojaire and his followers a charter after all?" Melinda asked.

"I have to admit I was surprised, but I gather from testimonies made at the meeting, concepts and beliefs can change after all, however slowly."

"Will Lozar and Xanthe honor Thayla's right to free choice?"

"I seriously doubt it. I have some important news for you."

"Oh, what is it?"

"The High Council has decided you will join the expedition to Lynnara to search for the colonists."

Melinda jerks in surprise. "What?" I know this expedition is very important to her. Ilene and Kaylya were Melinda's friends back on Earth. She wants to find out what happened to them and fears for their safety. "I'll be able to take Ilene her flute," she suddenly realized."

"We leave for Twala after a period of rest to locate a couple of boats to make the voyage. Be ready with your pack, we aren't likely to return here."

"It's been a long time since I've been on a boat," she said longingly. Melinda grew up in Southeast Alaska, mountainous country that hugs the coast. Her father was a fisherman and she has worked as a deckhand.

After the period of rest, we are all called to meet at the Academy. Quaylyn, Kaydra, back from Twaka, Melinda and I wait to meet and greet the Twakans as they arrive escorted by guards.

To facilitate the project, the Academy has provided us with the large airy meeting room with three arches in the eastern wall opened to a balcony overlooking the Golden Sea. Princess Xanthe and her warriors are the first to arrive. "Greetings, Princess Xanthe. How may I serve?" Quaylyn asked formally. We decided beforehand Quaylyn should do the formal greetings after my tangle with Xanthe.

"Greetings to you too, Councilor Quaylyn. I don't need anything right now."

"Greetings, Warrior Arpen and Warrior Rabiam," Quaylyn addressed the Twakans accompanying the princess. They both smile and nod in acknowledgement.

Xanthe notices Kaydra's presence, but doesn't make an issue of it. She also makes a concerted effort to avoid eye contact with me as she passes by. Then Prince Lozar arrives with Glisa and Yanzic.

"Greetings, Prince Lozar. How may I serve?"

"Greetings, Councilor Quaylyn. It is my honor to serve." The prince responded catching on quick. Glisa and Yanzic also accept Quaylyn's greeting warmly. Demeanors seem to have improved. Maybe they were just tired before and needed rest.

There are ten of us all together. It's time for us to get to know each other better. We may be together for a long time. We sit on the silvery cushions arranged around a low polished white stone table, located in the center of the large open space. An ancient navigational chart is spread out on the low table before us.

Quaylyn chairs the meeting. "We are gathered here in peace and united purpose for a common good. The more we work together, the more likely we will be successful. Are there any questions before we begin our journey?"

Xanthe looks over the navigational chart. "Is there nothing between here and there?" she asked moving a finger from where we are, across the sea, to the island continent Lynnara.

"No. There are only two land masses on Aaia. Mainland is the largest comprising most of the western hemisphere. Lynnara, much smaller is located half way around the world with nothing in between.

"How long will it take to make the voyage from Mainland to this Lynnara?" Lozar asked also studying the chart.

By our calculations, using crystal as our power source, it will take about five rotations to reach it," Quaylyn said.

"What is that in Twakan days?" Xanthe demanded. "Your days are so painfully long." Xanthe shutters in a dramatic show of the discomfort our long Aaian days cause her.

"That would be twenty Twakan days," Quaylyn said gently.

"Are you certain nothing lies in between? An island or a reef?" Lozar asked casually.

"Nothing, as far as we know."

"So you don't know?" I can hear the disdain rise again in Lozar's voice.

"Unless something has changed since the ancients have sailed the oceans, no substantial land mass exists between Mainland and Lynnara."

"I see. So this voyage may include some unanticipated surprises," Xanthe said with appropriate, though strained, cordiality.

"Perhaps," Quaylyn agreed without argument. "To find out we first need boats," he said changing the subject. "Councilor Zilka, Proctor of the Southern Communities, will meet us at the portal when we are ready."

"When can we leave?" Xanthe asked.

"We can leave immediately."

As promised, Proctor Zilka meets us on the stone paved square overlooking the village and docks. Her thinning white hair flutters gently in the sea breeze off the water making the air feel decisively cooler. A man I haven't met is with her.

Long sturdy golden brown wooden wharfs stretch out over the deep bluish green water with golden brown wooden fishing boats bobbing at their tethers. The village rises from the rose and lavender rocky shore.

Behind the village, tall dense quenka forest covers the hilly landscape with their golden brown trunks and purple crowns. The docks, the boats and the people's shelters are all built from the wood of the quenka trees creating a warm visual harmony. The southern provinces' rocky peninsulas, deep inlets and tall dense woods contrast sharply with Mainland's flat east coast of long sandy beaches.

"Look at all the boats," Melinda whispered gazing out toward the docks.

"Does it remind you of home?" I asked. Melinda generally evades references to "home." As usual my question is ignored.

"Welcome to Twala," Zilka greeted gathering us up. "This is Captain Jocko. He's not only an excellent sea captain, he's also a master ship builder. He will be your guide and answer any questions you have about the fishing vessels in the region."

"That I will," Captain Jocko said jovially. Captain Jocko's tall muscular build makes him a giant among men. "Looking for a couple of boats for a long journey, I hear. Well, I'm sure we will find something that will work for you." I like the captain already.

"Captain Jocko will take you down to the docks. Later we will meet to discuss what you found," Zilka informed us before rushing off. I sense the proctor would prefer not spending a lot of time in our company.

"How far out to sea do the boats go?" Lozar asked as Captain Jocko led us down to the wharfs.

"The fishing grounds for kana are half a day's journey out. We have to pack the holds with ice to keep the fish from spoiling before we can bring them back to port."

"How big are the fish?" Melinda asked.

"Oh, big!" Captain Jocko exclaimed. "As big as you or me."

"Are they good eating?" Xanthe asked.

"That you will find out for yourself. The proctor has a dinner planned for you after the boat tour. I'm sure kana will be included."

"How do you fish them? Net or line?" Melinda wanted to know.

Captain Jocko laughed heartily. "Well now, looks like we have a fisher here. Neither," he said. "We harpoon them."

CHAPTER 11

Quaylyn

Captain Jocko guides us down to the boat harbor, "Our ships are the sturdiest, best built boats anywhere. They are nearly unsinkable," he said speaking proudly of his boats. I like the sound of that. We head down the longest dock. Large boats and small are moored all along the dock with the smaller boats closer to shore. One must have come in recently, the crew is still busy scrubbing off the deck. I know little about boats and pause briefly to watch.

Captain Jocko continues to lead the group all the way to the end of the dock. I strive to catch up. "Now here are two fine ships," Captain Jocko said with heart felt praise. The two ships, their graceful beauty undeniable, sit majestically on each side of the dock. Flowing curves grace the boats from the high double bow to the delicately scrolled stern.

"Where are the masts and sails?" Lozar asked perturbed. Although we talked about how long it would take for a crystal powered boat to reach Lynnara, apparently it hadn't fully registered.

"They are not sailboats, Your Highness," Captain Jocko said proudly. "Our ships are equipped with crystal power technology. Come aboard and I will show you around."

The Twakan warriors wait on the dock while the rest of us follow Captain Jocko aboard, stepping over the bumper guards and jumping down onto the large aft deck. The dock is about level with the sides of the boat offering easy access at the moment. I don't know if the tide is rising or falling.

I look around while adjusting to the feel of movement. The wind has definitely picked up since our arrival. A low cabin, recessed into the hold of the boat, takes up much of the forward deck space with only walking paths on the starboard and port sides, graced with low spindled railing. A wheelhouse attached to the front of the cabin overlooks the bow.

Behind the wheelhouse, a tiny galley and a sleeping area with four bunks crowd into the rest of the space. Lozar insists that only four bunks are needed because someone will always be on wheel watch. The crystal powered drive system runs through the lower part of the hull.

There is a short mast attached to the rear of the cabin with a ladder leading up to a lookout platform. It must be used to spot the large kana that often swim near the surface. Hatches on the aft deck open to a large fish hold below.

"It smells like dead fish. What else have you got?" Xanthe asked crinkling up her nose.

"These are the best boats in the fleet, my princess," Captain Jocko said, a bit of the joviality loss in his voice.

The hairs stand up on the back of Xanthe's neck. "I am not your princess," she snapped back.

"No, Your Highness," the captain said with an apologetic bow.

"I want to see the other boat. Hopefully, it's better than this one."

"Yes, Your Highness. Let's hope so."

Kaydra, Melinda, Anthya and I remain aboard the first ship while Captain Jocko escorts Lozar and Xanthe to the other boat. "This is going to be some journey," Kaydra sighed when they were gone. Her dark animated eyes twinkle with amusement. "I wouldn't want to miss this." Kaydra's golden brown tanned skin and sun-bleached auburn hair attest to her love for sunshine.

Melinda is infatuated with the boat. "Isn't she beautiful?" Melinda exclaimed, practically jumping with joy over being on a boat again. I've never seen Melinda so spiritly alive before. I remember her on Earth, a demure young girl freshly rescued from Droclum by Rahlys, and later as a teenager devoting much of her time keeping little Leaf out of trouble. That wasn't so long ago, and now she is a woman stepping out of her shell. It seems like every visitor from Earth ends up going to Lynnara.

I continue to ponder on Lozar and Xanthe's true intentions. There seems to be more conflict than unity between them. Lozar is definitely easier to deal with than the fire spitting princess.

Before long Captain Jocko returns and signals us from the dock. "She chose the other boat," he shouted down over the wind. We climb back up to the dock to rejoin the others.

"I guess we should pick our crews," Xanthe said when we are back together. "I will have my personal warriors Arpen and Rabiam." Of course it's the rest of us she is referring to. "I'll take Quaylyn and Kaydra."

I find it strange Xanthe choses Kaydra and me since she despises us both. However, I did detect a condescending murmur about not having a pale ghost and a backwards Earthen on her boat. I have no doubt Anthya and Melinda are relieved by Xanthe's rejection.

"Do the boats have names?" Melinda asked.

"Names? Why do boats need names? They can't talk," Captain Jocko said confused.

"Where I come from people name their boats."

"I will name my boat the *Xanthe Queen*," Princess Xanthe announced immediately. "I require the name be painted on the bow immediately," she directed Captain Jocko.

Prince Lozar surprises us all by naming his ship the *Princess Thayla* after the sister he seeks. Not surprisingly, Yanzic and Glisa join his crew and Lozar doesn't seem to mind at all having Anthya and Melinda on board.

"If you will follow me, Proctor Zilka would like us to join her for dinner," Captain Jocko announced. He leads us back into the village and down a major avenue to a long boarding house used by crews who come to harvest trees from the forest. A large wooden table, capable of seating all of us, is already set.

The dinner with Proctor Zilka is a strained affair at best. Zilka had been adamantly against the colonists from the start. Her offer of help now is bound to her duty to the High Council, not out of concern for the ones we seek.

"Is all in order with the ships?" Zilka asked politely.

"No, everything is not in order," Xanthe piped up. "I require the hold of the *Xanthe Queen* be divided into private quarters for me and storage space for supplies for the expedition. And I require porthole windows in my cabin." Lozar gives her a hard, stern look.

"Is there anything else you require?" the proctor asked haughtily.

"That will do for now," Xanthe said backing off.

"We will do what we can."

It helps that Captain Jocko also attends the dinner, he's so much easier to converse with. Melinda has lots of questions about boats. "What do you use to preserve the wood?" Melinda asked. It's not a question I would have thought to ask.

"Quenka is naturally resistant to rot, but for added protection we make a preservative from the tree's sap."

"Who owns the boats?" Lozar asked.

"Well, I do, but ultimately they belong to the High Council."

"Who built them?" Lozar asked.

"I did," the captain confirmed. "With a crew, of course."

"So will you be compensated for them? What will you do for a fishing boat?" I'm surprised by Lozar's concern.

"The High Council provides all I need."

"What about joining us on the expedition?" I asked.

Jocko shakes his head. "I remember Rojaire and Kaylya coming to Twala looking for volunteers to become colonists to Lynnara. I said then and I say now, it's a fool's mission. Why would anyone want to return to the source of so much evil?"

"The land itself isn't evil. Droclum was evil and he's been destroyed. As to why they would go, maybe they wanted freedom to control their own lives."

"Strange speech for a member of the High Council, Councilor Quaylyn," Zilka said pointedly. I ignore the comment and instead offer thanks for all she has provided.

"The food is delicious, especially the kana. We are grateful for your kind generosity. The ships you have provided are excellent and will serve us well on our mission. The High Council will be pleased."

"Your gratitude has been noted. Now, if you will excuse me I have work to do." I believe we are all glad to see her go.

We are offered lodging in the boarding house until the ships are ready. The Twakans elect to stay on the water. The rest of us are each given a plain room with a bed, table and chair. With time on our hands, Anthya, Kaydra and Melinda go on a walking tour of the village. I teleport to the deck of the *Princess Thayla*.

As I walk along the port side, Lozar steps out the wheelhouse. "Greetings, Prince Lozar."

"Councilor Quaylyn, welcome aboard. You may call me Lozar."

"I would be honored if you would call me Quaylyn." Lozar nods in agreement. "Are you busy?" I asked casually.

"No, not especially." Lozar glances around. I sense a concern over being spied on by Xanthe. Does the princess always suspect conspiracy against her, even from her brother? The Twakan prince and I have made some progress in civility toward one another. I can't say the same about his sister.

"Well, I brought with me an elixir, highly acclaimed around here. I thought we could share it."

"Would you join me in the galley?"

"Or we could sit out here," I offered.

"The galley," he decided. "It will offer more privacy."

"Very well." I follow Lozar to the stern deck. The door to the galley is already hooked open. We descend two steps down to the galley floor and take our seats at the highly polished built in table.

"Captain Jocko and his crew do nice work," I said admiring the table and all the interior work of the cabin. "I'm impressed." I bring out the flask and two collapsible cups.

"I agree, the *Xanthe Queen* and the *Princess Thayla* are beautiful ships. If they sail as well as they look it should be a good voyage."

I pour out two drinks. "They certainly put Captain Setas' ferry boat to shame."

Lozar sniffs the emerald liquid. "What is this?"

"It's a very special drink made here in Twala. Captain Jocko helped me procure it."

He takes a cautionary sip, smiles, and then downs the rest of the cup's contents. "Tell me more about this Captain Setas. Her name kept coming up at the Crystal Table."

"Sure." I pour the rest of the liquor into Lozar's cup and take a sip from my own. "After the Dark Devastation, a millennia of cycles of seasons passed before the newly established High Council and Academy showed any interest in Lynnara. To understand one must remember, the Dark Devastation nearly destroyed our world. Few people survived. Certainly no ships survived. Nothing was left standing." Lozar is drinking slower after the first cup.

"After the Dark Devastation, it was no longer possible to teleport to Lynnara; at the time no one understood why. Now we know it is because of the formation of the Crystalline Landscape in the center of the continent."

"Have you seen this Crystalline Landscape I've heard so much about?"

"Yes, it is an incredible sight. If you feel you can trust me, I can telepath images of it to you." Lozar hesitates. It is obvious he is wary of the suggestion.

"I trust you," he said finally.

I can sense Lozar's wonder as he gazes in his mind upon a towering, jumbled landscape of crystals as far as the eye could see. "I would like to see this Crystalline Landscape for myself."

"Maybe one day you will." We both sip our drinks and I continue the story. The High Council may never have reached Lynnara if it weren't for Captain Setas. A survivor of the Dark Devastation, she once lived on a small island some distance away from Lynnara's shore. She claimed to have lived on a small island some distance away from Lynnara before the Dark Devastation. To everyone's amazement, when she attempted to teleport back to Alaia Island, she succeeded."

"A millennia later?" Lozar gasped at the reminder of the Aaians' long lifespans.

"Captain Setas decided to stay and over time transformed the island into a garden paradise. With the help of the Academy, a crystal powered ferry boat was built and Lynnara was finally reached. Captain Setas was appointed the guardian of access to the Devastated Continent, controlled by the High Council. But somehow Rojaire bribed Captain Setas for access. He spent decades of cycles of seasons exploring the continent without the High Council's permission."

"I see. And this is the same Rojaire that led the colonists to defect?"
"Yes."

"Rojaire is a brave warrior for defying the High Council."

"You could say that, or he is criminally foolish."

"What is your opinion?" Lozar asked.

"Between you and me, I tend to side with 'brave warrior.'"

CHAPTER 12

Lozar

Soon after Quaylyn leaves, a work crew arrives on the dock with lumber and tools. They must have teleported here, the dock was empty a moment ago. I still find teleportation a bit unsettling, but I guess I better get used to it for now. One of the shipbuilders jumps down to the deck of the *Princess Thayla* with a thump. I step out the galley to meet him. Glisa and Yanzic quickly appear beside me.

"We are here to remodel the fish hold, Sir," he announced.

"You have the wrong ship," I informed him. "Try the one across the dock."

"We have orders to remodel both ships, Sir. Do you have any special requests?"

"I don't need a private cabin." The builder opens the deck hatches and we stare down into the large fish hold, space not designed for our purpose. "We could use more living space," I conceded. "But how would we access it?"

"Leave that to us, Sir. How would you like the space divided?"

"Instead of a stateroom, could you put in a couple of private bunks? The rest of the space will be needed for the storage of supplies for a long voyage."

"Yes, Sir."

"You have my appreciation." The private bunks will be for Melinda and Anthya. That will give them some space. Yanzic, Glisa and I will have the existing bunks. I hear an uproar over the moan of the wind. I better check it out. "Give them a hand," I tell Yanzic indicating the work crew and climb the ladder up to the dock. The tide has dropped, it's a long climb.

Of course, Xanthe is at the heart of the commotion.

"What's the problem here?" I dare to ask.

"These shipbuilders," she said scornfully, "are trying to tell me how to remodel the fish hold!"

"They're shipbuilders, perhaps they know best," I said gently.

Captain Jocko comes to my rescue, appearing suddenly. "Greetings my friends. I thought we would take a boat ride to introduce you to crystal-powered technology."

"I would like that," I said immediately, eager to test drive one of these ships and get away from here.

"I don't need anyone telling me how to drive a boat," Xanthe said. "You go ahead, I'll stay here."

Captain Jocko wisely decides not to argue. "If you are amendable, Prince Lozar, I could teleport us to the ship we will take since these are being worked on."

I nod and quickly find myself on the deck of another ship, two docks away from the *Princess Thayla* and *Xanthe Queen*. Quaylyn, Anthya, Kaydra and Melinda are already here. This boat is built along much the same lines as the others, just a bit smaller.

"Well, if someone will tend to the bow and stern lines, I'll ease us out the harbor," Captain Jocko said stepping up to the wheelhouse. I step up to the bow and to my surprise, Melinda grabs ahold of the tie-off line at the stern. Captain Jocko starts up the engine. It is so quiet, I can barely hear it running over the slap of choppy water against the boat's hull. "Untie us," he shouted from the open door of the wheelhouse. Melinda and I work in unison and as soon as I indicate we are free, Captain Jocko pulls away from the dock. I quickly join the captain in the wheelhouse.

"Yes, come on in. It's choppy in here in the harbor. I'll take us around the point where we should find smoother water. Then I'll give you the wheel."

"So where is the power source?" I ask.

"In here," he said tapping a lit panel. "I'll show you all that later. Here is the throttle. To pick up speed you push the lever up like this." Captain

Jocko demonstrates by slowly throttling up. The ratio in increased speed per incremental adjustment of the lever is phenomenal. Then he settles on a speed that greatly smooths out the ride.

I look over to see Melinda standing in the doorway. "Come on in, Fisher Melinda," Captain Jocko invited. She doesn't hesitate, taking up a position before the console looking out. We quickly make it around the point and into calmer water, protected by the land mass.

Captain Jocko throttles down then steps away from the wheel. "Okay, Prince Lozar, you first."

Like a child with a new toy, I eagerly take the wheel. "Easy now," the captain cautioned. Following his advice, I ease the throttle up. The boat picks up speed and I grab the wheel to steer. I quickly become comfortable with the power. I reach over and increase the speed some more. The boat is so easy to steer, I have to be careful not to oversteer.

"How fast can it go?" I asked.

"A lot faster than this."

"Is it alright if I take it up a notch?"

"Yes, go ahead."

I do just that. Soon we are racing across the sound. Piloting this crystal-powered boat surpasses anything I have experienced before, its maneuverability is superb. I don't understand this crystal technology, but I respect it.

Soon the rest of the group shows up to see what is going on. "Alright, let's give Fisher Melinda a try," Captain Jocko said. I slowly throttle down and surrender the wheel to Melinda. She takes it like a pro. It quickly becomes obvious she is very comfortable driving a boat. I need to take her experience into account on the journey. Quaylyn, Anthya and Kaydra also take a turn, quickly showing their lack of experience. Captain Jocko takes the time to instruct them just the same.

The captain points out the panel display indicating the power level and shows us how to change out the crystal packs and recharge them. "Now let's head out into some rougher seas so you can get a feel for how the boat handles the waves. "Take her out, Prince."

"You can call me Lozar." I take the wheel and head out quartering the oncoming waves. The ship handles beautifully. "How rough a sea can she take?" I asked.

"She can handle most anything, if her captain is experienced."

I choose not to comment. Only Melinda wants to take a turn piloting the boat in the rougher water. Once again she proves her ability. The long Aaian day is finally waning when Captain Jocko gives me the wheel once again. "Take her home, Lozar."

I do so with ease. The wind is dying down and the sun is setting by the time we arrive back in port. Captain Jocko has me dock behind the *Princess Thayla*. He and Melinda secure the lines and I shut off the engine.

The *Princess Thayla* has changed. We all notice it. I jump up to the dock, the tide has come back in, and stare in wonder at the *Princess Thayla*. Except for walking space along the sides, most of the deck is covered with a low transparent roof, opened at the sides except at the corners where it is fastened to the deck, offering protection from sun and rain. Along one side of the canopy, a sloping wall and railing descends down to the newly built deck below.

I jump aboard to have a closer look. Glisa and Yanzic come out from below deck to meet me. "What is it like down there?"

"Have a look," Glisa said moving out the way.

Gripping a handrail, I step down into a well-designed storage area. Large storage bins are built into the wall opposite the stairs. A trap door in the floor offers access to the bilge. The center aisle continues to a tiny cabin with a bunk on each side. The sleeping spaces, complete with small porthole windows, can be closed off with a curtain. At the end of the aisle a ladder leads up to a trapdoor above for an emergency exit.

It is incredible work, completed incredibly fast. The smell of new wood permeates the area. On the way back through, I notice some of the storage bins are already stocked. My crew is waiting expectantly for my reaction when I emerge again.

"Your bunks are down below," I tell Anthya and Melinda. Go take a look."

I can't help but wonder about the *Xanthe Queen* and Princess Xanthe too. Crossing the dock, I see similar roofing protecting the aft deck. "She's down in the captain's quarters," Rabiam announced without me asking. "Quaylyn and Kaydra went with Captain Jocko." I descend the stairs.

"Where have you been?" Xanthe blurted out as soon as my foot touches the lower deck. "We should leave now," she announced without warning. "We have ships and we have supplies. I took care of that while you were out joy riding. We don't need the Aaians, and we certainly don't need the Earthen."

"What? Are you out of your mind?"

"I advise you not to speak that way to me."

I tone it down. "We have treaties with these people. You cannot violate treaties without reason or provocation."

"I care nothing for treaties. We have a right to rescue our sister."

"Is that what you want to do, Xanthe, rescue Thayla? The High Council granted Thayla the right of free choice."

"With my sword I deny Thayla free choice. You have allowed these people to soften your brain, Lozar," Xanthe spitted out with disdain.

"And you have allowed your heart to turn to stone," I retorted. Before I say more than I should, I leave the *Xanthe Queen*. Xanthe doesn't try to stop me. If I had any doubt before of her devious goal, I have no doubt now. I will watch her closely.

CHAPTER 13

Ilene

The whole community is solemnly gathered in the community circle to watch Rojaire, Thayla, and Traevus depart from us for a long time. The departure is especially hard for Kaylya and Rojaire and their two children. It is heartbreaking to see Jack and Setas cling to Rojaire as long as they can. At last the three explorers depart; twenty faces stare at their backs until they are swallowed up by the forest. Slowly, individuals break from the whole to return to their productive lives.

Many of us have developed an interest in some craft. Ollen, no longer able to do hard physical labor, has become our master weaver. It takes a tremendous effort to keep everyone in the village clothed, so we all help. Caleeza is a dedicated herbalist, cultivating a wide variety of medicinal plants in her herbal garden. In her spare time she spins thread from the silky white fibers found in peago pods. That on top of raising four children.

Kiril is the village chronicler and I bake most of the community's bread, but we also make paper, another commodity in great demand. Leave it to Caleeza to make the discovery. After extracting the fibers, she didn't want to throw away the pearly white, papery peago pods themselves, so she tried soaking them in water and then pressing the pulp. The experiment resulted in a fine creamy white paper. Thanks to Inventor Sulyan, the tools for paper production have greatly improved.

Edty is a wood cutter and toy maker. Tassyn has learned forging from Thayla. All the women and some of the men help with the sewing.

All of us are teachers; all of us are laborers. Each of us teaches either a subject or a skill. There is work to do; there is no time to pout.

I decide to work with the younger group of children. "I'll take Jack, Setas, Caponya and Alaia for an English lesson," I said getting their attention. "What do you say we have class at the pavilion, shall we?"

"Yes, yes," Alaia said dancing with delight. The children love going to the pavilion and the waterfall nearby. Jack is reluctant to leave his mother after watching his father walk away, but Kaylya knows he needs a distraction and urges him on. Setas and Alaia are always willing to hang out together. It will be hard keeping the children's attention after the earlier dramatic event, but I have to try and engage them.

"Well, I'll take the older group," Drak said. I think we will do some woodworking."

"Alright!" Halren said. Woodworking is his favorite activity and he reigns as Drak's star apprentice. Aurora, Theon and Selyzar are more reluctant, but they follow Drak to his workshop.

With little Sarus in hand, Caleeza turns to head home. "Come, little one, we're going to practice drawing our letters and numbers."

"I need to get back to weaving," Ollen said following her.

I gather up my group and lead them down the west trail from the center of the village west to the foot of the Crescent Mountains. On Earth we often referred to "purple mountains" as they appeared in the distance, but here the mountains are indeed purple, composed of dark purple and blue-violet rock that erodes into dark purple soil and lavender beaches.

"Are you going to tell us a story?" Alaia wanted to know. Alaia, is named for Captain Setas' garden island.

"It's a good day for a story, isn't it?" I agreed. The children love the classic stories I recall from my own childhood. Sometimes I have to adapt the stories to life in the valley, but they are a great tool for teaching English.

"Can we pick flowers?" Caponya asked when we pass by a patch of blue, white and green wildflowers. Caponya is named for a lost member of the exploratory expedition Caleeza and Ollen were once part of. Their son, Selyzar, is also named for a vanished explorer. They named their youngest son, Sarus, the last born in the village, after the expedition leader.

"We'll pick flowers on the way back," I promised.

"I don't want to pick flowers," Jack grumbled. Jack looks so much like Rojaire, same blue-green eyes and wavy dark hair. I know his namesake back on Earth. Jack Faulkner would be so pleased to know Kaylya named her son after him.

"You can look out for bear beasts while we pick flowers," I suggested.

The pavilion, as we have come to know it, is a large flat lavender rock formation, about 15 feet long and 12 feet wide. At the back of the pavilion, recessed into the mountain, is a partially collapsed cavern that served as a shelter for the first colonists before the big ground shake struck. Off to the right, a long thin waterfall flows down the mountainside about thirty feet away. The runoff stream flows east toward the river and forms the northern boundary of our little community.

The children become excited as the sound of the waterfall grows louder. Breaking out of the forest, they run toward the low stone pavilion, clambering up the broad naturally eroded "steps" to the flat stone deck.

After running up and down the pavilion a couple of times, the children run off to the waterfall. They need to expend some energy. The view between the pavilion and the waterfall is open, only grass and low shrubbery grows close to the mountain, the soil too rocky for large trees. As I step up to the pavilion, it strikes me how similar it is to a stage.

A stage! What an outrageous idea!

I could have the children put on a play. Setas, Alaia, Jack and Caponya are approximately six to nine years old in Earth-years, and somewhat dominated over by the four older children. They are fifth, sixth, seventh and eighth born, which according to Aurora, is low on the totem pole so to speak. Perhaps I can provide them with an opportunity to shine.

After giving the children a few moments to throw stones in the creek, I call them back to the pavilion. "How would you like to put on a play?" I asked after getting them settled down.

"What is a play?" Alaia asked. Both Alaia and Caponya have Caleeza's red-orange hair and violet eyes, but Alaia's hair is straight while Caponya's is a mass of curls.

"Well, it's like when we tell stories at the fire ring, except we will bring the story to life by acting it out. We could do the story of *The Three Little Kurpers*." Long ago, having no pigs or wolves in the valley, I adapted the story of *The Three Little Pigs* by changing pigs to kurpers and replacing the big bad wolf with a bear beast.

The bear beast is a misnamed reptilian creature, not resembling a bear at all. It was named originally by Edty. The name was based on the tracks it made and stories told by my father of bears in Alaska before anyone actually saw a bear beast. Nevertheless, the name stuck. Kurpers on the other hand, the silvery little hoofed grazers that feed on the valley's grasslands, actually resemble little pigs in appearance.

"I want to be the bear beast," Jack announced catching on fast.

"We will be the three little kurpers," Alaia said with glee.

"Why can't we be three little girls instead of kurpers?" Setas asked displaying her sophistication. Setas has Kaylya's thick auburn hair and golden eyes.

"Yes," Caponya agreed easily swayed. "I want to be a little girl."

"No reason, in fact, that's an excellent idea, *The Three Little Girls* it is."

"I'm still the bear beast," Jack said holding his ground, his spirit lifted for now. Time passes quickly as we share ideas about staging and props.

On the way back, we pick flowers for Jack and Setas to take to Kaylya, and for Alaia and Caponya to take to Caleeza. While we pick flowers, Jack decides to hide. Then he growls and threatens to attack the girls. They will have none of it.

"How can you protect us from bear beasts if you are a bear beast?" Setas asked her little brother.

"I can do both," Jack growled.

"No, you can't."

It has been a good outing. We return to the center of the community filled with excitement.

CHAPTER 14

Rojaire

Parting from the community is hard, but finally we are on our way. I don't want to think about how long it may be before I see Kaylya and the children again.

We quickly find our rhythm as we cross the waterfall stream and follow well established trails for the first few leagues of our journey. Tinsel trees and pocako trees dominate this part of the forest. The tall straight tinsel trees tinkle softly as their long curled green and violet leaves twirl against each other in the gentle breeze. The pocako trees provide the best shade. The tree's reddish brown mottled trunk fans out at the top into a wide thick canopy of blue and gold leaves, making the tree look like a giant mushroom. In season, the tree produces a tiny sweet brown nut. Between the trees, flowering bushes and aromatic herbs fill in the underbrush. Much of the flora of the valley remains unnamed.

We push hard to cover familiar ground quickly. By the time we approach the grasslands, the sun is arching high off the eastern mountains. The forest begins to thin and greenish yellow peago bushes take advantage of the sunlight, growing along the edge of the forest until grassland takes over. The bushes are loaded with the valuable fiber-filled creamy white pods we use to spin thread. The pods themselves we use to make paper. Kiril will be leading a team to pick these soon.

We take a brief rest while we have shade. The rush of the river, still swollen from the recent rains, can be heard off to our right. Across the river, some distance away, the northern tip of the plateau shimmers in the bright sunlight. A sea of shoulder high blue-green grass stretches out before us.

Before long we press on, determined to cross the grassland before taking a longer rest. As usual Thayla leads the way. "I'm the only one properly armed," she explained.

"We have the knives you made for us," Traevus pointed out.

"It is my job to protect you. I wouldn't want anything to happen to my little one." It is a well-known fact Traevus dotes on Thayla and she teases him mercilessly.

We startle a herd of kurpers, sending them scurrying through the tall grass, unseen except for the shivering grass and a few low squeals. The fat little silver creatures are our source of meat for those willing to partake. We render the fat to use in cooking and baking and for the oil to fill our lamps. The valley is wide here, the mountains east and west have receded into the distance.

The trek through the grassland seems endless.

Finally we reach the first trees again as we approach the ford in the river. The forest quickly thickens. I feel as though we are being watched, but when I look around I don't see anything. The feeling persists and I pause again. This time I think I glimpse movement through the brush. Thayla, who misses nothing, silently slips away.

"Where is Thayla going?" Traevus asked.

"I thought I saw something lurking among the trees," I said putting Traevus on alert. "Thayla must have seen it too, she's checking it out."

Traevus and I arrive at the river ford. Here, the river fans out into a braided stream that can easily be walked across. The broad opening offers a refreshing breeze after the hot, stifling woods. We will take a much needed rest here.

I approach the river, throwing cool river water on my face and the back of my neck. It feels soothingly cool and refreshing. A short distance away Traevus does the same.

"What kind of tracks are these?" Traevus asked locating strange prints in the soft river sand. "They look fresh, still wet from the river."

I hurry over to take a look. "There must be two of them, whatever they are. The tracks are different sizes." Traevus and I switch from on alert to high alert.

"I can't tell if they're four-legged or two-legged, or both," Traevus observed.

Then Thayla steps back out into the clearing herding two small creatures, standing upright, at sword point. I can hardly believe what I am seeing. Two small humanoid like figures, covered in brownish orange downy feathers, cower in fear before us. One is somewhat taller and obviously older than the other. They only reach Thayla's knees in height. The older one is wearing an ancient looking crystal floss sash across one shoulder cinched at the waist and an equally ancient looking medallion around her neck. Tiny feathers outline the exposed brown flesh of their foreheads and cheeks. Round dark violet eyes, and a little crinkled nose detract some from their humanoid appearance. Then I notice the palms of their little clawed hands are padded, but they don't look armed or dangerous.

"Thayla, I think you can put your weapon away now."

Thayla does so. "Should I dress them out for dinner?" Thayla asked jokingly. At least I hope she is joking.

"Greetings, Chitter and companion, how may I serve?" I greeted the visitors. Traevus' face lights up with sudden comprehension.

"You think this is the creature Caleeza met? I thought there was only one of them. Where did the other one come from?" Traevus asked. Where did they both come from? I wonder.

"Please, don't be afraid, we will not hurt you," I continued. "I am Rojaire and these are my friends Traevus and Thayla," I said pointing them out.

Chitter responds, at least I think it's Chitter with a long string of incomprehensive chittering chatter.

"You know this creature?" Thayla asked astonished.

"I know of her. Caleeza claims she visited Chitter in her valley before we arrived back from Mainland. I always thought her tale was just a feverish dream."

"Maybe we're dreaming," Traevus suggested.

There is more chittering and I think I hear Caleeza's name.

"Did you say Caleeza?" I asked. "Caleeza?"

"Caleeza," Chitter chittered quite clearly.

The Caleeza and Sarus story is a complex mystery. According to Caleeza, Sarus was somehow absorbed by the Crystalline Landscape and can actually control the forces within to transport people through space/time contingents. It was Sarus who found Caleeza on earth and transported her back to the Crystalline Landscape. When Caleeza traveled to Chitter's valley through a vanishing hole, it was Sarus who transported her back to our valley, or so she claims.

And if the Chitter part of Caleeza's story is true, does that mean that Sarus really has been absorbed by the Crystalline Landscape? Can Sarus actually control the forces in the Crystalline Landscape to transport people through space and time? How does one communicate with the Crystalline Landscape? These questions will definitely have to wait.

There are so many questions I want to ask Chitter. How did you get here? Where did you come from? Caleeza claimed she could communicate with Chitter. I don't see how.

"What do we do now?" Traevus asked.

"We have to go back. We can't just let these two arrive at the village without us accompanying them," I said stating the obvious. "We have to find out what is going on and if they are a threat to the community. It is another delay, but we have no choice."

"Do we get a chance to rest first?" Traevus asked. "It has been a long hike."

"We'll take a short break, maybe offer our guests something to eat."

Traevus pulls out a little sack of fruit and nuts from his pack and takes out a handful. "Want some?" he asked. He hands the little sack to the smaller chitter, then sits down on a log in the shade of a nearby tree. The little creature hesitates before opening the sack until Chitter nods her approval.

The rest of us pull nourishment from out packs and began to eat. It will be a long hike back to the village. Chitter tries again to communicate with us, but all we hear is chittering noise. Bracing ourselves for another long haul, we fill our water containers and prepare to leave.

"Let's go," Thayla said and again she leads the way. To our astonishment, Chitter and companion drop to all fours and lope after her, leaving Traevus and I to follow.

CHAPTER 15

Aurora

It seems like we have been working on these little wooden boxes forever. The boxes are just big enough to store a few little treasures. Only I don't have any little treasures. Well, I have one now, the star stone, but I'm not putting it in a box. Drak says today we will take our treasure boxes home with us. Good, I'm glad to be done with this project. Halren's box is so perfect with beautiful intricate carvings on the sides and lid. With the star stone I can sense Halren's pride in his work. He plans on giving it to his mother. She is going to love it.

My box is a different story. It didn't quite go together right from the start so the lid doesn't fit very well. I tried to carve my name in the lid, but it made it look even worse.

Theon and Selyzar's boxes look okay. I can read Theon's satisfaction with his work. He even managed to carve a couple of simple flowers on the lid.

Selyzar's finished piece is even better than Theon's. Still I can read his desire to do better.

I cannot read Drak's mind at all; nothing leaks out. It's the same for all the adults except Mother. Her mind is nearly as open as the children's. Is it because she is from Earth?

I really want to share my secret with someone; it's killing me keeping it to myself. But who can I trust to keep such an important secret? Certainly not my bratty brother. Halren? He's first born and so thoughtful and wise, he would probably want me to turn it in. Selyzar?

If I told Selyzar, he wouldn't be able to keep the star stone secret from Halren and Theon.

When Theon and I arrive home with our completed boxes, Mother is packing lunches for a community hike. I can read Mother's excitement over something about the younger children. I guess they had a good time at the pavilion. When Theon gives Mother his treasure box, her mind gushes with pride and pleasure. "Oh, thank you. It's lovely. I will treasure it always." I would have given her mine too, if it had come out better. Instead I spare her from pretending to treasure mine too.

"Don't go anywhere children. We will be leaving shortly to gather peago pods and yes, you are going," Father said counting a stack of gathering bags. "Have something to snack on before we go, it's a long hike."

"Who else is going?" I asked heaping jam on bread.

"Kaylya and the children, Zaloka, Wessid, Halren, and Caleeza is sending Selyzar."

Grabbing a handful of nuts, I take my box to my room and place it on the shelf by my bed. I spot the diamonds scattered on the shelf I collected from the cave at the plateau. I gather them up and drop them into the box, just to have something in it. Then I plop down on my bed and lay back, feet still on the floor, to think. Actually, I fall asleep.

"Aurora, let's go," Mother called. With great effort, I shake off the heavy drowsiness and rush out the door to join the group.

"Here's your gathering bag, Aurora," Father said handing me one. "What did you do, fall asleep?" Father asked noticing the puffiness around my eyes.

"For a little while," I admitted. Then Mother hands me my pack. I quickly overcome sleep drowsiness, springing alive to the occasion. I stuff my gathering bag into my pack and put it on. From a young age we are taught to carry our own food and water. It is a rite of maturity and a lesson in survival. Even Jack, the youngest in our group, seventh born, is wearing his little backpack.

With everyone ready, Father leads us to the waterfall stream where we fill our cylindrical gourd water containers corked with the soft pliable wood of the tuta tree. The water containers fit in a pouch sewed onto our packs.

Crossing the footbridge we are finally on our way to the peago bushes at the edge of the forest. There are eleven of us going, five adults and six children. As always, a group this large produces a merry outing. There is much chatter confusingly mixed with the fleeting thoughts and images I pick up from the children around me.

"We are going to do a play," Setas informed me with visions of kurpers and bear beasts in her head.

"What is your play called?" I asked.

"It's called *The Three Little Girls*. Alaia, Caponya and me are the three little girls," Setas said counting on her fingers, "and Jack is the bear beast."

"Who are the kurpers?" I asked.

"There aren't any kurpers."

See what I mean? Confusing. After a bit more chatter about the play, not all of it comprehensible, Setas skips off to join her mother.

Selyzar is really enjoying the hike after being kept indoors for so long. "We need to put together some tag ball teams," he said.

"We are a team," Theon said. "Who's going to play against us?" The boys discuss tag ball for a while, then Halren's thoughts turn to the schoolhouse.

"We're going to meet soon to make the final decision on the location of the new schoolhouse. I believe we should build it across the creek, opposite the giant nut tree grove. It would be close enough to everyone, we just need to build another bridge across the stream."

"That sounds like a good idea," Selyzar agreed. "It would be special being the first building on the other side."

"You should come to the meeting, Selyzar. We can argue the point together."

I can read Selyzar's reluctance, but he looks up to Halren and feels he can't refuse. "Yeah, sure," he said without enthusiasm.

"How about you, Theon? You want to come?"

"Who? Me? No thanks. Meetings are boring."

"Aurora?"

"Forget it."

The hike to the peago bushes is always longer than I think it will be. I spot a heart fruit tree a little off the trail with juicy ripe fruit hanging from its low branches. The boys and I rush off to pick the fruity hearts, then run to catch up with the others. I try to come up with a way to approach the topic of the star stone.

"Do you ever wonder what it would be like to live where you can teleport and communicate telepathically?" I ask casually nibbling on a sweet, red heart fruit.

"Not really," Selyzar said. No one else even bothers to respond and I can't detect any interest in the topic, so I say no more. Secretly, I reach into the pouch of my tunic and caress the star stone. During the rest of the hike, I try to imagine how Halren, Selyzar and Theon would react if they knew.

Finally, the woods begin to thin and the first peago bushes start to appear. The bushes are loaded. By now the sun has peaked and everyone is hot, tired and hungry. "A rest and a picnic before we start picking," Dad announced.

I'm more than glad to sit in the shade of a pocako tree. The boys plop down with me. We compare lunches and make food trades. All too soon, the adults are urging us up to get started. We make our way to the edge of the grassland where the bushes are plentiful, making the picking quicker and easier.

The dainty, yellow-green peago bushes are so loaded all I have to do is hold my bag under a bunch of the pretty creamy-white pods with one hand and pull off the palm-size pods from the delicate branches with the other. The pods detach easily. Despite the size of the pods, it takes a long time to fill a bag, because the pods pack down under their own weight. By the time the bags are full, they are surprisingly heavy.

I carry my bag to where I left my pack under the pocako tree. Before I can get my bag stuffed into my pack, I hear shouting. I hurry down the pathway to where all the commotion is taking place. When I break out of the trees, my jaw drops.

Rojaire, Traevus and Thayla have returned! And they brought with them two strange little people!

CHAPTER 16

Anthya

It has been challenging, but finally we are underway. Melinda, Glisa, Yanzic and I stand together on the aft deck and watch the shoreline recede as Captain Lozar steers us away from the dock. The sea is flat calm, not even a breeze rippling the surface. Seaa's light dances golden on the water. I didn't realize how much I looked forward to this voyage until now. Maybe I just want to get away from the High Council for a while. I have to admit I also feel a certain amount of apprehension, more than usual when facing the unknown. I'm not sure why.

From what we can see, it looks like Twaka's future queen is having difficulty handling the *Xanthe Queen*. We watch as the boat jerks forward, zigzags and stops suddenly. Yanzic goes to alert Lozar, but before he arrives, Lozar calls us to the wheelhouse.

"It looks like we have to go to the rescue of the *Xanthe Queen*," Lozar said already aware of the situation. From the tone of his voice, I'm not sure if he is referring to the boat or sarcastically referring to the princess.

"I can teleport you there," I offered.

Lozar gives my offer a brief moment's thought then looks over his crew. "Okay. Melinda, you have the wheel. The shock on Melinda's face is surpassed by Glisa and Yanzic's. I'm surprised too, but I see what he sees. Only Melinda has experience with power boats, regardless of the source of power.

Melinda quickly steps forward, "Aye, Captain."

I can teleport Lozar to the *Xanthe Queen* without accompanying him, but he doesn't know that. I want to be there. I take us directly into the wheelhouse, startling the princess in the process. Kaydra or Quaylyn could have offered her some guidance, but her crew is nowhere in sight. I suspect she has chased them away in a rage fueled by embarrassment.

"You should have come to the training session," Lozar admonished her right away.

"Who ever heard of a boat without sails," she grumbled. Captain Jocko convinced Lozar of crystal technology's superiority over sails, but not Xanthe.

I can detect the signatures of the absent crew members on the deck under the awning, so I join them, leaving Xanthe in Lozar's hands.

Arpen and Rabiam are startled to see me, but Kaydra and Quaylyn had detected our arrival. "I brought Prince Lozar over to give Princess Xanthe some guidance on running the boat," I told them. Kaydra translates and the Twakans nod their approval. Quaylyn or Kaydra could have helped Xanthe as calm as it is, they were on the training run, but Xanthe wants nothing to do with them.

Under Lozar's control the boat moves smoothly forward. We can tell when Xanthe takes over the controls, right away she presses too hard on the throttle. I'm sure there is some back and forth between them, but eventually Xanthe catches on and Lozar leaves the wheelhouse.

"We can go now," Lozar said. He tells Rabiam and Arpen something in Twakan. Kaydra translates telepathically.

Lozar told them to watch Xanthe carefully and make sure nothing happens to Quaylyn and me.

I take us back to the *Princess Thayla* and Lozar immediately calls for a meeting of the crew. "Here are the rules," Lozar states without ceremony. "First, everyone will learn to handle running the boat. In the event of an emergency, each and every one of you should be able to take the wheel. You will have wheel watch on a rotating basis, starting with Yanzic, followed by Glisa, then Melinda, Anthya and myself. I'll post a time schedule.

Second, when you are not on wheel watch, you are expected to take turns in the galley, as for scheduling, you can work that out amongst yourselves. You are also expected to help at any tasks necessary on deck when needed.

And finally, I am to be alerted to anything out of the ordinary, any and all incidences, regardless how minor, immediately. That includes waking me up if necessary." Lozar looks hard at each of us in turn. No one speaks. "Do I make myself clear?"

"Aye, Captain," we said in unison.

"Then everyone is dismissed except Yanzic."

Glisa, Melinda and I make our way to the roofed aft deck glad to be free. We sit on the bare deck enjoying the warm night and fresh sea air while Lozar instructs Yanzic on running the boat. As we watch, the *Xanthe Queen* catches up with us, and then passes us all together.

The wheelhouse door opens and Lozar steps out onto the deck, leaving Yanzic in control. Spotting us, he decides to join us. We stand as he approaches. "How strange, we can move so fast without wind," he said grinning slightly. Twakan faces rarely express pleasure. It's a shame because the smile looks good on him. Glisa and Melinda quietly slip away to the fore deck thinking to give us some privacy. They have it all wrong. I want to join them, but I stay.

I am struck again by Lozar's powerful presence. Seaa's light reflects off his bronze completion, his thin white tunic, open at the neck, the sleeves rolled up exposing his muscular form. Twakans' eyes range in color from almost white to dark red. Lozar's eyes are actually pink. I can detect some unease on Lozar's part over being alone with me. I can't help but wonder if he is in a relationship back on Twaka and what she is like.

Lozar and I watch as the *Xanthe Queen* stretches far ahead of us. Crystal propulsion runs quietly, leaving only the sound of water rushing under the hull.

"Princess Xanthe seems to be in a hurry. Does she think we are in a race?" I asked to break the silence.

"Let her go. She will be the first to run into trouble." I don't ask for examples of possible trouble.

As we continue to watch, the *Xanthe Queen* pulls farther and farther away. I sense more going on here than spoken. In cultures where siblings exist, brothers and sisters have spats. When the siblings are royalty, a spat can have important consequences.

"I haven't shared the spare crystal pacts Captain Jocko provided yet," Lozar admitted. "So we will be catching up to her eventually." I suppress a grin, impressed by his deviousness.

It didn't take long back in the Community of the High Council for Xanthe to demonstrate her dominance over Lozar when it comes to decision making. Between the two of them at least, her decision usually reigns final. But Lozar has begun to push back.

Twaka's culture and history is steeped in strong warrior women. Clearly Xanthe intends to inherit the throne. I have no doubt she would destroy anyone who might get in her way, but I feel she lacks compassion to be a leader. I wonder how her people feel about her. Perhaps I can question Kaydra about it. From what I can glean from Lozar's mind, he too is wary of Xanthe's ambitions and intentions toward Thayla.

"The princess seems very ambitious," I said as nonchalant as possible. My statement enables me to garner far more from Lozar's thoughts than his words.

"One might say so."

What did I expect? Transparency? Digging into Twaka's domestic affairs steps on established boundaries. Avoiding further awkwardness, I excuse myself as soon as politely possible to seek rest since I have the first watch after light.

Retreating to the privacy of my below deck bunk, how thoughtful of Lozar to provide Melinda and I with our own space, I contact Quaylyn telepathically. *Is Princess Xanthe trying to ditch us?*

Good question. The princess definitely has her own agenda.

I don't expect to fall asleep, but eventually I am shaking myself awake. I look out of my little porthole window, Seaa is high in the sky. I make my way up to the deck to find Melinda and Glisa in the galley preparing food before Glisa goes on wheel watch. "Smells good," I said. I speak English for Melinda's benefit since I don't speak Twakan.

"Yes, smells good," Glisa responded in English to my surprise. Melinda, who struggles with our Aaian language, is teaching Glisa English. What a great way to pass the time! Melinda has made a friend I realize watching them. Then I receive a telepathed message from Quaylyn.

The propulsion just stalled. You will be alongside us before too long.

When the boat slows, we make our way out on deck. Lozar is skillfully bringing the *Princess Thayla* alongside the *Xanthe Queen*. He certainly knows his way around boats. "What happened?" he asked shouting across the water to his sister waiting on deck. Like he doesn't know! I can detect the amusement in his voice.

"This crystal technology is cheap. It doesn't work," Princess Xanthe shouted back with hands obstinately on hips.

"You were going too fast, not conserving power," Lozar said. Then he sent Yanzic out on deck with a spare crystal pack. "I'm sending you over a charged power pack. Quaylyn or Kaydra can show you how to change out the depleted one and recharge it." He skillfully moves the boat in close enough for Yanzic to hand it over to her.

"You come show me," Xanthe demanded. Lozar ignores her demand.

"I'll scout on ahead while you recharge."

"Don't you dare, you stay right here." Lozar doesn't respond.

Then with the handover completed, not heeding Xanthe's warning, Lozar pulls away and speeds off leaving the temporarily stranded vessel behind.

Is the princess upset about something? I asked continuing my telepathic conversation with Quaylyn.

The princess is upset about a lot of things, none of which makes sense.

CHAPTER 17

Quaylyn

Xanthe watches with rage as Lozar pulls away and fades into the distance. Furiously she shoves the power pack into Rabiam's hand and marches off to her cabin without a word, slamming the door behind her. It is a relief for all of us to see her go.

Kaydra translates the exchange between Xanthe and Lozar for me. Then Arpen says something that makes the three of them snicker with suppressed laughter. I give Kaydra a quizzical look.

"I'll try to translate. Basically Arpen said the captain's face has changed places with her buttocks." I can't help but chuckle over the image it conjures up even if I don't understand all the nuances.

Kaydra has been Mentor to Twaka since our time as students together at the Academy. She knows more about Twakan culture than anyone else on the planet. Now, because of the incident with Thayla, she will no longer be Mentor to Twaka. What the High Council plans for her future after this is anyone's guess.

"I can show you how to change out the power pack," I offered Rabiam indicating the object in his hand. Understanding, we head up to the wheelhouse, with Arpen and Kaydra following. I show them how to remove the spent power pack and install the new one. It will be a slow charge by Seaa's light. When I go to put the spent cartridge to recharge, I find another fully charged cartridge. It's good to know we have two spare power packs.

Then Kaydra takes the wheel, starts the engine, and moves the boat forward. Kaydra shows Rabiam and Arpen what they need to know to drive the boat, then turns the wheel over to Rabiam. After that, we all stare out at the open sea glittering golden in the starlight. All the while I keep thinking about the royal sisters, Princess Thayla and Princess Xanthe.

"I didn't get to know Princess Thayla very well when she visited Mainland," I ventured as Rabiam gets the feel of the boat, "but she seemed quite different from Princess Xanthe."

"There is no comparison," Kaydra agreed. She would have said more, but with the *Xanthe Queen* underway again, Captain Xanthe comes up the steps to take back the wheel.

"Now everyone out," she ordered.

The four of us retreat to the galley to find something to eat. Arpen takes over encouraging the rest of us to sit. We offer to help, but she declines the offer.

"Tell me about Thayla," I said still wanting to know more. "She had to have known that her willful disappearance would eventually create diplomatic consequences."

"I guess. Thayla just wanted to be left alone. It's one of the things I admire most about her. She is unafraid to declare herself untethered." Kaydra politely shares the conversation with the others, then continues. "Thayla was quite young when the queen sent her away to a warrior training camp, far from any cities or settlements, as punishment for breaking rules of etiquette and decorum at the royal court. She was written off, then and there, as expendable, especially with four sisters and two brothers, all very ambitious, who have long been in intense competition for succession to the throne." Kaydra pauses again to translate our conversation to Rabiam and Arpen. They verify the facts.

"Turns out, Thayla thrived on the tough training and discipline, excelling in the martial arts. She also enjoyed the freedom of wide open spaces. When she returned, Thayla found life at the palace unbearable, its lack of substance and conniving pettiness maddening. So when I needed a body guard to travel with me around the planet, she saw her opportunity to escape court life."

"Therefore, you spent lots of time together."

"She and I became friends and eventually she wanted to visit my home world. It worked out great until she met Rojaire, Kaylya, Traevus and Kiril. I promised her family a safe trip and a safe return. I was terrified over returning to Twaka without Thayla, but they seemed almost glad to be rid of her. At least that's how it was at first."

I am fascinated. "Tell me more about the family. Is Princess Xanthe the oldest?"

"No, Prince Lozar is." Kaydra quickly translates for the others and Rabiam makes a comment. "Rabiam points out a more important fact, Xanthe is the oldest female."

"Doesn't that give her the right to the throne, being the oldest female?"

"Not necessarily. It goes to the most powerful politically."

"What about the other siblings?"

"One sister, Princess Sayer, died a mysterious death. The claim is she died of natural causes, but who knows? The second son, Prince Ockan, died in some confrontation, but I've never been able to find out much about the incident." Kaydra glances at our companions. "Should I risk asking them and see what they say? They have worked for the royal family most of their adult lives, as their family has for generations before them."

Go ahead, I indicate with a nod. As it turns out, Rabiam and Arpen are willing to talk. Kaydra translates. "According to them, the political strife in the family is murderous. Prince Ockan died defending Princess Ruthia's life. Her would-be assassin had been hired by Princess Sayer, Xanthe's younger sister."

"And Princess Ruthia?"

"She married and later died in childbirth."

"Xanthe, Sayer, and Ruthia; what about the other sister? "Didn't you say Thayla had four sisters?"

"The youngest princess, Princess Chayla, belongs to a religious order. She lives isolated in a remote temple where she prays for her people. It might be the only reason she is still alive."

"Nice family."

"Like I said, when I returned to Twaka without Thayla and explained what had happened there was little concern. Princess Thayla had been written off long ago. That is until recently. I don't know what changed, or maybe I do. The reigning queen's health is failing, making another succession to the throne imminent. Xanthe may want certainty the throne is hers.

The food is ready and it's delicious. Kaydra and I volunteer to cook the next meal. I'm thankful it is a partnership. I know as much about cooking as I do about boats. After eating, Arpen takes the captain her supper. The rest of us go out on the deck. The sea remains calm, but my thoughts are turbulent. To hear the stories, one would assume succession to the Twakan throne is based on last sister standing. This has turned into a very dangerous mission.

After all the drama, Captain Xanthe maintains a more sustainable speed, keeping pace with the *Princess Thayla*. Arpen doesn't return and soon Rabiam joins her and the captain in the wheelhouse. I retire to my bunk long before Seaa sets. Kaydra does the same. There is no reason for us to stay up. Xanthe does not consider us a part of the crew. We are unwanted passengers, and nothing more.

CHAPTER 18

Lozar

We have made great progress. An Aaian night and a day have passed, the equivalent of nearly two days on Twaka, and the sea has remained suspiciously calm. I don't like it; it's too calm. As evening falls once again, the sea is still velvety smooth. I can see the *Xanthe Queen* off to our starboard side. Things have remained calm there too. I haven't actually spoken with Xanthe since Yanzic handed over the power pack, but Anthya can communicate with Quaylyn and Kaydra across the distance. How is it they can do that and I can't? Is it something that can be learned?

We have traveled faster than we ever could by sail, especially in the calm. So far I really like this technology. I have gone through a wheel watch with each member of the crew, taking only short naps in-between. Naturally they can handle calm conditions like this, I worry about when the weather changes. The lack of land masses bothers me. There is no place to hide from storms. On Twaka, land and sea are more evenly distributed around the planet. Land of some sort is nearly always in sight.

"The *Xanthe Queen* is signaling for us to stop," Glisa called out from the lookout at the top of the mast.

I hand the wheel over to Yanzic and step out on deck. "Ignore it," I shout back. Glisa does a double take, but obeys my order. Anthya and Melinda come out on deck to see what is going on. They have been resting during the sun's last quadrant. We all watch as the *Xanthe Queen* slowly comes in closer. We can clearly see Rabiam shouting and waving from the lookout on top the mast. Anthya walks over.

"Aren't you going to stop the boat?"

"No," I said defiantly. I look at her earnestly, she stares back with quiet disapproval, her direct eye contact piercingly unsettling. I dislike her disapproval.

"Alright, see if you can find out what she wants," I tell her in surrender. I instruct Yanzic to slow the boat down to a steady crawl. "Don't stop when Xanthe pulls up to us, unless I tell you to." Anthya can give Xanthe the benefit of the doubt, but I am well passed that. I know what she is capable of. Any action Xanthe takes may have devious intentions, even if it appears innocent.

"Quaylyn says Xanthe just wants to take a break and talk."

"Tell her there is no reason to stop, the sea is calm, the evening is young and there is nothing here to stop for."

I shout my order to Yanzic to resume speed. Xanthe appears on deck releasing a string of curses and insults vowing revenge and deadly consequences. I'm glad Anthya, Melinda, and Quaylyn can't understand a word of it, but of course Kaydra will eventually fill them in. Her rage finally spent, Xanthe returns to her wheelhouse and we continue on.

Night sails in smoothly leaving only starlight reflecting off the water. Anthya enters the wheelhouse reporting for duty. The others have retired to their bunks. "I'll stay at the wheel until Seaa rises," I tell her. "You can help me keep watch until she does."

Anthya is actually attractive in a pale sort of way. The councilor is an inexplicable mystery of opposites. Her light gray eyes are soft, yet they can be piercing I learned today. Did she take over my mind? I can't help but wonder. She is so soft spoken, calm, even serene, yet so powerful. She doesn't fit the description of a warrior, but she easily overcame Xanthe's attack. She definitely intrigues me.

"What made you choose to become a councilor?" I ask.

"I didn't choose, I was chosen by the Runes of the Crystal Table."

I couldn't help but roll my eyes a little at mention of the Crystal Table, a theatrical show at best in my opinion. "Are you married?"

"We don't marry or have families."

"What about procreation?" I blurted out without intending to.

"Our population is kept at a minimum. When needed, the High Council selects a chosen mother and a chosen father to produce a new person for a village to raise."

What? I almost shout, but think better of it. And these people are supposed to be an advanced race! I change the subject before I say something I can't take back.

"Your navigational charts are questionable," I said getting back to the task at hand.

"Why do you say that?"

"There are a few features, strangely marked 'improbable,' on the boat's chart I didn't see on the navigational chart at the Academy. One such feature is directly ahead of us. At this rate of speed we should be upon it sometime tomorrow. I'd show you if there were enough light."

Then with a wave of her hand a glow globe appears overhead. I would like to be able to do that! The glow globe in the cabin blinds us from seeing in the darkness ahead, but there isn't anything out there to hit anyway. I quickly pull out the chart drawer. "Right here," I said pointing out the location while securing the wheel.

"The Pinnacles," Anthya read out loud. "I've heard about The Pinnacles before in stories. They are believed to be a thing of legend, a myth from long ago. After viewing the chart, Anthya extinguishes the glow globe and our eyes gradually readjust to starlight.

"Is it a place we might go ashore?" I asked.

"I don't think so. According to legend, the Pinnacles rise up from the ocean floor from Seaa rise to Seaa set once every one hundred cycles of seasons. Supposedly they glow beckoning sailors to them. In the stories, the Pinnacles cover so vast an area, it is impossible to go around them in a day, so sailors would try to go through them. But if a ship is caught within the Pinnacles when they sink again, the ship will be sucked down to the depths of the ocean in a giant whirlpool."

"When was the last time this event supposedly occurred?"

"It's only a legend. I don't think it's anything to worry about."

"You people don't go out on the water much, do you?"

"Sure we do, about this far. Fish is an important part of our diet. Beyond this point, the continental shelf drops off to great depths. Another reason to doubt the legend."

As we watch, Seaa rises brightly in the night sky casting her light on the sea and on Anthya's light features giving her a ghostly appearance. The *Xanthe Queen* continues to follow a safe distance away. There is little reason for me to remain. Anthya can take over from here. Melinda will follow her, followed by Glisa and Yanzic. It's time I get some rest.

CHAPTER 19

Ilene

Kaylya's shout sends everyone running toward her. Then we see Kaylya rush to Rojaire's side, almost stumbling over two small feathered creatures, to get to him. Their tender reunion makes me want to reach out for Kiril and touch him. Traevus and Thayla are also here.

Jack and Setas run out to greet their father, but pause upon seeing the strangers. I can't say as I blame them, they are a sight to behold. The strangers seem just as surprised to see all of us. Eager to hug his children, Rojaire dashes forward and scoops them up into his arms. They continue to latch on to him after he sets them down.

I scan about for my children. Theon is closing in with Halren and Selyzar. Aurora has just arrived from stashing away her harvest. The shocked look on her face is something to see. Slowly she moves in closer.

"Welcome back, Rojaire," Kiril greeted. "I see you brought guests. Did you find a route out the valley so quickly?"

"Greetings, Kiril, Ilene and everyone. We came across these two at the river ford. Is Caleeza with you?"

"No, she didn't come," Kaylya said. "Why do you ask?"

"We believe the taller one is Chitter." We have all heard the story of Chitter. "We need Caleeza to verify her identity and communicate with her if she can."

"You look tired, Rojaire," I couldn't help observing.

"We're all tired. It was a hard push to the ford, and then we had to turn around." Thayla and Traevus continue to stand guard over the strangers a short distance away. Rojaire waves to them to join us.

The crowd opens up, allowing Traevus and Thayla to bring the visitors amongst us. "Welcome back," we greet them warmly. Having them back makes the community whole again. Traevus begins introducing us to the little creatures. I feel the effort is meaningless until I hear the strangers make a questionable attempt to repeat our names.

"Where did you come from? Would you like something to eat?" Zaloka asked offering them food, which they took from her hand.

Chitter chitters what may have been an answer, but no one understands it. "Caleeza claimed she could communicate," Wessid said. "I don't see how."

"I guess we should pack up our harvest while Rojaire's group takes a rest break," Kiril suggested. "Should we send a couple of runners ahead to alert the others, especially Caleeza?" he asked.

"That might be a good idea," Rojaire agreed.

"Selyzar and I will go," Halren volunteered.

"Tell Caleeza we are on our way back, we intercepted Rojaire, Traevus and Thayla while gathering peago pods, and they brought company. We think it's your friend Chitter."

"I want to go, too," Theon said.

"Go, go!" Kiril urged. I watch as the boys nudge Aurora before taking off. With some hesitation she turns to follow them. She seems stressed out about something lately. Aurora is hiding something. But what? I've tried probing the problem, but she shuts me off.

When we are ready to move out, Rojaire has our group go first. It's a long hike and we are anxious to reach the village. When we finally arrive at the village circle, the rest of the community, Tassyn, Edty, Drak, Inventor Sulyan, Ollen, Caleeza and the children are all there waiting for us. The children did a good job of spreading the news.

Caleeza rushes up to us to confirm what she can't believe otherwise. "Where is she?" We split off revealing those behind us.

Seeing Caleeza, Chitter rushes to her and bursts into a chittering monologue that conveys little meaning. Nevertheless, Caleeza grabs the little feathery creature up in her arms and spins her around in delight. Rojaire retreats to the sideline with Kaylya and the children. Traevus and Thayla also give them room.

"Chitter, I'm so glad to see you!" Caleeza squealed. Chitter chitters violently in protest of the swinging about and Caleeza sets her back down. "I told you Chitter exists!" she exclaimed to the rest of us.

"I've never before seen the likes of these two." Inventor Sulyan said puzzled. "What are they?"

"These are the life forms pictured on Great Grandfather Vestan's map of the second valley," Drak declared.

Chitter is now highly animated and chatters on excitedly. "I'm receiving some mental images," Caleeza said, as the rest of us continue to gawk in amazement.

"I think she is saying this is her daughter," Caleeza said pointing to Chitter's companion. As though she understands what Caleeza said, Chitter seemingly agrees. Then Chitter points to her daughter and repeats her name several times.

"Kitca. Kitca. Kitca," Chitter enunciated, indicating her companion.

"Kitca," several of us repeat. All the children stare in stunned silence, with mouths agape. That is all except Aurora.

I see Aurora creeping up closer to Caleeza, Chitter and Kitca. She is always putting herself where she doesn't belong. I move to intercept, but Kiril holds me back. We watch as Aurora walks up to Kitca.

"Hi Kitca, I'm Aurora."

Kitca becomes excited, takes Aurora's hand and speaks at length for the first time.

Aurora jumps back startled. Did Kitca convey something to Aurora? If so, what? I'm not the only one puzzled by her reaction.

"What did she say?" Caleeza asked.

"I don't know."

Then Kitca speaks again.

"Do you know what she said?" Caleeza asked suspiciously.

"No, of course not. I just wanted to say hi," Aurora said a bit shaken. I can see the puzzlement in Aurora's face, but I can't explain her reactions. I feel she is not being completely honest.

Rojaire steps forward as Aurora slips away. "I guess we can put them up in First Shelter for now," he suggested.

"Good idea," Kiril agreed. "What are they going to need?"

"I believe their needs are simple, probably just some bedding," Caleeza said.

"Ask them how long they have been traveling." Rojaire said. Caleeza speaks to Chitter and she answers something.

"Two cycles of seasons. I believe that's what she means," Caleeza said with uncertainty. "That's a long time."

"You mean they have been traveling for years?" I butted in startled. I've never understood why Aaians refer to a year as a cycle of seasons when they only have two seasons—two seasons that don't vary much at that. Coming from Alaska, it all feels like summer to me.

"How is it you can understand anything?" Rojaire asked.

"I'm not sure, it's seems to be a form of telepathy, but I don't know why it just works with me."

Rojaire would have continued asking questions, but Caleeza intervened. "Perhaps Chitter and Kitca would like to rest some before meeting everyone and answering questions. I will show them where they will be staying," Caleeza said.

"I'll go with you," Zaloka volunteered.

As they leave, I look around for Aurora, but she is nowhere in sight.

CHAPTER 20

Rojaire

I expect to see Chitter and Kitca drop down on all fours and lope along behind Caleeza and Zaloka as they did traveling with us, but they remain upright. So many questions left unanswered. How did they get here? Where did they come from? Do they know of a route to the sea?

"Should we call for a gathering with food and cheer?" Kaylya asked.

"Probably, eventually. Maybe we should consult with Caleeza first." How will Chitter and Kitca change the dynamics of the community? Are they a threat in any way?

"Are they going to live here? With us? Forever?" Jack asked.

"I don't know. We'll have to wait and see what happens. They will be staying here for a while at least. Is that a problem?" Kaylya asked our son.

"No, it's just they are so strange looking."

"They really are strange looking," Setas agreed.

"You will get used to how they look," I said. I realize these are the first strangers the children have ever seen. It is the first time their minds are being stretched to accept anything outside our valley.

"Maybe they will want to be in our play," Setas suggested ready to give the strangers a try.

"Yes, they can be in our play," Alaia said agreeing with her best friend.

"They are not children just because they're small," Kaylya explained.

"Can Kitca be in our play?" Setas asked Ilene with the one track mind of a young one.

"Yes," Alaia seconded. "Can she?"

"Sure," Ilene said. "If she wants to."

"I'm still the bear beast," Jack piped in.

"What play?" I asked yawning and rubbing my eyes. Exhaustion is starting to catch up with me.

"I'll tell you about it later. First thing you need to do is get some rest."

"Not quite yet. Let's go see what's happening at First Shelter," I said yawning again. Ollen and the younger children follow Kaylya and me down the pathway to our little meeting house. Upon arriving at the shelter we encounter Zaloka and Caleeza stepping out.

"We're just going to gather up a few things for our guests," Zaloka said. "They seem to be happy to be here."

"That's good, so what are you finding out?" I asked Caleeza casually.

"Not much. It seems they have been traveling a long time to reach us. I sense they are looking for something, although I don't quite understand exactly what it is they are searching for. Maybe they don't want me to know."

"I thought you said Chitter was the last of her kind. Where did the daughter come from?"

"I've been wondering about that myself," Caleeza said. "I tried asking, but I didn't receive a clear answer."

"We need to show them our maps," I suggested. "Perhaps they can show us how they got here. They may even know a way to the sea."

"When will you be leaving again?" Ollen asked.

"Soon, I hope. After we see if these two pose any kind of threat."

"I'm sure Chitter would never hurt anyone," Caleeza said coming to Chitter's defense.

"How should we welcome the new arrivals?" I asked her.

"Well, after they have rested, I suppose we could have a simple gathering around the fire ring with food and drink and introduce everyone," Caleeza said.

"What do you need me to do?" I offered trying to be helpful.

"You're not doing anything, you need to get some rest," Kaylya protested.

"She's right," Caleeza agreed. "Let Zaloka and I take care of that. We'll round up some help. You need to listen to Kaylya and get some rest. We've already sent Thayla and Traevus home to do the same."

I can't remember the last time I slept so hard. I pry open my heavy eyelids and find Kaylya sitting beside me. There's sweat on her brow, she has obviously been out and about, probably helping with the welcoming feast.

"How long have I been out and what have I missed?"

"You have been out as long as your body needed you to be and you haven't missed anything," she said kissing me sweetly, "but you will if you don't start moving."

It takes a while to get moving, but eventually I stand dressed and ready to go. "I'm so lucky," Kaylya said, "I get to escort the guest of honor."

I offer her my arm. "I'm the lucky one." The walk to the village circle is a short one. We arrive to a celebration already in full swing. When we break out of the trees, the entire community rises, cheering and applauding. I didn't expect a standing ovation and it moves me to tears. Imagine if we would have actually accomplished our goal!

I notice right away, Kitca and Chitter are dressed in light blue frocks, making them look even more human. The women have been experimenting with natural dyes and embellishing their garments with embroidery. Even some of the men are dressed in fancy tunics.

"We have an excuse for a celebration," Drak announced, "a welcoming celebration for Chitter and Kitca and a welcome home gathering for Rojaire, Thayla and Traevus."

"Drak, you can make an excuse for a celebration out of anything, but this time you are on the mark," Kiril said.

The Chitters prove to be party animals. They sample every food— and drink—presented. Then we remember Kitca's age, although we have no idea about the development of a Chitter, and cut her off from the potent drink.

Then Ilene brings out her flute, a much finer one Drak and Sulyan worked on together to replace the cruder first flute Sulyan made, which replaced the flute she brought from Earth and left behind in Mainland when she fled with the colonists. The flute is exquisitely made from native materials including the reeds, which creates a sound as vibrantly alive as the valley.

The Chitters love the music, vivaciously jiggling with the rhythm and keening soulfully with some notes which brought on uproarious laughter and many toasts. How will the Chitters fit into our community? Should I even be pondering this question when I should be celebrating instead?

CHAPTER 21

Aurora

I slip away from the house to the nut tree grove and climb up one of the massive trees. Most of the village is resting after the celebration. I did my best to avoid any contact with Kitca during the party. It wasn't hard to do with all the attention on them and not on me. I've been avoiding Mother, too. Even worse, I've been avoiding the boys. The secrets are killing me. I have to do something about the situation, but what? Is it really the star stone that makes it possible for me to understand Kitca? It has to be, there is no other explanation.

The giant nut trees, we haven't given them any other name, are tall and massive with huge branches. The branches grow parallel to the ground and are covered in rough greenish brown bark, making them easy to climb. This is the same grove that serves as our tag ball playing field. There are seven trees in all, we have given many of them individual names. This one, the Fort, is one of my favorites, the largest tree in the grove.

I hear the boys coming and climb up to the next level of branches to avoid detection. It doesn't work.

"We know you are here, Aurora," Halren called out. "Come down, we want to talk to you."

I don't want them invading my special space so I work my way down and drop to the ground. "What do you want to talk about?"

"Crystal shards, Aurora! That was quite a show!" Theon exclaimed.

"Yes, very impressive," Selyzar added. "What did her paw feel like?"

"What's going on, Aurora?" Halren asked. "What are you hiding?"

They are on to me. "Look, we need to talk, but not here. What I need to tell you is very important. Let's go to the pavilion."

"Okay," they all agreed.

The pavilion is another place we aren't supposed to go to alone and without telling someone. At least I'm not alone. We quickly arrive and as I hoped, no one is around. Then I remember something I gleaned from Mother about working with the little children on a play at the pavilion. Now I understand, we climb the two short, rough lavender stone steps to the large flat rock stage. The pavilion is a fascinating place. We peek into the cave at the back and pace around a bit before sitting down. The waterfall beckons a short distance away.

"Okay, talk," Halren demanded.

"First, I need the three of you to swear to secrecy."

"We swear," Selyzar said.

"I need each of you, one at a time, to swear, seriously swear, that you will never tell anyone what I'm about to tell you."

"Oh come on, your secret can't be that important," Theon said. Brothers are so annoying!

"You first, little brother. Swear by Seaa's light that you can be trusted—or you can leave right now."

"Okay, okay. I swear by Seaa's light your secret is safe with me."

"Halren?"

"I swear by Seaa's light your secret is safe with me," Halren said.

"I swear by Seaa's light your secret is safe with me," Selyzar said. Their thoughts say they are sincere.

"Now what is your secret?" Halren asked.

"I have something to show you."

Slowly I pull the star stone out of my pocket and soak in the boys gawking stares. I definitely have their attention.

"Crystal shards! You stole Mother's star stone?" Theon accused.

"No, I did not. I found a star stone. It's mine. I didn't steal it, I found it. I'm not guilty of anything except keeping it a secret, if that's a crime."

"Where did you find a star stone?" Halren asked.

I told them the story of how Mother accused me for Halren's fever and how I ran off to the yicil forest in anger. "While I was there, I spotted a pykee playing with something shiny on the ground. When I startled him, he zoomed up the tree without it. The shiny object turned out to be a star stone. Also, I should give you fair warning, I can read your thoughts."

"What?" Immediately I can feel them attempting to shield their thoughts. They succeed to an extent, for a while. I guess it takes practice.

"Can you read everyone's thoughts?" Theon asked.

"Just Mother's and the other children's when they are standing close by.

"So what are you going to do with it?" Selyzar asked.

"I'm going to keep it. That's why you can't tell anyone."

"Can I hold it?" Theon asked.

"If you prove you can keep a secret, you may eventually have a chance to experiment with it." Now I have something to bind their loyalty.

"We have all sworn to secrecy," Selyzar reminded me.

"There's more," I added.

"More? More than finding a star stone?" Theon asked incredulously.

"When Kitca held my hand something happened."

"You mean, you really did understand her?" Halren asked guessing the truth.

"Yes, sort of. It's not exactly speech, more like impressions."

"That's why you drew back the way you did! So what did she say?" Selyzar asked excitedly.

"It wasn't like that. I didn't understand what she said. It was more like thoughts. She seemed glad to be here and she knows I have a star stone."

"Really? Just like that?" Selyzar asked.

"Chitter and Kitca are so strange, so different," Theon said. "Thayla looks different from us, but these people are really different.

"How does Kitca know you have a star stone?" Halren asked.

"I believe she can sense it. She was really excited about it." I pause recalling the experience. "I think she wants my star stone!"

"What?" the boys shouted in unison.

"What do you suppose she wants it for?" Halren asked.

"For the same reasons we do, I guess."

"We need to find out. This could be very important. We have to find out why Chitter and Kitca are here. What are they looking for? And we need to do it in secret, without adult interference."

"We should form a secret club," Theon suggested.

Now, I've never known Theon to have a great idea before, but this time he came up with one. The others think so too.

"Yes," Halren agreed. "A club is a great idea. We need a name."

"We could be the First Four Born Club," I said.

"That sounds dumb. How about the Powerful Four or the Special Four?" Theon suggested.

Several possible names were shouted out, each sillier than the last. "Maybe we need a name that doesn't include the word 'four,'" Selyzar said.

"How about Secret Warriors?" Halren asked. We silently consider the suggestion for a moment.

"Secret Warriors. Yes, I like it," I said.

That sounds good," Theon agreed. Selyzar's approval makes it unanimous.

"Our first mission as Secret Warriors is to learn all we can about Kitca and Chitter. We need to find out why they are here," Halren said.

"But that will require me to spend time with Kitca. What if I don't want to?"

"You have to, the safety of our community may depend on it. You are a Secret Warrior," Halren explained. "We will help."

"I guess it's pretty special to be the only one who can communicate with Kitca. But eventually someone will find out about the star stone and take it away from me."

"We won't let that happen. We need a plan, an activity we can all participate in so you have unsuspicious contact with Kitca," Halren said.

"We'll be shucking peago pods after everyone is rested. Do you think Kitca will be there?" Theon asked.

"Why don't we just invite Kitca on a picnic?" Selyzar asked. "Then we don't have to deal with a bunch of adults around."

"What if Kitca really does want my star stone?"

"Don't let her have it and report back to us. We'll figure out something," Halren said. "Remember, we are all bound by secrecy."

Great! Another secret to keep secret.

CHAPTER 22

Anthya

Wheel watch continues on uneventfully as Seaa arches a quarter of the way across the sky and Melinda joins me. Being well rested, I stay up. Melinda welcomes my company.

"Do you think we will find Ilene?" Melinda asked quietly.

I know it would be a wonderful thing for Melinda to be reunited with a friend from Earth. How alone she must feel. "Yes, I believe we will find her and the others. We have to keep our focus positive," I reminded her.

"You're right of course. But I'm afraid Princess Xanthe will do something that will put us in danger. I think she means to harm her sister."

"Quaylyn, Kaydra and I won't let anyone come to harm," I promised. I hope I can keep my promise. "You didn't have a chance to meet Princess Thayla, since they left before you arrived. I think you will like her. Thayla exudes strength and independent-thinking without being cruel and self-centered. The idea of colonizing an uninhabited country suited her."

"I would have joined the colonists given a chance," Melinda said.

"Maybe you still can."

"I'm glad Thayla isn't like Xanthe. I would hate to imagine the colonists putting up with someone like that."

"Xanthe must have some redeeming qualities. Perhaps we just haven't found them yet."

"That's optimistic thinking."

After Seaa arched halfway across the sky, Glisa joins us. "Blaka," Melinda greeted her in Twakan. To my surprise she spoke even more.

"What did you say?" I asked.

"I told her all is well."

"You're learning Twakan, I'm impressed."

Soon after, I leave so the two young women can freely pursue their English/Twakan lessons. On the way to my bunk below, I encounter Lozar standing barefoot on the deck in front of the galley door wearing only breeches and an open vest. "Blaka," I said somewhat bashfully.

"Blaka. Join me please," he invited. Apparently he just woke up. He looks almost vulnerable rubbing sleep from his eyes. I can't decline; his invitation is warm and earnest. I slip into the bench across the table from him.

"How are things on the bridge?" he asked.

"Melinda and Glisa have things well under control," I said with a smile.

"That's good." I smell his special wakeup brew simmering on the stove. "Want some?" he asked rising from the table.

"Half a cup. I want to sleep, not stay awake." Lozar sets a cup before me, its steamy aroma fills the cabin. "It does smell inviting."

"Watch it, it's hot," Lozar warned as my lips come close to the cup. He sits down across from me with his own cup, his rosy bronze skin glowing even in the pale light of the galley. I sip my drink in silence for a while, allowing Lozar to fully awaken. Slowly he comes to robust life. "Xanthe still with us?" he asked.

"Yes. Quaylyn doesn't seem to think she will try anything else until we arrive." That sends Lozar on another track.

"This communicating with the mind, do you think you could teach me that?"

I couldn't help but smile, but I have to hand it to Lozar, he is willing to learn anything from crystal propulsion to telepathy. "I don't know. Maybe, over time, with some practice. Anything is possible."

"And what does Quaylyn think Xanthe will do when we arrive?"

I face Lozar head on. "You might be able to answer that question better than Quaylyn can."

He actually ducks his head in a moment of humility, then quickly recovers. "You can read my thoughts, can't you?" It is my turn to look away. I don't answer; I don't have to.

"You can learn to shield your thoughts." I feel I may have offended him.

Then he smiles. "I need you to teach me how to guard my thoughts, too," he said.

"We'll work on it," I assured him.

We sit quietly sipping our tea, then Lozar speaks. "It is no secret our mother is failing and as you know, Xanthe is ambitious."

"Yes, we noticed that. The naming of her boat was a subtle hint." Lozar rewards my facetious comment with another smile.

"My family has a long painful history of fighting to the death for the right of succession to the throne. Xanthe plans on killing Thayla, I have no doubt about that." The admission takes a lot out of him even though it is a fact we already knew.

"What am I thinking?" I asked, telepathing the answer to him.

"You are thinking it's time to let me know that you can telepath messages to me, too. I guess that could be useful. Why didn't you let me know before now?"

"I had to find out if you are worthy of my trust."

"I see, so now I'm deemed worthy?"

"You have my respect, Prince Lozar."

"Please, just Lozar.

"Alright, Lozar, and what is your plan?" I asked.

"I will protect Thayla."

"Of course, but what do you plan on doing after this is all over? Are you married? Are there little ones on Twaka waiting for the return of their father?" Lozar actually blushes.

"I see. I apologize, Councilor Anthya, if I was being too forward before."

"Please, just Anthya."

"Alright, Anthya, I am not married and have no children. I would like to have a family someday. Will that suffice?"

"For now." Again we drank a while in silence.

"Tell me about Melinda, she's sort of a mystery."

"Melinda is a warrior in her own right. She has humble beginnings. After her mother died she lived with her father on their fishing boat."

"You can tell she has spent a lot of time around boats."

"She was still a girl when Droclum killed her father and held her a captive underground until she was rescued by Rahlys, Guardian of the Oracle of Light. The experience left Melinda deeply scarred. She became a member of the group of warriors on Earth who defeated Droclum, playing a major role in his defeat."

"This Droclum is the same evil sorcerer who nearly destroyed Aaia?"

"In essence."

"What about Quaylyn? What's his story? Can we trust him to keep a watchful eye on Xanthe?"

"Quaylyn is honest, trustworthy, dependable, and a trained warrior. I can assure you he and Kaydra have things under control on the *Xanthe Queen*." I don't feel it is my place to tell Lozar, Quaylyn is Droclum's son.

"Good to hear," he said rising from the table to refill his cup. I decline his offer of a refill and notice for the first time how stress is taking a toll on him.

"You really care about Princess Thayla," I said.

"We were very close as children," Lozar said. "I would give my life to save hers."

"You need not worry, we are all on your side. Xanthe will not be allowed to harm Thayla."

Departing cordially, I leave the galley for my bunk. For the longest I can't sleep, then later I wake to a change in the boat's movement, indicating the sea is no longer calm.

CHAPTER 23

Quaylyn

The sea has turned rough. As the sun rises, so do the waves. I've learned I am no sailor. Drawing a little energy from the elemental forces, I manage to keep the nausea down. The princess, on the other hand, thrives in her element, exhilarating over riding the waves. I imagine the sea gives her something to take her hostilities out on.

Rabiam laughs at my unstable sea legs. "This isn't rough," Kaydra translated for Rabiam, although I notice Kaydra also looks a little green.

Fortunately the sea doesn't grow any angrier during the long blustery day. Rabiam and Arpen take turns on wheel watch, relieving Xanthe from time to time. Kaydra and I often join them in the wheelhouse, Kaydra makes communication easy. The companionship is great, but there is only water to see. Not even flotsam rides the waves.

As the seemingly endless day approaches sunset, the storm and the sea become even more violent. Dark clouds wipe out the sun and lightning flashes followed by rumbling thunder accompany pelting rain. An ominous feeling I can't dispel, permeates my psyche, and I'm certain it's not all storm related.

The storm passes quicker than I expected it to, although the sea continues to roll. Xanthe resists relinquishing the wheel as long as she can, perhaps she also senses something, but eventually she lets her warriors take over while she rests.

"Relax," Kaydra translated for Rabiam. "This isn't so bad."

"It's terrible to me." The clouds part as the sun disappears behind the mounting waves. Darkness quickly follows, forcing Rabiam to turn on the running lights. Is it better to see or not to see the rolling sea? I wonder, as bile rises in my throat.

Just as Seaa peeks over the watery horizon something begins to happen. The movement of the waves changes drastically. Instead of a rolling sea, the water surface suddenly starts to shudder violently like a boiling cauldron, a deep vibrating rumble assaults our ears.

"What's happening?" I asked concerned. I've never seen the sea behave this way before, and judging from the shocked expressions on my companions' faces, neither have they.

"Maybe it's an underwater ground shake," Kaydra said. Rabiam and Arpen have no answers.

The shuddering sea becomes increasingly more violent, impeding any forward progress. Then lumps in the sea begin to rise and the *Xanthe Queen* slides sideways as a lump rises beneath her. I see Rabiam gripping the wheel tightly as the *Xanthe Queen* surfs off the rising edge of water into the trough below, only to be lifted up another watery slope.

Xanthe rushes up to the wheelhouse, "What's happening?" she shouted over the maelstrom, holding on to the cabin door frame for support. No one has an answer. Xanthe stares momentarily at the sea in shocked disbelief before taking the wheel from Rabiam as the *Xanthe Queen* rises ever higher, threatening to tumble down the slope. She is more subdued than before, even fearful. I take that as a bad sign.

"Help me stabilize the boat!" I shouted to Kaydra.

We step out of the wheelhouse onto the upper deck, I take starboard and she takes port. Holding fast to the handholds and the railings outside the wheelhouse, we draw energy from the elemental forces that roar around us. There is no lack of energy to draw on. Whatever happens, we must keep the boat from capsizing and sinking.

"Something is breaking through the water," I shouted. Could it be the Pinnacles rising up from the bottom of the ocean? Of course not, the Pinnacles are a thing of legend. I can't see the *Princess Thayla*, which worries me. Anthya doesn't have anyone to help her.

We survive one monster wash over after another while all around us pearly white pinnacles of stone rise skyward shoving aside water that comes crashing down upon us. "Watch out," Arpen shouted in Twakan, but the urgency in his voice translates to all languages as a deluge of water washes over the boat.

Kaydra and I strain to keep the boat upright as we hold on, practically lifting the boat out the water. We resurface in a deep trough among rising monolithic pinnacles of white stone. We are trapped, with no way out. All we can do is watch as the sea continues to tumble down upon us. Kaydra and I draw on vast amounts of energy to keep the boat above the drink as the Pinnacles continue to rise. I don't know how long we can hang on.

Then finally the Pinnacles stop rising. The agitated sea sloshes back and forth for a while, then settles down into a quiet calm. It's over. Seaa's light reflects eerily bright off the stark white monuments of stone towering above us, dwarfing our boat.

I search for the *Princess Thayla,* urgently telepathing Anthya. I can detect life signatures, including Anthya's. *Is everyone all right?*

We are all safe. Soon I spot the boat coming around a pinnacle toward us.

Then Anthya telepaths a message that chills my spine. *We have to move on, and quickly. If a ship is caught in the Pinnacles at Seaa set, it will be sucked down in a giant whirlpool when the Pinnacles sink back into the ocean.*

We survived, but if this is true, our nightmare has just begun.

We pull up alongside the *Princess Thayla.* "We have to get out of here!" Lozar shouts to Xanthe.

"Why? What's the urgency?" Xanthe asked. "The rocky points keep the water calm; we can rest."

"Those rocky points will sink back into the sea when Seaa sets creating a giant whirlpool," Lozar explained.

Anthya repeats the story of the legend of the Pinnacles, and Kaydra translates in Twakan so everyone understands.

"You're going by a legend?" Xanthe asked incredulously.

"She's telling you the truth," I said. "We cannot question it after what we have already seen and experienced."

"I know you are tired," Anthya said compassionately, "we all are. But we have to go on. The powerful suction of the whirlpool will be too strong for Quaylyn, Kaydra and I to counter."

CHAPTER 24

Lozar

" You heard Anthya, there is no time for rest. We don't know how far the Pinnacles extend. We can't waste any time, we have to go now!" Having seen the Pinnacles rise I have no doubt they will sink again and I don't want to be here when they do.

"Try to go as fast as you can without draining the crystal. Watch your gauge. When the power bar is low, switch to the auxiliary crystal pack before you lose power. There is a spare charged crystal stored in your console if you need it."

"You could have told me that before," she snarled back.

"Have luck!" I shouted ignoring her retort.

"Have luck!" she replied and speeds on ahead.

It is easy going in the calm water, but impossible to travel for long in a straight line, the random spacing of the pinnacles of stone forcing us to weave around one obstacle after another. I strive to keep the *Princess Thayla* in a generally easterly direction to stay on course. It wouldn't pay to go in circles.

Anthya returns to the wheelhouse after changing into dry clothes. She looks even paler than before, if that is even possible. "What are you doing back here? You should be resting, you look exhausted."

"Not until this is over."

"You saved us, it was you alone who kept us afloat. I thank you." How she did it remains a mystery as incredulous as the Pinnacles themselves.

I race against time, speeding and weaving through the towering white spears, seeking a route to freedom. Half way through the long

Aaian night the Pinnacles continue to stretch before us, ghostly in the starlight. We take shifts on steering and on lookout so others can rest, but I can't rest.

Still the night continues on, and so do the Pinnacles. How much further do we have to go? My stomach cramps with anxiety as I watch the fatal star reach for the horizon. The whirlpool will be huge. How will we ever escape it?

Shortly before Seaa prepares to set, open water breaks before us. I watch as the *Xanthe Queen* breaks free of the Pinnacles behind us and comes to a stop. Instantly I swing around. "Keep going!" I shouted. "Don't stop now! Go! Go!" I don't stay to argue and speed off again. To my relief Xanthe follows as Seaa inches toward the horizon with the Pinnacles still visible in the distance.

We speed into the wind, the boat bumping over the chop. All too quickly, Seaa touches the horizon. "The *Xanthe Queen* seems to be losing ground," Melinda shouted from her lookout.

"Find out what's happening? Tell them to speed up."

"They're switching crystals," Anthya reported.

As Seaa drops lower, the *Xanthe Queen* closes the gap. Soon they are speeding ahead of us. I nudge the throttle forward, for we are running the race of our lives. A quick glance back, and to my horror, I watch as Seaa dips below the western horizon in the first glow of morning to the east.

"Something's happening!" Yanzic shouted in Twakan from the deck.

"Something happen," Glisa translated roughly in English. I've been only vaguely aware of Glisa and Melinda's Twakan/English lessons.

The sea behind us begins to swirl and the monstrous edge of a phenomenal whirlpool forms threateningly close. "Go! Go!" I shout to the ether, terror gripping my soul. I bare down on the throttle, crossing the line of caution. The sea swirls faster tugging at our progress even at this distance. Then the Pinnacles begin to sink. The whirlpool's suction pulls us back, canceling our forward progress. We are going to lose after all.

Anthya stands beside me, entranced with power, pure energy crackling around her. She will not give up the fight, and neither will I. Urging the boat forward at full throttle, I watch mesmerized, as Anthya directs the energy surrounding her to the boat's crystal power unit. The boat's console begins to glow.

Powerless to intercede, I can only watch. Slowly the *Princess Thayla* gains ground, a boat length at a time, as the Pinnacles sink back into the sea, but at what cost to Anthya I can only imagine, it has to be tremendous. I look for the *Xanthe Queen* and panic when at first I can't find her, but finally I spot her far off to the port side. The nightmare seems endless, but gradually the whirlpool's suction releases us. We race on, nearly flying over the water until the Pinnacles are far behind us.

Then abruptly the boat comes to a stop. I rush over and catch Anthya as she collapses toward the floor and carry her in my arms to the captain's chair.

"Did we make it?" she asked in a barely audible whisper.

"Yes, we did, and you were wonderful," I said holding her in my arms, probably longer than needed. I want to hold her and protect her forever.

Soon the *Xanthe Queen* circles around us and pulls up to our port side. Yanzic and Melinda catch the lines Rabiam and Arpen toss to them, securing the boats together. I would carry Anthya down to the deck if I still had the energy, but somehow she finds the strength to stand, though somewhat wobbly, holding on to my arm for support. With Glisa in the lead we leave the wheelhouse.

Xanthe and her crew are waiting for us. I've never seen Xanthe look so physically and mentally depleted before. All the anger has drained out of her. Quaylyn and Kaydra look as empty as Anthya does. They seem to be holding up each other. If one should topple, they would both fall. Rabiam and Arpen look just as tired.

Glisa, Anthya and I make it down to the deck, and Melinda and Yanzic join us at the railing. We are alive, but too exhausted to dance and cheer. Instead we look at each other in silent joy.

"My brother, we have survived," Xanthe said softly.

"Yes, my sister, now we can rest."

Then Xanthe spoke again. "Kaydra, Quaylyn and Anthya, thank you." The words seem to drain her of what little energy she has left. "When I return to Twaka, I will see you are greatly rewarded." With that, she turned and with Arpen's help descended the stairs to her private quarters to rest.

For now we are united by survival.

CHAPTER 25

Ilene

Most of the community is gathered in the village circle shucking peago pods. I feel I should be helping, but Kiril asked me to take notes at the meeting with Chitter and Kitca. We had Caleeza arrange the meeting as a planned visit, we don't want our visitors feeling as though they are being interrogated, but Chitter and Kitca's arrival is the single most important event in the history of our community. We need reassurance they pose no threat. Rojaire, Traevus and Thayla are seeking information for their journey and Drak wants to learn more about his great grandfather Vestan who made first contact with Chitter's ancestors.

We arrive at First Shelter carrying gifts such as bread and fruit jelly, some useful household items, and two new child size frocks for them to wear. They have rejected our homemade sandals of woven tree bark with wooden soles, preferring to go barefoot. Caleeza greets us at the open door.

"Please be seated," she said after a traditional round of greetings. Chitter also chitters something in greeting. Some of the chairs have been removed to provide more living space, but there are still enough to go around. Kiril and Drak spread the two crystal floss maps we brought with us on the table and we gather around. Chitter studies the maps with interest, then chitters with laughter over Drak's great grandfather Vestan's crude drawing of one of her kind, drawn so long ago.

"This is a map of our valley," Caleeza explained. "We are located here. And this is a map of your valley. Can you show us where I met you?" To our surprise, Chitter reaches over and rearranges the maps so Chitter's valley is to the left of ours. Why had we always assumed it was the other way around? Then she pinpoints for us where she found Caleeza on the map of her valley.

Chitter and Caleeza must be bonded in some way, but no one knows how or why. Chitter understands Caleeza when she speaks and can impress thoughts and images to her in answer to our questions. But it doesn't work with anyone else.

"How did you get here?" Rojaire asked.

Chattering away, Chitter draws an imaginary line with her finger from where she met Caleeza, across her valley, then along an obscure zigzag line off the map to the edge of the table.

"The route to the edge of the table is a mountain pass to the coast line," Caleeza explained. "Chitter describes a long and arduous journey."

"Of course," Drak reasoned out loud. "Grandfather Vestan must have found a route to the valley from the sea."

Then Chitter's finger traces a line back across the table, right up to the unexplained markings at the northeast corner of the map of our valley.

"So what do these symbols stand for?" Rojaire asked indicating the mystery markings. When Caleeza poses the question, the reaction from Chitter is explosive. She trembles visibly, protectively clutching Kitca tightly to her as she screeches at invisible demons. After much discussion Caleeza tries to explain.

"The best I can understand, it is some kind of stairway, very old, dating back before the great devastation, and very dangerous. Some sort of evil magic lurks there."

"Did they use the 'stairway'?" Thayla asked.

"Yes, but she's not happy about it. I can't understand what she is trying to convey, but something terrible happened there. One thing is certain, the passage is dangerous."

"This could be another nightmare like the ruins of the Temple of Tranquility," Rojaire said.

I shudder at the thought. I was a member of the team, along with Rojaire and my father Theon, to find Caleeza, Ollen, Traevus and the rest of the members of their expedition. Anthya and Quaylyn were also with us. We discovered the ruins of the Temple of Tranquility where

Councilor Zayla met with a horrible death. Cremyn, a member of the expedition we were searching for, also met her demise there.

"How old is Kitca?" Kiril asked changing the topic.

"The best I can figure, Kitca is about Halren's age."

Where's her father?" Traevus asked. "Didn't Chitter tell you she was the last of her kind? Don't you think an explanation is needed?"

"I've asked these questions before," Caleeza said frustrated, "but I can't understand the answer. I will keep trying."

"Why did they come here if the journey was so hard?" Kiril asked. It's a good question, one on all our minds.

"To find me," Caleeza said after Chitter's response.

"But why?"

"I think they hoped to find more of their kind," Caleeza said after questioning. "I don't know where they got that idea from."

"How is it possible for you and Chitter to communicate?" Traevus asked.

"That's another question I haven't been able to get an answer to," Caleeza said.

"The crystal floss strap over there once belonged to my great grandfather," Drak said pointing to the discarded sash. Chitter abandoned wearing the strap after Caleeza provided her with a dress to wear, but she still wears the medallion. "I wondered if I could have a look at it."

When Caleeza asks, Chitter immediately jumps off her chair and fetches it for him. She chitters something as she reverently hands the strap to Drak.

"She said it is yours to keep, as a gift."

"Thank you," Drak said graciously surprised by her generosity. "I will treasure it always." He takes the gift examining it carefully. Worn across one shoulder and cinched at the waist, the crystal floss sash had to have been made for Chitter's ancestor, probably by Drak's great grandfather. It is too small for anyone else to wear. It is a tool belt of sorts with pouches to carry an assortment of things. The crystal floss material is darkened with age and ground in dirt, but it endures. Drak inspects the pouches still in tack. They hold dried fruit, seeds and nuts, as well as some stone implements.

"Do you want these?" Drak asked offering Chitter her tools. Chitter declines indicating the new utensils they have been provided.

Drak's maps have proven to be invaluable aides and Rojaire was right all along, there is a route to the sea. But there are still so many unanswered questions. I have copious notes from the discussion and so does Kiril. I'm sure between us, we have it covered.

"Maybe Chitter and Kitca have questions they would like to ask us," I suggested to maintain a balance.

"Good idea," Kiril agreed. Caleeza asks and Kitca speaks up for the first time and Chitter repeats for Caleeza's benefit, which raises an interesting question. How come Caleeza can understand Chitter, but not Kitca? Don't they speak the same language?

"She wants to know if she is allowed to leave the shelter when she wants," Caleeza said with some shock. "Of course," she answered immediately. "You can go outside whenever you want, wherever you want. This is your shelter for now. It's a place for you to rest and have privacy. You are not a prisoner here."

It's time to bring this visit to a close. "Should we join the peago pod shucking party and give them a hand?" Kiril said when there were no more questions. Everyone volunteers to help, even Chitter and Kitca. I gather our notes and Kiril rolls up the maps. Drak is still looking over his gift. Together we stroll to the village circle.

The peago pod shucking party has made great progress. There are bags of the silky white fibers ready for spinning and bags of empty pods for making paper. More helping hands will make quick work of what is left.

As we enter the circle, Setas runs up to her father. Rojaire picks her up and carries her in his arms back to the group. "I need to ask Chitter something," I hear her say.

"What's that?" Caleeza asked.

"Can Kitca be in our play?"

"I'll ask."

Caleeza quickly discovers Chitter has no concept of a play. "Well, Alaia and Caponya are really excited," Caleeza said. "I would be glad to give you a hand with it."

"That would be wonderful."

"Let me know when you want to meet, I'll bring Chitter and Kitca."

CHAPTER 26

Rojaire

We slip away from the community by Seaa's light, without fanfare this time. Leaving Kaylya and the children is the hardest part of this journey.

I still feel some unease about leaving those strange creatures with the community, despite Caleeza's reassurances they are harmless. Or something else could happen or go wrong. Of course there really isn't any need to worry. I know there are many capable men and women in the village who can handle any situation that arises.

I tried again to learn more about the "stairs." Caleeza gave me all she could from Chitter's confusing information. Hopefully some of the things she mentioned will make better sense when we are there. For her, the crossing had been terrifying and she vowed never to make the journey again. But one thing is certain, there is a route to the sea and I intend to find it.

We reach the edge of the forest and the now mostly harvested peago bushes just before Seaa sets. It is dark in the brief span of time between Seaa set and sunrise, so we take a brief rest break while waiting for daylight. Refreshed and eager to hike, we rise with the break of daylight, giving us an early start across the grassland before it gets too hot. We leave the forest behind and head northeast across the grasslands.

As usual Thayla leads. "How can I protect you if I don't scout ahead first? As you may recall, it was I who flushed out the Chitters." I can't argue with that. To argue with Thayla against the need for so much protection is futile. So Thayla leads and naturally Traevus follows. Therefore, I've taken the position of rear guard.

Right away we stumble upon a herd of kurpers at their morning feed, the little silver-furred hoofed animals make a hasty retreat before us. The rustling and waving of the tall blue-green grass, hiding them from view, marks their passage.

The day quickly grows warm. Seemingly endless grassland stretches out languidly before us, shimmering in the sun. The promise of eventual cool forest shade remains in the hazy distance. Journeying across the grasslands wears us down and eventually we have to rest. Thayla chops down an area of grass, large enough for all of us, with her long curved blade then sits down to sharpen it again.

So far we have sustained on prepared trail food and water. The forest, when we reach it, may offer fresh forage. But Thayla is thinking meat. "I'll see if I can sneak up on a kurper for our dinner while you two rest." I wave her off and lay back in the grass to take a quick nap.

It isn't long before Thayla startles me by appearing silently with a gutted, headless kurper in hand. How can such a massive woman move so quietly? "I see you had a successful hunt."

Thayla kicks Traevus awake. "Time to get up my precious one. We need to make it to the forest before we sleep. I have our dinner," she said proudly holding up her kill for Traevus to see. "We don't want it to spoil before I have a chance to cook it."

"What a woman!" Traevus said with admiration.

"And a princess, too!" I couldn't help adding.

Coaxed by Thayla we march on. The land begins to rise slightly. Berry bushes and scrubby trees gradually replace the prairie grass. Soon we are back in forest and the sound of the river reaches our ears. Finally we arrive at the ford in the river, our turn around point before. We set up camp, refill our water flasks and gather dead wood for a fire while Thayla preps the meat.

"Do you think the High Council has ever sent out a search for us? It's been a long time." Traevus said as we sit around a little fire, the aroma of roasting kurper assailing our senses. Dripping fat sizzles in the fire creating an occasional brief flare up.

"Good question, I've often wondered about that myself." I think about it for a moment. "They probably have by now, don't you think? They can't be that disinterested."

"Well, they didn't find us, that's for sure. I wonder who replaced Captain Setas on Alaia Island."

"They would have had to replace Captain Setas' ferryboat too," I added. "The ferryboat is at Lavender Beach."

"That wouldn't be so hard to do with all the wood available on Alaia Island," Thayla said. She removes the spit from over the fire and we tear into the meat. It tastes so good, I'm really hungry. Apparently, so is everyone else. We reduce the little roasted creature down to skin and bones fairly quickly.

"If we find a route to the sea and build a boat we will be able to return to Mainland," Traevus pointed out. "What will you do, Thayla, love of my heart, if we make it back to Alaia Island? Will you leave me to grieve a life alone, or will you take me with you to be your prince?"

Thayla gives Traevus a shove, far too gentle to ever hurt him, which says more about her feelings for him than she usually cares to show. "Don't think of me that way. It can never be."

Traevus moves closer to her, his feelings for her never veiled. "Why can't I think of you that way? Is it because I'm Aaian?"

"No."

"Is it because I'm shorter than you? I can make taller shoes."

"No," she said smiling over the implied image.

"Is it because you are a princess?"

"No."

"Please, tell me why."

"Because I don't want to put you in danger. It is my job to protect you."

"Protect me from what?"

"From my family who may want to assassinate you."

"Is there anyone you get along with in your family?"

"Just my brother Lozar."

"Would he beat me up? Let me know, I'm ready to take him on. I'll take my chances," Traevus said kissing her on the cheek. Thayla didn't resist.

"Why, Traevus, I think you're wearing her down," I chuckled moving off to get some sleep.

The sun is high in a cloudless sky when we ford across the river to continue our hike. Fortunately the forest provides some much needed shade. Gradually the landscape changes. The flatland rises into gently rolling hills. Soon we are walking into a dense forest of large trees. The sound of gurgling water indicates a creek nearby. Locating the creek, we douse our arms and faces with cool refreshing water.

"You know what I miss most?" Traevus said as we hike on.

"What's that?" I asked.

"Fish. Remember the fish dish Captain Setas used to serve us during our ferryboat crossings?"

Actually I miss Captain Setas far more than her fish dish, but I say nothing, letting Traevus continue to reminisce as I turn my thoughts toward Kaylya, Jack and my own little Setas. What are they doing now?

CHAPTER 27

Aurora

"**Y**ou want us to do what?" I asked Mother shocked by her suggestion.

"You heard me, Aurora. Kitca is about the same age as you and the boys. You should include her in some of your activities." This is bad, really bad. And there will be no getting out of it. Theon and I exchange horrified looks. But then again we need to spend time with Kitca to learn more about why she and her mother are here.

"Chitter and Caleeza are going herb gathering, and I'm going with them, so I thought you could spend some time with Kitca and show her around a bit."

"But Theon and I were going..." I paused. I almost gave it away. Our meeting of the Secret Warriors will have to wait.

"Going where?" Mother asked.

"Play tag ball," I quickly substituted.

"Excellent. You can teach Kitca how to play." Oh no, this is getting even worse. Theon and I exchange looks of dismay. Mother has us trapped. "By the way, Halren and Selyzar have some news to tell you."

"What news?" Theon asked.

"I'll let them tell you." We finish our chores and the math assignments Zaloka and Wessid gave us. Then grabbing our bag of tag balls, we dash off to let Halren know what we had gotten ourselves into.

Our family is the only multi-generation family in the valley. Mother says Halren is my uncle, which doesn't make sense at all. When we arrive Zaloka lets us in. Zaloka is our grandmother, although we don't call her grandmother like Mother says they do on Earth. Still we love her dearly. She always has special treats made for all the children. I guess you could say Zaloka is everyone's grandmother. Grandfather Wessid and Halren are engrossed in a miniature building they are constructing out of wood, clay and rocks.

"What's that?" Theon asked.

"It's a model of your future schoolhouse," Wessid said grandly. "What do you think?" The model doesn't have a roof yet, so you can see inside. There is an entry way, then a wall dividing the building into two rooms. "We would have built the model at First Shelter, but since it is being lived in at the moment we decided to build it here."

"And guess what? Selyzar and I have convinced the school committee, and the rest of the community, to build the school on the other side of the creek, directly across from the tag ball grove."

"That's the big news. I thought everyone said across the creek was too far away. How did you change their minds?" I asked.

"Father suggested we could build more foot bridges. With the school across from the nut tree grove, it will be centrally located, and with another foot bridge, it will be easily accessible. We start work on the foundation after the next period of sleep."

I realize since I live next to the tag ball course, the school will actually be closer than before with a bridge across the creek. Halren and Selyzar have influenced an important decision, the location of our school. I probably should have volunteered to be on the committee after all.

"Why do we need a schoolhouse anyway?" I asked.

"Because it will make educating all you children easier, a place to teach and learn," Wessid said. Zaloka and Wessid have been teaching all the math instruction from the oldest to the youngest. Only a few books and scrolls made it to the valley, all highly valued, but no math textbooks. So Zaloka and Wessid, both math enthusiasts, are writing the textbooks as we grow. Zaloka even does pre-math activities with Caponya and Sarus, as she did with all of us, giving Caleeza some quality free time.

"We better get to Selyzar before Chitter and Kitca arrive so we can tell him what's happening," I said as we leave Halren's house."

"Why, what's happening?" Halren asked.

"Instead of a meeting of the Secret Warriors, we are to teach Kitca how to play tag ball," Theon quickly explained.

"So let's invite Kitca to play Tag Ball. This could be the break we've been looking for. It's our mission to gather information from Kitca, here is our chance. Very little is known about these people, maybe we will learn something. The information we gather could be very important," Halren explained.

Put that way, playing tag ball with Kitca isn't such a bad idea. We have a secret mission. We are the Secret Warriors.

"Plus, it could be a lot of fun. Imagine Kitca playing tag ball," Theon said giggling.

Arriving at Selyzar's house we find Chitter and Kitca are already there and Mother arrives right behind us. It's always fun going to Selyzar's house. With so many siblings around there is always something happening.

Taking advantage of the situation, I graciously invite Kitca to play tag ball with us. Mother nods her approval, but of course, she is unaware of my ulterior motive. Caleeza translates and Kitca is delighted to join us. There, it's done.

Then Ollen decides, "It's such a beautiful day, how about if Alaia, Caponya, Sarus and I join the game."

"That would be great," the boys agreed. Can this get any crazier? We gather all the tag balls we can find into a sack and head out to the grove of nut trees between our house and Halren's where we play. The nut grove has always been a favorite playground, second only to the village circle. The trees, so big and easy to climb, are irresistible to a child and the scattered brush growing between them makes the grove great for sneaking around and hiding. Eventually, utilizing both features of the grove, the game of tag ball evolved.

On the way, Theon pulls Selyzar aside to quietly explain what led to a tag ball game instead of a club meeting, I can sense his excitement. Watching them, I totally miss Kitca's approach until she touches my hand. Startled, I involuntarily jerk away as I feel the mental connection.

"I know you have a life seed, but you don't have to worry. I will keep your secret."

I gape at her, mouth open, but speechless. A life seed? Well, I know I'm not pregnant. Does she mean the star stone? Wait till I tell the Secret Warriors about this! Not knowing what to do, or say, I hand her a tag ball which she examines with interest. "That is a tag ball."

We quickly arrive at the grove and empty out our bags of tag balls, ready to pick teams. "Who should be the captains?" Selyzar asked.

"How about this? Let's have Halren, Theon, Aurora, and Kitca on one team, and Selyzar, Caponya, Alaia, Sarus and myself on the other," Ollen suggested. That's four against five, fair enough?"

Why not? We lose Selyzar from our dream team to play with his family, but we are left with only one weak player, Kitca, who knows nothing about the game, while Ollen and Selyzar have three weak players to deal with because of their young age.

"You're on our team," I told Kitca.

"Are we playing tag ball?" Edty asked appearing out of nowhere at the edge of the grove with several new tag balls in hand. I don't know how he does it, it's like he can smell a tag ball game forming.

Tag ball wouldn't exist without Edty, he makes all our tag balls and has laid out most of the rules. He also loves watching, playing and refereeing the game. Tag balls are fist size balls made of kurper fur stuffed with dried grass. Edty makes sure all the balls are the same size and weight, keeping them light enough not to hurt on impact, but heavy enough to throw a short distance. Abusive throwing disqualifies a player from the game.

While Edty and Ollen distribute tag balls, I try to quickly explain the game to Kitca. "The rules are simple. Each player is given two tag balls. Teams start at opposite ends of the grove and make their way to their opponent's end trying to take out the enemy while avoiding being taken out themselves. If you are hit with a ball, you are out of the game. A team member who is tagged out can give any balls he or she has in possession to another player. Balls once thrown, whether they hit or miss their target, can be claimed by any player who comes across them. Survivors of the first run compete again until there is a victor. Got it?"

Only confused thoughts hit my brain. "You'll see," I said brushing it off.

Seeing we were already divided up into teams Edty makes a decision. "I'll play on this team," he said joining Ollen.

"Wait, six to four isn't fair," Theon protested. "If you have Edty, we want Selyzar."

"Alright, Selyzar, you can join your friends," Ollen agreed.

We were satisfied. The four of us and Kitca against two old men and three little children seemed fair. Edty is a great player, but so is Selyzar. "Go!" we hear Edty shout from across the grove and the game is on.

We spread out making our way deeper into the grove. I try to keep an eye on Kitca, but she is gone, I don't know where. I make it to the center of the grove and start to climb the tree we call The Castle to look for her. A tag ball flies by my head causing me to pause. Before I can spot Caponya on the tree branch above me, Ollen jumps out of the brush and takes me out. The boys don't fare any better.

As luck would have it, Kitca is the only player on our team to make it through, and she does it without throwing a single ball. Apparently, running to the other side of the grove is all she understood about the directions I gave her.

"What happened?" Theon asked. We gather together on the sideline, tagged-out losers, in shattering disbelief. The defeat of the dream team is a hard blow for the boys to take.

"We still have one player," Halren pointed out.

"That's just great," Theon moaned.

"Can you give Kitca some instruction, Aurora?" Selyzar asked.

"I'll try, but it won't do any good."

"Hey you losers, are you ready for the second round?" Alaia gloated, her team still in tack.

"Kitca against five?" I found myself protesting vehemently. "Ollen and Edty cheated by putting the little ones up in the trees. They should be disqualified."

"That's right," the boys cried out joining the protest.

"That would leave Caponya, Alaia and Sarus against Kitca. At least they are closer to the same size," Halren pointed out.

"It would be a fairer match," Selyzar agreed. To my surprise Edty and Ollen agree with our logic and bow out of the second run.

I grab Kitca's hand and nearly drag her to our end of the grove while pumping some strategy in her head. "Now listen, stay low and move quickly. Don't let anyone see you as you sneak across the grove. You also have to take out the enemy. Hide in the tree branches or in the bushes as you sneak up on the others and when they are in range, hit them with a ball, not too hard, gently. Can you throw a ball?" I doubt Kitca understands a word of it, but she chitters with enthusiastic eagerness.

"Then go!" I urged her when Edty shouts start.

Kitca shoves her two balls into—a built-in pouch! At least that's what it looks like to me. To my added shock, she drops down on all fours slinking low and soundlessly through the brush like a predator on the hunt.

To our amazement, without Ollen and Edty's help, the younger children don't have a chance. She flushes them out one by one, and due to their poor aim, in no time at all, Kitca becomes the victor of the game.

CHAPTER 28

Anthya

"**A**re you sure these are the right coordinates?" Lozar asked solemnly.

"Yes," I said weakly walking away. Dread and horror tightens my stomach as I think of Captain Setas and the colonists. Silently I leave the wheelhouse and make my way down to the deck. Grief overwhelms me. I clutch the deck railing as I watch the *Xanthe Queen* bobbing around on open water where Alaia Island should be. Nothing marks the spot. How devastating a seismic event it must have been to break up Alaia Island, sending it to the bottom of the sea! How could anyone have survived?

Amongst us, only Quaylyn and I have met Captain Setas and seen the beautiful, densely foliated tropical island she cultivated. Now she is gone. Quaylyn and I share our grief and our joy of having known Captain Setas in life as the *Xanthe Queen* bobs in place beside us.

"What about the colonists?" Melinda asked joining me at the railing. I don't know what to tell her.

"There's no island here. Should we move on?" Xanthe shouted across the water to Lozar. The princess has toned down her rage some after our near death experience, her attitude toward Quaylyn and Kaydra, Twaka's former Mentor, somewhat changed since they saved her ship from the Pinnacles. She has even softened some toward me. Hopefully it will last for a while.

"Yes, we go on," Lozar agreed. "Lynnara is a continent. There must be something still standing."

Our journey since our run-in with the Pinnacles has been uneventful until our discovery of the demise of Alaia Island. The last leg of the voyage is now excruciating as anxiety over what we will find intensifies. I'm really looking forward to stepping on land again. I just hope Lavender Beach is recognizable. We should reach our final destination by sunrise.

Melinda and I stand at the bow gazing east toward a land mass we can't yet see. The sea ripples under the starlight, glistening lazily in a dance of reflected light. Glisa soon joins us.

"Do you think we will find any land left standing?" Melinda asked.

"Of course we will. Lynnara is a big place, Alaia was only a small island," I assured her, but I too will be relieved to see land. I'm starting to have doubts myself. Of course, I don't tell her that.

"We find Princess Thayla, I stay," Glisa announced in English. "I not go back."

Her announcement hardly surprises me. Life under the thumb of Twaka's royal family can't be all good. I would want to leave too after having met Xanthe. And Glisa knows Melinda doesn't intend returning to Mainland if she finds Ilene. But I wonder what Yanzic's position is on this since Glisa and Yanzic have exhibited great interest in one another. Then I realize with shock, the others see Lozar and me in the same light.

We continue to gaze, sharply focused, on the eastern sky seeping daylight over a dark purple line rising above the sea. It's impossible to tell from here if it is land or a cloud bank. Yanzic climbs up to the lookout platform.

"Rofk topah!" Yanzic shouts back dashing our hope.

"No land," Melinda translated. Climbing back down, Yanzic joins us at the bow railing. He greets me with a gentle tip of his head and a hint of a smile. He and Glisa leave after a while, so does Melinda. I don't even notice them leaving. I also don't hear Lozar's approach until he is standing beside me. Looking around, I note we are alone.

"This is the longest I've ever been at sea," I said to start a conversation. "I miss land."

"I miss seeing land on the horizon," Lozar said. "On my world the sight of land is never that far away."

"Is there a lack of water on Twaka?"

"We have plenty of ocean. It's just that our land masses are broken up in more pieces and spread out."

"I would like to visit Twaka someday."

"I will be your guide."

This time he does smile, freely and openly, then grows more solemn. "Do you think Thayla and others are still alive?" he asked.

I answer honestly. "It's getting harder to believe they are, but we must. Melinda and I carry with us a flute that was left behind on Mainland and a charter for a colony on Lynnara from the High Council, and we intend to deliver both," I said with force.

Then suddenly I see morning glow glint off of something floating in the water. "Debris!" I quickly warned pointing starboard. Glisa swerves the boat avoiding a collision. The debris turns out to be a floating log.

"Well, that's the first sign of land we've seen. How strange there are no birds! You better warn the others to watch for obstacles."

I try to send a telepathic message to the *Xanthe Queen* through Quaylyn or Kaydra about the need for caution, but I can't make contact. "I can no longer contact the others telepathically," I informed Lozar. "We are under the aura of the Crystalline Landscape."

"So that means the Crystalline Landscape still exists?"

"Apparently. Therefore, we can probably assume, so does the continent it dominates."

As the sky continues to lighten, Yanzic climbs up the ladder to the mast once again. "Topah!" he cried out from the lookout platform. Early morning light reveals the distinct outline of land looming before us. We gaze out mesmerized as we watch a continent rise out of the sea. It beckons mercilessly. Lynnara's contour sharpens in the strengthening daylight, then burns in fire as the sun rises above her. If I could teleport, I would be there already, but the influence of the Crystalline Landscape prevents it.

As we approach the shore, several fish breach the water before us. "At least the fishing should be good," Lozar said.

Vertical cliffs surround most of the continent's coastline, with Lavender Beach offering the only easy access to the interior of the continent. As we approach, I notice drastic changes to the landscape. The long curving peninsula that served as a protective breakwater to the bay is eroded away leaving Lavender Beach exposed to the ravages of the sea. The beach we approach differs greatly from the pristine lavender sands I remember. Instead, a tangled pile of wood debris covers the beach and extends far into the valley.

The *Xanthe Queen* pulls up alongside us. We tie the two boats together and inch in toward the shore.

I can hardly wait to get off this boat. The last leg of the voyage has taxed my patience.

"Land is a welcomed sight," Xanthe said standing on the deck. For once I have to agree.

CHAPTER 29

Quaylyn

At long last I stand on solid ground. At first, the land undulates in my vision as my body continues to compensate for the roll of the sea, slowly the land starts to settle down. After helping to securely anchor the *Xanthe Queen* and *Princess Thayla* to the beach, I make my way up the beach through the maze of debris to the mouth of the Zayla River and follow it while the others get organized. I want a little time alone.

If the colonists settled near Lavender Beach, I fear they may have died in the tsunami. There would have been lots of incentives for living near the shore: the view, the climate, access to the sea for fish, plus Captain Setas had introduced many food producing plants in the area to supplement the devastated continent's sparsity of plant variety.

What am I looking for? Signs of life? Human bones? Will I find skeletal remains mixed in with the jumble of wood? Only thin clumps of wispy blue-green grass and a few knee-high spiky zan fruit bushes dot the desolate landscape. The zan fruit bushes' round golden leaves and bright orange fruit add cheerful splashes of color to the bleak landscape.

Zan fruit is the most prevalent plant on the continent, a survival food if one becomes stranded. The small, round orange fruit serves as a valuable source of nutrient rich water. And they are easy to find, the gold/orange zan fruit bushes contrast strikingly with the continent's dark purple soil. For old time sake, I pluck a zan fruit off a bush, tear it open and suck on the juicy pulp.

I can see undisturbed ground unreached by the waves in the distance. Looking even farther into the distance I see what looks like a forest. Only there are no forests on Lynnara. My heart springs with eternal hope. Could the colonists still be alive?

Having recovered my land legs, I head back to the beach. Lozar meets me half way. "So what's the plan?" I asked.

"Glisa and Yanzic have volunteered to stay with the boats. The rest of us are to follow the route on the map."

We have in our possession the journal Kiril turned in documenting Rojaire's mapping expedition and the resulting map. I suspect much has been left out of both, but I'm not sure what they are hiding. There is also a good chance the colony went inland to the Cremyn River Valley, much talked about in Kiril's journal and named after a member of the lost expedition.

"What did you find?" Lozar asked.

"I haven't found any skeletons yet, if that's what you mean. A large swath of land has been stripped of vegetation, but I see a tree line on a rise to the northeast that wasn't there before."

"I guess that's encouraging. Maybe the colony is there."

"Maybe. There is always hope."

"Any wildlife to hunt here?"

"No wildlife, no animal life, not even insects. Just fish in the sea."

"No wonder it looks so dead."

By the time we return to the beach, the team is ready to go. I tell the group about the line of trees I spotted on a low rise in the distance. "I think they are trees planted by Rojaire's mapping expedition. I don't recall seeing them the last time we were here."

"We know Captain Setas had the mapping expedition plant trees along the way. Perhaps the colonist are there," Anthya said.

"Oh, I hope you are right," Melinda gasped.

"The shade will be a welcome relief from the sun," Xanthe added. "Let's get moving."

What a pleasure it is to walk on solid ground again! The debris field thins as we make our way northeast where zan fruit bushes are once again claiming the land. "What's this?" Xanthe asked.

"Zan fruit, a survival food that provides both water and nutrients. Here try one," I said plucking the fruit off the bush and offering it to her. To her credit, she took a bite and chewed.

"I wouldn't want to have to survive for long on this," Xanthe growled spitting out zan fruit pulp. Fortunately we have enough trail food and water.

"There are more desirable edibles to be found once we clear the scoured area," Anthya assured her.

The ground rises gradually as we continue to hike angling away from the beach and the river toward the forest we can now clearly see, shimmering in the hot sun on a rise of higher ground. Then Melinda turns our attention in the opposite direction.

"Look, over there!" Melinda called out pointing to something different off to our right.

"It definitely looks like something constructed," I said gazing at the mound of debris. Melinda, Anthya, Lozar and I rush toward it.

"It's Captain Setas' ferryboat," Anthya announced.

"I hope she wasn't on it at the time," Lozar said.

Wide holes yawn from the bottom and one side of the ferryboat where I assume it was rammed hard by floating debris. The ferryboat's other side burrows deeply into the sandy soil piled around it.

"Does that mean Captain Setas made it off the island before it sank?" Anthya asked.

"I think so. If the ferry had been at Alaia Island it would have been sucked down when the island sank. My guess is the ferryboat was anchored at Lavender Beach when the tsunami struck. It could mean the boat was still here after bringing the colonists across."

"Let's hope Captain Setas stayed with the colonists and they all escaped the tsunami. Surely Rojaire warned her the High Council would come after her for helping the colonists escape if she stayed at Alaia Island," Anthya speculated.

I have to agree with her. Rojaire would have convinced Captain Setas to leave the island for her own protection.

"We're wasting time here," Xanthe complained coming onto the scene huffing with impatience. "Let's move on."

I'm surprised Xanthe didn't take the opportunity to plow on ahead without us. Her curt commands are a constant reminder of her intention to find Thayla and remove her from the line of succession. A knot of anxiety grips my stomach. What will happen when we do find the colonists? I shouldn't have let Xanthe out my sight, even if Kaydra is keeping an eye on her.

We move on, the hot sun bearing down on us. Climbing out the flood plain, we step over a high water line of small debris and onto land that hasn't been disturbed for centuries. Though the foliage still seems sparse across the lavender landscape, Anthya points out pinkberry, waist-high pink and orange spiky leafed bushes with thumb-size pink teardrop fruit, and ground nuts, a small unassuming plant with dull gray and silver leaves that produces a delicious nut underground. And of course there's the ubiquitous zan fruit bushes.

As we approach the edge of the trees, Kaydra and I move in closer to Xanthe. I notice Anthya and Lozar are close at hand, so are Arpen and Rabiam. Whether their intent is to protect Xanthe from us or Thayla from Xanthe, I'm not sure.

We crest the rise to find hundreds of trees stretching before us all the way to the distant hillside. But it quickly becomes obvious the colonists are not here.

"I didn't expect to see a whole forest of trees," Anthya said in awe.

"Some are already bearing fruit!" Kaydra exclaimed.

The forest, young and thriving, has obviously been planted by human hands. Fruit and nut trees, as well as ornamentals and hardwoods, well-spaced, but starting to fill in the space, covers all the level ground of the rise.

But there is no sign of habitation, no evidence of shelter building. No evidence of human presence.

"Alright, Quaylyn, so where are they?" Xanthe demanded.

"Somewhere other than here," I said walking away to enjoy the shade and fruit of the forest.

CHAPTER 30

Lozar

Thayla isn't here and there are not clues to her whereabouts. I almost feel relieved. At least a confrontation has been avoided. How can I get Xanthe away from here? For Thayla's safety, I need to convince her to give up the search and go home.

I stroll to the edge of the forest. The rise provides an excellent view of the broad river valley sloping up to the foothills and mountains in all directions. Looking out over the landscape, I can see the farthest point the flood reached inland. As I continue to study this strange land, Quaylyn steps up and points out something else. "You see those groups of mounds out there in the distance? Those are zaota trees, an incredible specimen native to the land. I suggest we camp there. The trees will provide us shelter for a period of rest."

"Sounds like a plan, let's share it with the others."

Before leaving, we stroll through the forest loading up on fresh food, while still searching for clues. But there are no clues to be found. Obviously no one has been here for a long time, possibly not since the trees were planted.

Finally we are on our way again. The sun has gotten even hotter and the distance to the small grove of zaota trees proves to be far greater than it looked from the forested low rise overlooking the valley. By the time we arrive here, everyone is ready for a rest.

I have to admit, these trees are quite amazing. For a land of such sparse growth, the zaota tree is a noble surprise. Reaching three times my height, the tree's thick trunk is hidden under a dense umbrella-shaped canopy of long thin blue-green and gold streaming leaves waving in the breeze. Apparently all the growth is from the top, yet the leaves reach all the way to the ground. And the space under the canopy is large enough to shelter a half dozen people—two or three comfortably.

"You call this a tree?" Xanthe asked upon close inspection.

On cue, Quaylyn and Anthya walk up to the tree and pull back the canopy of leaves, creating an opening. "Your quarters, your Highness," Quaylyn said bowing gracefully. "The trees are living grass huts offering dry circles of ground cushioned with old leaf growth around their trunks for bedding."

"And you can tie off the opening if you want a view," Anthya said. For once Xanthe actually smiled.

After Rabiam, Arpen, Melinda and Kaydra finish exploring the zaota grove, we gather in the shade of Xanthe's shelter and feast on the bounty we harvested from the young forest.

"So where do we go from here?" I asked when we were all settled.

Anthya unfolds the map created by Rojaire's mapping expedition and locates our position. "We are here," she points out. The zaota tree groves are clearly marked on the map. "From here we need to go northeast to intercept the Cremyn River, then over this ridge to reach the Cremyn Valley."

"Kiril's journal indicates the Cremyn Valley would be an ideal place for settlement," Quaylyn said.

"Then that is where we will go," Xanthe said and retires to her tree. Totally exhausted, everyone else soon does the same. Since there are seven trees and eight of us, Melinda and Anthya decide to share a tree. While the others sleep, I rest outside in the shadow of my shelter keeping guard over them.

The sun is high in the sky when we continue on again. Anthya walks apace with me on the hike from the zaota tree grove to the Cremyn River. More zaota groves loom in the distance, but in the direction we are headed, the landscape rises gently into rolling hills.

"Away from the coast, the land seems unchanged since our journey several cycles of seasons ago seeking the lost expedition, so empty, so lonely," she said after a long period of silent walking.

"And you returned."

"Honestly, the more I see it, the more I'm drawn to it."

Although I'm not ready to admit it, there is something compelling about this place, it can easily swallow you up. Where are you, Rojaire? Where's my sister and your other followers? Is the colony in a secret, hidden location as Quaylyn suspects? Or has the continent swallowed you up?

I have a hard time understanding Thayla's motive for joining the colonists. I know Thayla is no fool, so why did she join? Was she running away from Xanthe or toward something she wanted? One thing is certain, she went on her own free will.

"What are you thinking about?" Anthya asked.

"I was thinking of Thayla and the lost colonists," I answered. Not a complete lie. "Why does Quaylyn suspect that the journal and map are incomplete?"

"Well there are several reasons actually. We don't believe the journal Kiril turned in to the High Council is the actual journal he kept on the journey. It was too clean, too polished, lacking the spontaneity of actual time entries. Also three members of the mapping expedition voluntarily stayed behind, but there is no indication on the map, or mention in the journal, where they stayed. Plus, snatches of poorly concealed thought were picked up from Kiril, the youngest member of the group, when they returned that indicated a great secret."

"I see, something to consider."

The land becomes increasingly rocky, and the journey evolves into an exhausting hike across overlapping hills. Finally we reach the Cremyn River, a trickle of a stream meandering through a narrow dark blue rocky chasm, where we take a welcomed break.

"Not much of a river," Xanthe said.

"Most of the water takes an underground route to the sea. Only a small amount of the water comes through the canyon to join the Zayla River," Quaylyn explained. We fill our water containers, splash cool refreshing water over faces, and lean back against dark blue boulders covered with plush iridescent pink and orange mosses.

"We will have to hike over that mountain," Quaylyn said pointing out the route to the north as the sun eased off toward the west.

"Why can't we follow this little stream?" Xanthe asked.

"Too dangerous, even impassable, through the canyon according to Kiril's journal," Quaylyn explained. "Kiril probably got that information from Rojaire and knowing Rojaire, he's probably tried it already."

After a brief rest and some refreshment we head out again. Quaylyn and Anthya lead the way, soon stretching far ahead of us with Xanthe stomping after them followed by Rabiam and Arpen. Melinda and Kaydra, in less of a rush, keep pace with me in the back of the pack.

"I've heard so many tales of the Devastated Continent from Anthya and Quaylyn, it's fascinating to finally see it for myself," Kaydra said.

"I like it because it is so open and free," Melinda said.

"Like Alaska?" Kaydra asked.

"No, this is nothing like Alaska."

We push ourselves harder to catch up with the others. The warmth of the sun and the mostly uphill exertion soon drench us in sweat. We pause briefly when the ground levels out, enjoying the view. A gentle breeze helps to cool us off. Eventually, we catch up with Xanthe and the others as we crest the highest point and look down into the Cremyn Valley, the Cremyn River cutting through it, and a stone shelter nearly hidden in another young forest on the opposite bank of the stream.

The only thing keeping Xanthe from charging down the mountain to attack her sister are the others all around her. We head down the mountain as a group, keeping a close watch on the nearly growling princess. There is no answer to our shouts as we wade across the shallow river and approach the shelter. It doesn't take long upon our arrival to ascertain the area is deserted and has been for a long time.

CHAPTER 31

Ilene

The atmosphere is always festive when the village gathers, regardless how hard the work may be. The entire community, children and adults, have turned out to work on the foundation for the new schoolhouse. But such gatherings also emphasize Traevus, Thayla and Rojaire's absence.

Kiril, Theon, Aurora and I arrive together, carrying food and tools to the chosen site across the creek from the giant nut trees. A log bridge has already been constructed using the trees cleared from the foundation site. "Thank you so much for your help," Kaylya greeted us.

"What's the goal for today?" Kiril asked.

"The committee is hoping to finish the foundation work so we can start the framing. I know that's ambitious considering the size of the building and with three of our strongest workers away."

"We'll just have to do what we can," Kiril said.

The site is lovely, surrounded by mixed forest, berry bushes and the babbling stream. One lone giant nut tree, seemingly rebuked by the larger grove on the other side, dominates the area. At a safe distance from both the stream and the roots of the giant nut tree, Zaloka, Wessid, Caleeza and Ollen are squaring off the ground, staking it off while the others wait with homemade shovels to start digging.

"That's it," Inventor Sulyan called out when the cross measurements agreed. After driving in the corner stakes, Edty and Tassyn tie a string connecting the four corner stakes to mark off the perimeter.

"Well, there you are. It's a lot of digging," Tassyn said.

The dimensions look to be about fourteen feet by twenty-four feet by my estimate. I didn't adapt to the metric system on Earth and I haven't adapted to the Aaian system of measurement here. I guess I'm just a slow learner. We need to remove about four inches of topsoil to reach the hard pack underneath. With ridiculous eagerness, seven manned shovels begin digging with seven pairs of waiting hands ready to relieve them. The topsoil is piled off to the side to be claimed later for gardens.

Eventually Inventor Sulyan calls for a shift change and hands his shovel to Kaylya. I hand my shovel to Aurora and Kiril presents his to Theon. Edty and Tassyn switch out, so do Caleeza and Selyzar, Zaloka and Wessid, and Drak and Halren. Ollen, Chitter and Kitca aren't physically capable of digging, but they cheer us on, keep watch on the young children who are enjoying the growing mounds of dirt, and supply fresh drinking water.

The sun, long pass its zenith, slowly descends toward the west promising the eventual end to another long Aaian day. Seaa's light will be a cool relief from the heat of the Aaian sun. Just as my stomach starts to growl, Kaylya calls for lunch break. Before surging off to the picnic stashed under the giant nut tree, we stand around the foundation's perimeter to judge our progress, which is phenomenal considering. We will definitely manage to finish after lunch.

"How is the play coming along?" Kaylya asked after we sit down.

"We haven't had a lot of time to work on it with all that has been going on. I would have invited you to join us in the production, but I figured you already have a project, plus Jack and Setas want you to be surprised when you see it."

"You and Caleeza should take the little ones to the pavilion during the next work session here to work on the play. We will be hauling gravel and there are only three gravel carts, the small children will just be in the way."

"Alright with me. We can bring it up to Caleeza when she gets here." We both glance to where Caleeza is still washing dirt off the little ones at the stream, so they can eat.

"Do you think Thayla, Traevus and Rojaire have reached the end of the valley yet?" I asked. Kaylya and Rojaire have explored and mapped more of this continent than anyone.

"They should be getting close. We can approximate the coordinates of the valley and we know the latitude of the northern coastline. If the valley is as long as we estimate, the end of the valley won't be very far from the sea, barring a few mountains."

We wolf down sandwiches, fruit, and baked treats, then the men drift off to shade closer to the site to discuss the next work session's task, hauling in gravel fill from the river. After lunch, we make quick work of the rest of the excavation and go home weary, but with a warm sense of accomplishment. The children are tired and ready for sleep after a light supper. So are we.

After sending Kiril, Theon, and Aurora off to work on the schoolhouse, Caleeza and I meet with the children for a play rehearsal. She brings along Chitter and Kitca and Little Sarus. Setas, Alaia and Caponya want Kitca to be in the play too. After much explanation including the gist of the story, Kitca decides to join the cast and Chitter volunteers to help with communication.

I didn't know what I was getting into when I decided to do a play with the younger set. The production of "Three Little Girls," now "Four Little Girls," has grown into a huge project. I have to admit the four little girls together make for a cute picture. Even though Kitca is twice their age, she fits in perfectly.

Jack is a whole different story. He takes his role as the bear beast to heart, terrifying the girls on and off stage. Then little Sarus starts following Jack around growling and soon we have two bear beasts in the play. I have to admit, we have an enthusiastic cast.

"So where are we?" Caleeza asked settling down on one of the stone levels leading up to the pavilion while the children run around burning off some of their excess energy.

"Well, I've written up some lines for actors to practice." I said handing her a copy.

She glances over the paper. "Good. What are we going to do for props?"

"That's the question. Now we need to construct four shelters instead of three." The word 'houses' in the original story has been changed to 'shelters.'

"Why don't we pair them up since we have four girls?" Caleeza suggested. "That way we only need to construct two shelter props."

"That's a great idea! We can make one out of stick and one out of stone. The bear beasts can blow down the stick shelter, but not the one made of stone."

"We can't expect these little ones to build these shelters."

"What if we pre-build a little stick shelter just big enough for the children to crawl into at one end of the pavilion and the stone shelter at the other end? The children can then place the last two pieces of construction onto their shelters in the play. And so no toes get smashed, we can construct a couple of light-weight fake stones."

Then Chitter starts chittering and Caleeza interprets. It seems Chitter can follow our conversation somewhat by her telepathic connection with Caleeza. "Chitter suggests we use the entrance to the cave for the stone shelter."

"Another great idea," I exclaimed impressed. "The cave will easily accommodate all four children at the end of the play. We can build a little fake front wall in front of the cave entrance for the stone shelter. And of course the bear beast can't get them there."

"Makes things a lot easier," Caleeza agreed. "Let's have the littlest girls, Alaia and Caponya, in the stick shelter and Kitca and Setas in the stone shelter. That will leave one end of the pavilion free for action. We need something to help the children stay on cue and knit it all together."

"We could have a narrator," I suggested.

"And a flutist," Caleeza said. "I'll narrate if you provide the music."

"Agreed. I think we need a role for Chitter too."

Then Chitter had another idea. Caleeza laughed. "Chitter wants to scare off the bear beasts at the end."

"Excellent! That will get lots of laughs. We already know Chitter can be the life of the party."

"We certainly have our work cut out for us," Caleeza said indicating the rambunctious cast running and playing between the pavilion and the stream.

"We have time to get it all together, Jack and Setas want their father home for the performance. Besides we need more people in the audience. At the rate we're going, half the village will be involved in the production."

"I wonder how Rojaire, Traevus and Thayla are doing. They should be nearing the end of the valley by now," Caleeza sighed. Then Chitter began chittering vociferously.

"Chitter is sending me images again of the Stairs. She still insists the Stairs are darkly dangerous and strangely powerful, and she is upset over Rojaire's rejection of her warning."

"I don't think he rejected her warning, I'm sure he is taking it into consideration. Thayla will protect Traevus and Rojaire."

"I miss Thayla," Caleeza sighed. "It's strange, but even though she hasn't had to actually defend the village, I just feel more secure with her on guard."

"She did save us once. You weren't with us, but she drove off a bear beast in our path when we first arrived in the valley," I reminded her, relating the story.

"Even Thayla isn't invincible."

I stand up. "Worrying isn't going to solve anything. Let's corral in the little ones and get started." Of course, now I have to explain the words 'corral in.'

CHAPTER 32

Rojaire

"**W**hat is that?" I heard Traevus ask.

Oh no, what did she find this time? I wonder as I shake myself awake. Apparently, Thayla has just returned from scouting out the area, a routine she performs at every camping spot before we set out again. The woman never sleeps. The little short-haired, bluish gray questionable object Traevus referred to, follows Thayla at her heels.

"Shoo!" she shouted turning and pointing her blade at the hand-high, four-legged creature that seems determined to win her affection. The little animal takes Thayla's rejection hard, lowering its triangular head and whining piteously.

"Crystal shards, what a strange looking animal!" Traevus exclaimed. "It's so geometric." Two back legs hinge out from its triangular body and five short tails with triangular tips hang like a tassel from its pointed rear end. "Where did you find him?"

"I found him up in the hills under a bush, whining like he's doing now. It's been following me ever since." Thayla sounds annoyed.

"He might have gotten lost from his family."

"Family? I didn't see any others."

The little creature pleadingly inches toward Thayla. "Should we have it for dinner?" she asked.

"No!" Traevus shouted, roused into action. Probably a perfectly normal question coming from Thayla, but seemingly inappropriate in this case.

"You can't kill him and eat him," Traevus protested. "Look at the little fellow. He's so sad."

"Then make him go away."

"Come here little fellow," Traevus coaxed with an offering of trail food. The sight of food instantly catches its attention. Twirling its five tails it runs up to Traevus, then folding in its back legs, sits on its pointed back end. Two little pointed ears stick out of the top corners of its triangular face, its mouth forming the bottom point of the triangle.

"Watch it doesn't bite you," I warned not sure what to make of this.

Heeding my caution, Traevus breaks off a small piece of trail food and places it on the ground. Consolidating its five tails into one, the little creature stands and sniffs at it first, then cautiously picks it up with its mouth and chews appreciatively. Immediately it wants more. The five tails snap apart twirling in utter joy while its highly expressive triangular blue eyes watch Traevus intensively.

"You like that, don't you, Gyro?" Traevus said.

"You named him? We're not traveling with pets," I reminded him. Ignoring me, Traevus breaks off another piece of trail food. Without hesitation, Gyro takes the morsel directly from Traevus' hand and begs for more.

"You're still hungry? Do you want to feed Gyro, Thayla?" Traevus asked tossing her a nut bar.

"What am I supposed to do with this?" Thayla asked catching it.

"Feed him."

Gyro immediately runs to Thayla in expectation and what looks like adoration, his five little tails twirling with joy. Reluctantly, Thayla extends the food out to him which he takes eagerly from her hand and chews with delight. Then in appreciation, Gyro curls up contentedly on her foot and starts to go to sleep.

"Get off of me," Thayla protested kicking up her foot. Her action sends Gyro flying. Traevus jumps up with concern, but to our astonishment, Gyro extends out his four little clawed feet revealing a flap of skin along each side of his body. We watch amazed as Gyro glides safely over a long distance before disappearing into the landscape.

"Amazing! Well, let's get started," I said, certain we have seen the last of Gyro. "The Stairs await us." The mountainous valley wall looms close at hand with rough up and down terrain in between.

The going gets tougher with the hills growing steeper as we continue to head northeast toward the formidable mountains. On the map these mountainous hills are indicated as lumps on the landscape. We can see farther ahead of us now with the tree and brush density thinning, and each hard won summit offers a spectacular panoramic view. We should reach the end of the valley before the next period of darkness. I can't help but wonder what we will find there? Why did Chitter try to talk us out of using the mysterious Stairs?

One hill rolls into another in seemingly endless secession. The hike drains us, and eventually we stop to rest by a rivulet of fresh spring water in a shady depression between hills where we find an abundance of ground nuts and fruit laden berry bushes to snack on. Greatly refreshed, we push forward, on the last stretch to the Stairs.

Each hill grows rockier than the last and reaches a higher elevation as the dark purple wall of the Crescent Mountains draw close. With dragging step, we crest yet another hill and look down into a narrow high elevation valley extending to the base of the mountain. Before us appears a threateningly dark, forbidding structure built into the mountain itself, its upper reaches shrouded in dark swirling mist.

"Let me guess," Thayla said with unmasked dread, which was scary in itself, "This must be the Stairs."

"Doesn't look very inviting, does it?" Traevus said. "It looks like parts of it are missing," he added staring up at the monstrosity as far as the shrouding mist permitted. Following his gaze up the dark purple face of the mountain I see what looks like black voids.

We have finally reached the end of the valley, but instead of rejoicing the mood is subdued. "The sun has already set, soon it will be dark. Should we wait for Seaa's light?" I asked.

"I don't think it will make any difference," Thayla said. "Someone built this, but why? It's certainly not a natural formation."

"The answer has been lost to antiquity. I wish Drak's great grandfather would have left a journal to go with his maps."

"Should we try it?" Traevus asked. "Maybe we should look for another way out the valley."

We gaze upon the dark, forbidding sheer walls of the Crescent Mountains barring the way with more saber sharp towering peaks pressing in from behind. "It is unlikely we will find another way out. I'm not going to ask anyone to do this who doesn't want to."

"Well, it is getting dark, are we going or not?" Traevus asked after a moment of silence.

"Those chittering feather balls made it, I can too. Let's get started," Thayla said boldly heading down the hill. With some dread we approach the Stairs. I can feel the aura of darkness on approach and have no doubt Chitter's warnings are well founded.

Without further hesitation, Thayla ascends the bottom steps and Traevus and I quickly follow. Then to our shock, we hear a howling roar and the swirling dark mist descends to the ground with a thud, entombing us in. "That can't be good," Thayla said.

My first instinct is to turn and flee, but I fear the Stairs may not release us.

"I already hate this place," Traevus groaned.

It is not totally dark, more like late dusk. Slowly our eyes adjust to the dim light and with pounding hearts, we move on. "Stay close together," I cautioned.

The first half dozen steps recess deeply into the mountain, then the passageway begins twisting every which way. I keep my eye on Thayla ahead of us, disappearing and reappearing like a wraith through the tendrils of roiling mist, a big achievement for the mighty warrior, as she weaves around curving corners. Then I don't see her at all.

"Thayla is getting ahead of us," I pointed out.

"Thayla!" Traevus called. "Wait for us." There is no answer.

Suddenly we round a turn to find ourselves in a long, straight tunnel faintly lit by an unknown source, but there is no Thayla in sight.

CHAPTER 33

Aurora

Building a foundation is hard work. Seaa is already high in the sky providing ample light for the job. We have three push/pull carts designed by Inventor Sulyan and Drak for hauling gravel. Drak, Kaylya, Wessid and Zaloka form one team and Kiril, Tassyn, Edty and Inventor Sulyan make up the second team. And the boys and I, the third team, have a cart to ourselves, giving us a chance to finally talk.

"We need to have a meeting," I grunted from the pushing end of the cart to Halren up front on the pulling end. The wooden, perfectly balanced two-wheel carts aren't very big because gravel is heavy. They are designed so two people can easily handle them with one person pulling from the front and another pushing from the back. With four people on a team, two workers can rest between loads. This is our third load. The trail from the river to the foundation is already hard packed from abusive use. "It's really important, I have a lot to tell you."

"I agree we should have another meeting, it's just between working on the schoolhouse, lesson assignments, and sleeping there hasn't been time for anything else."

"Seriously, Halren, I have some important information to share."

"Yeah, what is it?"

"Not here. It's something the Secret Warriors need to discuss together."

"We'll meet as soon as we can," Halren promised as we arrive at the foundation site. Kaylya and Zaloka have finished dumping their load and are ready to head back to the river.

"Good job, Halren and Aurora, you are a big help," Zaloka praised.

"We are all grateful for your help," Kaylya added.

The work session is long and hard, but finally the twelve of us stand around a gravel filled foundation ready for the next step, the three carts abandoned off to the side for now. "I want the four you to take off the next work session to do some schoolwork," Kaylya said speaking to the four of us. "We'll bring you back on crew later when the walls are going up."

For once, time off to do schoolwork sounds like a good idea. The Secret Warriors will finally have a chance to meet. Satisfied, we trudge home tired.

When I rise again, it is all about schoolwork. There is always schoolwork to do. There will be no meeting with the boys until it is done, so I get right to work.

I have a decision to make. Do I take Kitca to our Secret Warriors meeting for questioning? Or should I meet with the others first and then we can decide what to do? Kitca achieved some admiration with our group after winning at tag ball. At least she has been less of a nuisance since she became involved in Mother's play. But there are far more important issues to consider.

Kitca and I can communicate in the same way Caleeza and Chitter do, but no one knows except the Secret Warriors. And then there's the star stone. Kitca calls it a seed of life. I'm certain this is important information.

I decide to consult with the others first. Play rehearsal is over and the actors are gathered at Caleeza's house so our meeting place should be free. Having completed my chores and schoolwork, I dash off to collect Halren and Selyzar. It doesn't take long to find them, they are already headed our way.

"Where's Theon?" Halren asked.

"He's still working on his essay, he'll meet us there."

"What is he writing about?" Selyzar asked as we headed down the trail.

"I don't know," I said dismissively. "Dad was helping him so it must be something about history."

"I wrote about building our schoolhouse," Halren volunteered.

"Ugh! I still don't see why we have to have a schoolhouse. We will just lose all our freedom!" I complained. The idea of a schoolhouse has been hard for me to accept, yet like everyone else, I've been working hard to get it built. It just wouldn't do to protest.

"My essay is about Mother and Chitter," Selyzar said. "What did you write about, Aurora?"

I hesitate to answer, fearing their reaction. "Star stones," I finally admitted biting my lip.

"You didn't! Aren't you concerned about drawing suspicions?"

"What do you mean? I didn't say I have one."

"Still, considering you're hiding one, the subject is best avoided," Halren explained.

We quickly arrive at the pavilion. As expected, it is deserted. A pile of sticks has been gathered, for what purpose I don't know, but I'm sure it has something to do with the play. Theon didn't lag behind long. As soon as we finish walking around, he arrives.

"We need an opening ceremony," Halren suggested.

"Like what?" I asked.

"Repeat after me. This is a meeting of the Secret Warriors," Halren formally announced.

"This is a meeting of the Secret Warriors," we repeated.

"Everything we say and do is held to secrecy," Halren continued.

"Everything we say and do is held to secrecy," we dutifully repeated. With opening ceremony completed, all eyes turned to me.

"I might as well go first," I said answering their stares. "Let me remind you, I can read your thoughts if you don't practice protecting them." Immediately I feel the wall going up, blocking their stream of thoughts. It will be an important skill for them to have if we ever go to Mainland. "Let me begin by saying, Kitca definitely knows about the star stone."

"Are you sure?" Selyzar asked.

"She confirmed it on the way to the tag ball game."

"What? How did she find out? Did you show it to her?" Theon asked.

"No, I didn't show it to her. I don't have to. I think it's what makes it possible for us to communicate."

"What do you mean?" Halren asked with scientific interest.

"Look at it this way. From the time I welcomed her here we have been able to communicate, like Chitter and Caleeza," I said. "It has to be the star stone. Kitca calls the star stone a seed...a seed of life."

"You mean like a seed that grows into a plant?" Selyzar asked.

"Not quite." I hesitate to continue, my theory is so bizarre. "I think the star stone is more like an egg."

"You mean it can hatch into an animal?" Theon asked incredulously. "Crystal shards, Aurora!" Theon exclaimed. "This is big."

I bring out the star stone and hold it up for inspection. The smooth round golden stone seems to hold a spark of light within. Is this spark of light more than just reflected light? What if it is a spark of life?

"I think a star stone can hatch into a Chitter," I blurted out. "I believe Kitca was hatched from the star stone Caleeza lost." The boys stare at me in silent astonishment. I'm sure they think I've lost my mind.

"How?" Theon finally belted out.

"I know it sounds crazy. I don't blame you if you don't believe me," I stammered in my defense. "I hardly believe it myself." For a moment no one spoke.

"I believe you," Halren said. "At least I'm willing to consider it." I let out a sigh of relief and glance at the other two.

"What makes you think Kitca was once a star stone?" Selyzar asked.

"If you recall, Caleeza lost a star stone when she first met Chitter. Caleeza said Chitter was the last of her kind. Now there is Kitca."

But how can Chitter hatch a star stone?" Halren asked. "It just doesn't make sense."

"Kitca has a pouch."

"So?" Theon asked.

"I'm not talking about a homemade pouch. She has a pouch that is part of her body. Chitter has one too." I describe in detail the tag ball experience.

"Let's go back to how?" Theon said.

"I told you. She can sense it."

"No, how did she hatch?"

"I believe Kitca hatched in Chitter's pouch." We have all seen Chitter affectionately touch her belly when referring to Kitca.

"So Kitca can communicate with you because of the star stone. And Kitca is female and has a pouch. Has it occurred to you that Kitca may want your star stone to hatch it?" Halren asked.

"It has," I admit.

"Maybe Kitca isn't old enough to hatch a star stone yet," Selyzar said.

"How old does she have to be?" Theon asked. Of course, no one knows the answer.

"I think we should invite Kitca to join our group," I said after a contemplative moment of silence.

"You mean make her a secret warrior!" Selyzar exclaimed.

"Have you gone mad?" Theon asked.

"Hold on now," Halren interrupted. "We need to consider our mission goal."

"Our mission goal?" Theon asked.

"Yes, our mission is to learn more about Kitca and Chitter. If we bring Kitca into our group we are bound to learn more than if we shun her," Halren reasoned.

"I didn't suggest we shun her, but can we trust her?" Selyzar asked.

"We are going to have to. She already knows about the star stone," I reminded them.

"If she knows about the star stone, the secret is out," Theon said.

"No," I burst out, surprised I'm taking her side. "She promised to keep it a secret."

"And you trust her?" Theon asked astonished.

"Look, I didn't tell her I have a star stone, she told me!" I said in exasperation.

"So do we ask Kitca to join us? Yes or No?" Halren asked for clarification. With mixed feelings, we all vote. The decision is unanimous. We will invite Kitca to the next Secret Warriors meeting. What else can we do? I didn't tell the boys, but she knows about the Secret Warriors too.

CHAPTER 34

Lozar

"Where are they?" Xanthe demanded.

"Obviously not here," I said. I can tell she is running out of patience, she doesn't like her objectives thwarted. I notice Melinda walking off, silently weeping for the friend she assumes is dead, but I refuse to believe Thayla is dead, although I would like Xanthe to believe she is gone.

The crude stone shelter looks lonely, despite the beauty surrounding it. Tall, untrammeled grass covers what once was a clearing around the shelter, reaching up to vacant windows and right up to and into the open entrance. There is no door. Inside, stored nuts and grains, breaking down with age, sit undisturbed in covered clay pots. There are piles of supplies neatly stacked, probably brought from the sunken island and hauled in to wait for someone who never returned.

So much effort has been put into starting a settlement here, even to the point of constructing a kiln. With fresh water readily available and a young forest, already producing food, stretching to the north, why aren't they here? Everything the colonists needed to survive is here. So where did they go? Did they find a better place? Surely they didn't all return to Lavender Beach only to be wiped out by a tsunami, someone would have stayed behind. Suddenly I feel certain Thayla is still alive. Thayla would have fought hard to survive, certainly seeking higher ground after a major seismic event.

"You're hiding something," Xanthe accuses Quaylyn to his face.

"That is false," Quaylyn said simply.

"Search the forest," Xanthe ordered Rabiam and Arpen. Following her orders, Arpen and Rabiam leave to beat the woods. When she moves to follow her own directive, I intercede to block her.

"Let her go," Quaylyn said. "The colonists aren't here." I know he is right, but I hate her arrogance. Nevertheless, I back off.

"Who do you think built this?" I asked Quaylyn after they left.

"I don't know, but it wasn't the colonists. The seismic event that wreaked so much destruction occurred soon after the colonists departed from Mainland. If they died in the tsunami, they wouldn't have had time to achieve so much so quickly."

"Maybe they built the shelter after the tsunami," Kaydra suggested.

"Then where are they?" Anthya asked.

"If not the colonists, then who?" I asked. "You said the continent was uninhabited."

"Could it have been built by members of the lost expedition?" Kaydra asked.

"Maybe," Quaylyn said. "There are five still unaccounted for, which brings us back to the question, where are they?"

"Is there anything in the journal about this place?" Melinda asked.

"Kiril describes the valley and planting trees, but there is no mention of the shelter. As we always suspected, he left a lot out of his report. Probably for good reason."

"Then maybe whoever built this joined the colonists," Melinda said.

"I guess that could be a possibility," Quaylyn agreed.

"What do we do now?" I ventured to ask. Before anyone can respond, Xanthe reappears without her warriors. Rabiam and Arpen are apparently still scouting out the area.

"We move on," Xanthe said answering my question.

"Where do you want to go?" Quaylyn asked.

"Through the mountains to the interior. You spoke of an underground passage through the Crescent Mountains. You carry the map showing the way."

"Do you really think any underground passageway is still open after all the destruction you have seen?" I asked, my anger rising again.

"Lozar is right. You don't want to go underground," Quaylyn said. "The Crescent Mountains are just that, a crescent, not a circle. If you want access to the interior you will have to go around."

"The colonists would not have settled in the interior," Anthya said. "The land encircled by the Crescent Mountains is dry and nearly barren. It is not an ideal location for a colony, not like right here."

"I give the orders around her, Councilor," Xanthe said as Arpen and Rabiam return shaking their heads.

I almost draw my blade on the spot. The Aaians have promised no one will get hurt, but now they no longer have any special powers. Without powers or weapons, there is little they can do.

"Enough!" I shout. I need to convince Xanthe to end her search. "Thayla is gone. There is no one to challenge you. We return home." My voice hissed with anger. I would prefer Thayla had died struggling for survival in the flood than murdered by her sister.

I see Quaylyn and Kaydra coming in closer, Xanthe disregards them completely. Arpen and Rabiam look to me for guidance, but with a wave of my hand, I indicate for them to stay out of it.

Then Xanthe draws her blade. "We go where I say we go," she threatened.

"Don't be a fool! Why do you want to prolong this? You will be queen. No one stands in your way. We have to accept Thayla's death for what it is. At least she died free," I added.

Not open to reason, Xanthe moves to strike. In one smooth motion Quaylyn and Kaydra move in and disarm her, before I can even draw my blade. Again I underestimated them.

I pick up the fallen weapon as the enraged princess struggles for her freedom. "You can let her go now." I said calmly.

Kaydra and Quaylyn ease their grip. Xanthe shrugs them off and faces me defiantly. "You are supposed to protect me!"

"From what, yourself?" It occurs to me, if I want Xanthe to leave, I need to lead by example. I make up my mind.

"I'm leaving," I announced throwing her sword on the ground.

"You can't leave!"

I stare at her hard. "I'm leaving and I'm taking my crew with me. I suggest you do the same." Xanthe gapes back in disbelief.

Ignoring her, I turn toward Anthya and Melinda. "Let's go," I said gently, beckoning them to follow and walk away.

CHAPTER 35

Anthya

"**G**o," Quaylyn whispers to me. "Use this opportunity to take Melinda safely away from here. Kaydra and I can complete the mission. Xanthe isn't going to leave until she is convinced Thayla isn't here. You can report back to the High Council."

I am torn between loyalty and agreement. As much as I would like to leave, I can't just abandon Quaylyn and Kaydra to Xanthe's whims.

"Go!" Xanthe ordered. Quaylyn and Kaydra nod in agreement. I'm sure Xanthe will be glad to be rid of me. "Go!" she ordered again when Melinda and I hesitate.

Having barely rested after the day's long trek, we don our packs and Lozar, Melinda and I turn our backs on the Cremyn Valley. After cresting over the mountain, despite my feelings of guilt over leaving Quaylyn and Kaydra, a weight seems to lift, releasing the depressing mood Xanthe constantly foments. No one speaks as we trudge along.

"Can we rest?" Melinda asked when we finally reach a level shelf of ground overlooking the Zayla Valley. In response Lozar calls for a stop and Melinda gratefully plops down, wiping sweat from her eyes. The sun burns hot overhead. For Melinda, it will be the length of another Earth day before it sets. There is no place to avoid the sun, no shade.

Then Lozar points a short distance down the slope where a small indentation into the side of the slope offers a bit of shade. I make Melinda hydrate before helping her back up. The move is well worth it. The shallow depression in the hillside offers cool sanctuary with enough room for us to stretch out. Lozar paces around deep in thought, still agitated over Xanthe's behavior and grieving over the loss of his sister, Princess Thayla. Melinda is already asleep.

Inactivity provides time to reflect. My heart silently weeps for those we lost, I knew them all. I realize Lozar is as deeply affected as Melinda and I. "I'm sorry for your loss," I said when he finally settles down beside me.

"Thayla is not dead," Lozar said emphatically. "Neither are your friends. I just wanted to convince Xanthe Thayla is dead so she would call off the search." He says it with such conviction, I want to believe him, but it's hard to convince myself.

"I don't understand how you can be so sure."

"Thayla is still alive, I can sense her presence on this continent."

"So where is she?"

"I don't know, but think about it. The colonists are defying the rule of the High Council, which is a treasonous act, therefore, they wouldn't settle in a place as obvious as the Cremyn Valley, because they don't want to be found. Plus, as Quaylyn pointed out, there are obvious omissions in the journal by this Kiril fellow, like he is hiding something.

I am moved by Lozar's certainty Thayla lives, it gives me a surge of hope. "Then aren't you worried Xanthe will eventually find Thayla?"

"No, if Thayla doesn't want to be found, she won't be. Are you worried about Quaylyn and Kaydra's safety?" he asked.

"Yes, even though I know they are capable of carrying out their mission. So what's next?"

"Well, if it's all right with you, instead of returning to Mainland, I think we should stick around for a while. Go back to the boat. Maybe take a cruise around this island continent."

"If it's all right with me? I have a say in this?"

"Of course you do, so does Melinda. We are partners. You want to find the colonists, don't you?"

"A cruise would be nice," I agreed with relief we aren't abandoning the others completely. Conversation lags and soon I too drift off into a much needed nap.

When we stir again, it is cooler. A bank of clouds has moved in from the west promising rain. Melinda too looks recovered, so we head out immediately hoping to reach the zaota trees before the storm. I would have been willing to push for the coast, but the distance is just too great. By the time the valley curves back to the west and the zaota groves are in sight, it begins to rain. The sky continues to darken as wind-driven rain showers down in sheets onto the deserted landscape, darkening the lavender soil as the moisture soaks in.

Once we are as wet as we possibly can be, we halt the rush for shelter. A beautiful display of lightning cracks across the clouds. Then a reverberating rumble of thunder sends Melinda momentarily cringing on the ground. I stoop down and put my arms around her for comfort. Lozar turns back, when he notices we have lagged behind.

Melinda recovers quickly from her fright, and I urge her on. We meet Lozar halfway. "Is she all right? Melinda, are you okay?" he asked concerned.

"Yes," she said nodding. "Thank you." We finally reach the zaota trees and dart into the crispy, dry interior of the closest one. Lozar doesn't join us so I assume he chooses his own shelter to give us privacy.

"I'm sorry for that moment of weakness back there," Melinda said softly after we change into dry clothes. "Melinda, you have nothing to apologize for. Things will continue to get better as you embrace life again."

"It was a reflex reaction. Droclum twice spoke to me through lightning and thunder."

"You have been through so much. And you are so strong. You faced up to a great evil, sprung from our world to yours, and won.

"Earth is no longer my world."

"Of course it is. You are a young woman, one day you may want to go back...at least for a visit." I was pleased to see her smile at that.

"I heard what Lozar said, about Thayla and the colonists being still alive. Do you think it's true?"

"We can always hope, can't we? I think Lozar has some kind of filial sense when it comes to Princess Thayla."

Exiting our natural shelter again, it is late afternoon, the sun finally dipping toward the horizon. I breathe in deeply the freshly washed air and the aroma of Twakan tea. Lozar squats by a small fire.

"Greetings, Melinda and Anthya. I hope you rested well. Grab your cups and have some tea."

"You're in high, good spirit!" I observed.

"Of course, I am. If we get a quick start, we may be able to reach the beach by sun set," he said. "What do you say?" We quickly pack our things.

Following the Zayla River we reach the debris pile marking the furthest reach of the tsunami. More plant life than we previously thought has taken root along the river, in some places nearly covering the scar, another hopeful sign of the continent's healing.

We make good progress, arriving at the beach in time to see the sun sink into the Golden Sea. Glisa and Yanzic, greeting us warmly, do not attempt to hide their pleasure in seeing our return, and Yanzic prepares a celebratory meal which includes fresh fish. The five of us gather around a low make-shift table on the deck, eating and conversing in three languages, like friends on a pleasure trip reunited, sharing all the details of our adventure.

"We're leaving," Lozar said once the meal is over. "We're going on a cruise."

"What about the *Xanthe Queen*?" Yanzic and Glisa wanted to know when Lozar announced the cruise. They had been left with the responsibility of watching over both ships.

"Leave it," Lozar said.

Then by Seaa's light Lozar eases the *Princess Thayla* away from shore.

CHAPTER 36

Quaylyn

With a sense of relief, I watch Anthya and Melinda leave the Cremyn Valley. I trust Lozar will keep them safe. I understand Lozar's strategy. We have to convince Xanthe Thayla is dead, although I know he doesn't believe it himself.

So are Thayla and the others really still alive? I'm not sure what I believe any more. Regardless, Kaydra and I can better focus on Xanthe without worrying about Melinda's safety, although we lose Lozar and Anthya's added strength.

Once the others are out of sight, Xanthe relaxes her shackles and decides to move into the shelter. She has Rabiam and Arpen clean it out, repair the roof and build a comfortable sleeping area for her, like she plans on staying for a while. For her I guess, it's a step up from a zaota tree. Without a doubt, regardless of the weather, Kaydra and I will be sleeping outdoors.

Getting out of their way, I follow Kaydra to sit in welcoming shade under the young trees. Staring back at the shelter, I notice some details I hadn't noticed before. "The shelter has been around for a while," I pointed out to Kaydra. "It's older than the new forest around it."

"What makes you say that?"

"Well, look at it. The walls are starting to crumble and a lot of soil has built up around it."

"So who do you think built it?"

"I think you and Melinda may be right and it was built by members of the lost expedition."

Kaydra and I attended Academy with Sarus, Ollen, Caleeza, Caponya and Selyzar. We share many fond memories and stories of these friends no longer with us. Could they still be alive?

"If they are still alive, why didn't they meet Captain Setas at Lavender Beach and return?"

"Perhaps they didn't want to return. This land has a way of affecting people in strange ways."

"So where are they now?" Kaydra asked.

"With the colonists," I say with conviction. It's the only answer I can come up with. Kaydra gives me a puzzled look so I explain. "We know Rojaire's mapping team passed through here, the trees are hard evidence. Kiril doesn't mention the shelter in his journal, because he is protecting their secret."

"Wouldn't it be wonderful if they were still alive, living here on the continent? Where might they be?"

"Wherever Rojaire left Theon, Tassyn and Edty when the rest of the mapping team returned, another secret the journal protects."

"So what is the strategy from here?" Kaydra asked.

"We try to get Xanthe to end her search and go home. Xanthe will leave only when she is convinced Thayla is dead. Xanthe going home would be best for everyone, especially the colonists, assuming they are still alive."

"That may take some doing. I know Xanthe better than you do. She can be quite stubborn."

We spot Rabiam collecting brush to replenish the roof of the shelter in case of rain. Apparently, Arpen is keeping busy setting up Xanthe's room.

"Let's go give Rabiam a hand," I suggested.

The confrontation with Xanthe earlier would have been quite different if Rabiam and Arpen had chosen to counterattack when we disarmed her. And Lozar won't be around the next time Xanthe blows. I need Arpen and Rabiam to understand we are not a threat to their princess, in fact, we are on the same side as far as no one getting hurt.

"How long is Princess Xanthe planning on staying here?" I ventured to ask.

Rabiam actually chuckled before he spoke. "He said Xanthe is waiting for the colonists to come back," Kaydra translated.

As we cut and gather, I share our goal to convince Xanthe to leave. "We need to work together on this." Kaydra translates and Rabiam readily agrees.

With roofing for the stone shelter secured, Kaydra and I set out to build a shelter of our own, cutting brush for a lean to under the trees. Rabiam gives us a hand. By the time we finish, dark clouds are rolling in. The fast moving storm drenches the valley, watering the growing forest and parched grass. But Kaydra and I sleep through it warm and dry.

During this time of leisure, we continue to build on the rapport we established with Rabiam and Arpen during our voyage across the Golden Sea. We haul water, gather food and prepare meals together. Sometimes Princess Xanthe even joins us.

"I can't understand why anyone would want to live in such an empty place," Xanthe said as we share a simple meal. "There's no entertainment."

"It's not palace life for sure," Kaydra said. "It's more like lots of hard work, but it offers freedom."

"I don't understand all this talk of freedom. People can't be left to themselves, they need guidance. They need to be told what to do."

"Government is supposed to protect the people, not control them," I said. Where did that come from? Then I remember the long political discussions I had with Vince Bradley in Alaska, so many cycles of seasons ago.

"Peculiar talk for a councilor of the Crystal Table, isn't it?"

"Living under these conditions wouldn't be my choice, but I can understand the desire to determine one's own destiny. I experienced living in such a place once, on Earth."

The others avoid participation in the toxic topic and I look to change the subject, but Xanthe does it for me. "The colonists may have gone to the crystal landscape you talk so much about," she said.

"What for? The Crystalline Landscape is a dangerous place. It's not habitable." I can only imagine how the landscape of giant crystals faired during the epic ground shake, yet it still prevents us from drawing energy from the elemental forces.

"Go home to your palace. Lozar is right. To continue the search is a worthless use of time and energy." Lozar's leaving must have planted a seed in Xanthe's mind to give up the search. I need to find a way to nurture it. "Are you going to let Lozar report back to Twaka instead of you?" That should get her thinking. "Aren't you concerned about what he might say?"

Xanthe stands abruptly and Kaydra and I go on high alert. I notice her warriors tense up too. "Don't attempt to tell me what to do, Councilor Quaylyn. I will decide when we will leave," she said her voice threatening. Fortunately, she then turns and leaves the gathering for the privacy of her shelter.

CHAPTER 37

Rojaire

"Thayla! Where are you? Thayla!" Traevus shouted repeatedly to no avail. "We have to go back and look for her, she might have taken a wrong turn, or we took a wrong turn." Traevus' desperate concern for Thayla blinds him from what is happening around us. Dark tendrils of mist, icy cold to the touch, drift in from behind us, driving us away from the entrance.

"Traevus, listen to me. There were no other turns."

"You don't know for sure, we might have missed it."

"Thayla is somewhere ahead of us. We have to move," I shouted giving Traevus a gentle push toward the far end of the tunnel. "We can't leave the way we came." The icy tendrils quickly thicken around us. "Run!" To my relief he moves in the right direction. We take off running to avoid the sting of the icy cold wisps. But there doesn't seem to be an escape route.

"We're running toward a wall," Traevus said slowing down. The thickening dark mist obscures the light and turns the air freezing cold.

"Keep going. There must be a way out."

The way out, we discover, is up. We reach the end of the tunnel to find the ceiling open above us. Powered with adrenalin, we quickly scale the rocky wall to the ledge above. The dark mist does not follow.

From here, the Steps transform into a strange vertical maze. It becomes increasingly difficult to determine the next step, and not all options work. Then suddenly we are on a misty ledge surrounded by a wall of blackness. Momentum plunges Traevus forward and before I can grab ahold of him, he vanishes into the void. I hesitate to follow.

"Traevus! Where are you? Can you hear me?" I shouted into the wall of darkness. The intensity of the answering silence instills skin-crawling alertness. How did we get separated so easily?

Being cautious, I stretch out my hand, extending it beyond the edge of darkness and watch with horror as it disappears from sight. Shocked, I jerk my hand back, breathing a sigh of relief to find it still attached to my arm. Stay rational I remind myself. Think of it as a puzzle needing solving. Like Thayla said, Chitter and Kitca made it through.

I toss a loose rock into the darkness. There is no corresponding sound of the rock landing on the ledge or tumbling down to what could be my death if I venture forward. No sound escapes the dark zone.

Is that what happened to Traevus? Does the ledge end at the edge of the void? It can't be so. I have to find out.

Holding on to the wall at the shelf's edge, I get down on all fours and reach out to feel for an extension of the ledge beyond the edge of darkness. With some hesitation, I slide my hand forward, once again watching it vanish from sight, the dark line of division cutting sharply across my forearm. Relief sweeps over me when I feel the extension of the ledge. Traevus may still be alive.

I continue to crawl forward, closing my eyes as I stick my head through. Opening my eyes, I strain to see, but there is no light, the cold blackness is absolute. I continue to feel my way, with eyes closed in an attempt to heighten my other senses, until I discern some light penetrating my eyelids and open my eyes to gray mist and Traevus standing over me.

"It's about time you arrived," Traevus complained.

"Why didn't you come back for me after disappearing like that?" I demanded getting to my feet. "I thought you fell to your death. Why didn't you answer my calls?"

"Look," Traevus said nodding to the wall behind me. I turn quickly and come face to face with a solid rock wall. The dark void has vanished. "It seems to be a one-way passageway," Traevus explained as I inspect the wall that proves to be solid indeed.

"I'm really getting to hate this place. Where's Thayla?" I asked dismissing the void.

"I haven't seen her. I've tried calling, but she doesn't answer," Traevus said obviously stressed over her disappearance. I try to continue to believe we will meet up with her somewhere. "And we have reached another rock ledge that doesn't seem to offer a way forward."

I look around. High above us stretches a vaulted ceiling and before us yawns an open chasm, too wide to jump, its depth lost in misty darkness. Across the chasm I can see an open ledge and pathway beckoning from the other side. "I see what you mean."

"Now what do we do?" Traevus asked after an extensive search for a way out and finding nothing.

"There has to be a way to reach the other side. We might as well rest for a moment while we figure this out," I suggested.

"Maybe Thayla will find us eventually," Traevus said hopefully. "Maybe she has already found a way out."

"Maybe." But I have my doubts, I add silently. I sit down at the edge of the chasm, with my feet dangling over the edge, and look for a way to cross. Either out of frustration or sheer boredom, I start tossing pebbles into the chasm. Unlike in the void, the pebbles make a soft tinkling sound as they strike rock somewhere far below in the roiling mist. Then a stone lands on something solid directly in front of me. To my surprise, a floating stone step appears out of the mist and makes its way toward me.

"Do you see that?" I asked jumping up in excitement. Traevus quickly joins me at the chasm edge and together we watch in astonishment as the stone slides into place at our feet with a soft click.

"Can we trust it with our weight?" Traevus asked.

"I don't know." I press down on the step with my hand. It doesn't move, offering solid resistance. "It appears to be stable."

"We are going to need far more extensions to the bridge than this before we can cross," Traevus observed.

"Let's toss some rocks." In a joint effort, we toss dozens, then hundreds of stones in all directions, near and far, listening to their distant ping as they land in the misty gorge below. Despite all our effort, we can't contact another addition to the bridge.

Running low on loose stones to toss, we eventually give up in frustration and settle down to think of another strategy. Meanwhile the one link to the bridge remains in place. Then we hear a familiar whining sound and searching through the swirling mist, we locate the source across the chasm.

"Gyro!" Traevus shouted.

Overjoyed to see Traevus, Gyro dashes across an invisible bridge that solidifies under his feet and flies into Traevus' open arms. I stare dumbfounded from the strange little creature to the bridge crossing the chasm and back again. "Where's Thayla?" I asked on a whim.

At the mention of Thayla's name, Gyro springs out of Traevus' arms and rushes back across the bridge, then waits for us to join him on the other side.

"Let's go," Traevus urged.

We rush across the still visible bridge half expecting to plummet to our deaths with each step, but make it to the open passageway without incident. Looking back after landing safely, I notice the bridge has already vanished from sight. I reach down to touch the now invisible stone bridge, but my hand meets only air, causing my stomach to do a double somersault. "Let's get out of here."

"Gyro, where's Thayla?" Traevus asked and once again Gyro dashes off. The little creature can certainly move fast.

We try to keep up as best we can crawling through tight tunnels, jumping narrow gaps, and sliding up a curved slide. Beyond questioning at this point how we could slide up, we continue to hurry after Gyro. Fortunately the little guy stops occasionally to wait for us to catch up or we would have surely lost him. There is no way of knowing how far up the Stairs we have gone by now or even if we are making any real progress. Time seems meaningless here. Then Gyro turns a corner and emits a joyful shriek. Thayla reluctantly catches him as he springs into her arms.

"He found you," Traevus said with relief.

"No, he found you. Where have you been?" she asked setting Gyro down. Immediately Gyro runs back to Traevus.

"We have been trying to get through this maze. Where did you disappear to?" I asked.

"I didn't disappear, you did," Thayla continued to insist. Finally reunited once again, we decide to eat and rest a bit while describing our separate terrifying adventures.

"Let's not get separated again. We have to stick close together if we are ever going to get out of here."

"Gyro, you are amazing," Traevus praised him sharing his food.

Searching for the next step, we find only one way out and once again, that way is up. "It looks like we will have to do a bit of rock climbing," Traevus observed eying a series of protruding nubs and narrow ledges that lead up into an opening above us. "Do you think you can find the way, Gyro?" Traevus asked. In response, Gyro struggles out of his arms and we are off again. My body is so tired I can hardly move, but I want out of here. Gyro leads the way.

"After you," Traevus offered. I don't hesitant and start the climb. He and Thayla follow closely behind. We want to be certain no one vanishes again. The climb becomes even more arduous as the Stairs steepen. The maze is broken apart in places leaving scarred bare rock and jumbled piles of debris. Then suddenly the Stairs become a stairway again, stretching above.

"Is that sky up there?" Traevus asked.

Exhausted we all pause in our climb to look up to see what looks like sky far above us. Could it be an illusion? We mount the steep curving steps as fast as our weary bodies will let us. Eventually our heads emerge out of the mist into open air and we gaze out from a high peak overlooking the coastal range and the Golden Sea glimmering under Seaa's light in the distance. We all gratefully drop down onto the rocky ground, even Thayla looks drained, and breathe in deeply the fresh sea air.

"I can almost taste fish already," Traevus said longingly.

"We still have to find a way down there. How long do you suppose we were in the mist?" Thayla asked.

"Too long." I look out toward the west where Seaa has already begun her descent. Though grateful to have survived the Stairs, we are too tired at this point to move on. Finding a spot sheltered from the wind, we set up camp.

"You watch over us, Gyro," Traevus said before closing his eyes as the little triangular creature curls up beside him.

CHAPTER 38

Ilene

"The schoolhouse is coming along great!" I exclaimed astonished by the progress when I drop off bake goods for the crew.

Among the many oddities this valley has to offer is the square tree forest across the valley to the east. The four-sided trunks of the rose wood trees grow tall and spindly to about four to six inches square with few branches and no bark making them ideal logs for framing. Star-shaped silver leaves sprout from the tips of the upper branches.

"The framing is almost done and we will be ready to start filling in the walls next work session," Kaylya said glowing with the success so far. "Since the beams were cut and stacked to dry ahead of time, this stage of construction went fast. We just had to bring the logs to the site to get started. Of course we will have to replace what we use for the next construction project."

"Rojaire is going to be so proud of you when he returns," I said. I regret bringing him up when I see her joyful mood dampen, but she recovers quickly.

"If the older children have caught up with their schoolwork we can put them back to good use again."

"I think the children may be glad to get back to work. I'll make sure the family is here next work session. I'm sorry we took Edty off the project to help us, but he has been incredible with the props."

"I wouldn't dream of keeping Edty from what he loves. And as you can see, we have been doing fine without him. So how is the play coming?"

"Surprisingly slow, but we are making progress. We meet for another rehearsal in a little while."

When Caleeza, Chitter and I arrive at the pavilion with the children, Edty is already there. "Edty!" the children called out, running up to greet him.

The stage prop shelters he has built look fabulous. The children excitedly run around inspecting them. Of course, Edty is eager to help, his immense love for the children adding to his drive to go over the top. Now he has become a big part of the production. We wouldn't have it any other way.

It takes a while to settle everyone down. With some effort, we finally are ready to start. "Alright, performers, from the top," I called out, after positioning everyone in their assigned places. Taking my place at the base of pavilion I begin playing the flute and Caleeza walks up onto stage left as she will opening night. As narrator, it is up to Caleeza to start the action.

"In a beautiful lavender valley in a land far, far away, there lived four little girls," Caleeza began. "The four little girls are strong and smart and the best of friends. One day they set out to find the ideal place to build their shelters."

While Caleeza narrates, Alaia, Caponya, Setas and Kitca enter stage right and look around. Again I improvise on the flute and Caleeza steps off the stage.

The music stops and Caponya, the youngest girl, has the first line. "What a beautiful place. Let's build our shelters here."

"I agree," Alaia said. "Let's build a shelter of sticks. It will be quick and easy and will protect us from the rain." The two girls go skipping off to a nearly complete stick shelter (stage left) that Edty has built for them. They go to work adding a pile of sticks to the roof.

"A shelter of sticks is not strong enough," Setas said from center stage. "A good strong wind could knock it down. We will build our shelter of stone. Building with stone may be harder work, but our shelter will be strong and protect us from the wind."

Kitca chitters in agreement. They skip off to a stone wall (back center stage) and work on their stone shelter.

I play another musical interlude on the flute while the girls work at adding the sticks and light, pretend stones (also provided by Edty) to their structures. While the girls are putting the finishing touches onto their shelters, Caleeza walks back on stage left. The music stops.

"The four little girls work long and hard until their shelters are complete," Caleeza narrated. "Then they enter their new homes to have tea." I begin playing again while the girls crawl into their shelters. Caleeza remains at the edge of the stage, the music fades, but continues softly, and Caleeza speaks again.

"The four little girls live happy lives visiting, laughing and playing together, and drinking tea." The music rises in volume and tempo and Alaia, Caponya, Setas and Kitca leave their shelters and join hands center stage laughing and dancing in a circle to the music of the flute. The music swells while the children play, then fades out and Caleeza narrates.

"Then one day two big, bad bear beasts come to the valley."

Edty produces some dramatic sound effects with reeds and blocks of wood as Caleeza exits stage left. Every rehearsal Edty adds a new feature to the play and he has warned us he has some new surprises in wait. On cue Jack and Sarus come roaring on stage in beastly masks, also made by Edty. Edty's sound effects reach a crescendo then fade out for the bear beasts to speak.

"I'm a big, bad bear beast," Jack growled running around the stage.

"Me too," said little Sarus following him. The girls scream and run into their shelters with the bear beasts in pursuit. When Edty's sound effects stop again, the big, bad bear beasts approach the shelter of sticks.

"Little girls, little girls, come out and play," little Sarus said.

"No, no, big, bad bear beasts, go away," Alaia cried out.

"We don't want to play," Caponya followed.

"Little girls, little girls, come out and play. If you don't, we will huff and we will puff and we will blow your shelter down," Jack said with little Sarus joining in on the "we will huff and we will puff" part. The boys huffed and they puffed practicing their blowing, then to everyone's amusement, the huffing and puffing, skillfully enhanced by Edty operating a bellows type gadget, roars like a hurricane. The affect sends us doubling over with laughter. I'm guessing Inventor Sulyan had a hand in this.

From within the stick shelter, Alaia and Caponya release the latches Edty has set up, dropping the stick wall facing the bear beasts to simulate the shelter being blown down. While the bear beasts prance around in glee, celebrating their success, Caponya and Alaia run screaming to the shelter of stone at the cave entrance.

"Let us in. Let us in," they cried.

"The big, bad bear beasts huffed and puffed and blew down our shelter of sticks," Alaia said. Setas and Kitca appear from behind the stone wall in front of the cave entrance.

"Come in," Setas said with Kitca motioning them in. "You will be safe in our shelter of stone." The four little girls retreat into the cave and shut the door. At least Edty produces the sound of a closing door.

Then the big, bad bear beasts approach the shelter of stone growling.

"Little girls, little girls, come out and play," Jack said.

"No, no, big, bad bear beasts, go away. We do not want to play." Setas said.

"Little girls, little girls, come out and play," Jack said again. "If you don't, we will huff and we will puff and we will blow you shelter down."

The little girls laugh. "Go away, go away," they chanted. "We are not afraid of you. You can't blow down our shelter of stone."

Then the big, bad bear beasts huffed and they puffed, and they puffed and they huffed to the steady accompaniment of Edty's bellows until the boys are on hands and knees panting out of breath and the rest of us are rolling with laughter.

The stone shelter does not come down.

"We told you," the girls chanted peeking around the stone wall.

Then Chitter runs up on stage toward the huffed and puffed out bear beasts brandishing wooden swords and chittering violently. Jack and Sarus make a mad dash off stage, I'm not sure all the fear and effort to escape is acting, with Chitter chasing after them.

Cautiously the children come out to play. "The bear beasts are gone," Setas announced.

"Hooray, the bear beasts are gone," the others rejoiced.

Then the music starts up again as they join hands and dance and sing, "Who's afraid of the big, bad bear beasts? Not I." Music fades.

Caleeza, Edty, and I applaud jubilantly. It is the first time we have made it through the whole play without stopping, a major achievement. The children are excited too.

"Next rehearsal we'll have them practice lining up on stage at the end and taking a bow," I said.

"They did great, don't you think so?" Edty asked bursting with pride for the children's success.

"Absolutely," Caleeza said. "And, Edty, you were great too. I don't know what we would do without you."

Proud of the children and pleased by the praise, Edty goes right to work resetting the props for the next rehearsal.

CHAPTER 39

Aurora

The boys and I are hanging out at the village circle waiting for the play crew to return from rehearsal. "Kitca wants to be in the club. Actually she knows all about the club. She knows we are the Secret Warriors. And she knows our secret mission is to learn all we can about her and her mother," I informed them.

"We're sunk," Theon groaned.

Then we see them coming. It's a large group, even Edty is involved, and they are jubilantly energized.

"Have you finished all you school work?" Caleeza asked Selyzar right off.

"We just finished our math assignments with Zaloka," Theon confirmed.

"You children will be going back to working on the schoolhouse next work session," Mother informed us.

Good. I've had enough of school work. "We thought we would see if Kitca wanted to hang out with us for a while now you are back," Halren said. The surprise expressions on the faces of the adults are almost comical.

"Of course," Caleeza confirms with Chitter. I can read Kitca's excitement to be included. "Do you want Chitter and I to stay too?"

"No, we'll manage," Selyzar said.

"How will you communicate?" Mother asked.

"We'll find a way," Halren assured her.

"Well, I'm taking my little actors home and feed them," Caleeza said leading Alaia, Caponya and Sarus in that direction. "Don't stay out too long, Selyzar." Chitter and Edty also disperse in different directions.

"That goes for you two also. Don't stay out too long, and don't go wandering off. Your father will be home soon." Mother said. Then she too leaves with Jack and Setas in tow, and for the first time, the five of us are alone. It's an awkward moment.

"Should we meet here or go to the pavilion?" I asked.

"To the pavilion," Theon said. We all agree, even Kitca.

Weaving our way down the short trail in silence, I wonder how we are going to ask the questions we need answers to. Soon we arrive at the pavilion.

"What's that?" Theon asked rushing up onto the stage to check out a structure made of sticks. Kitca is faster. Dropping to all fours, she lopes up the stone steps and across the stage to stand between Theon and the stick prop, chattering furiously.

"She doesn't want you to touch their props," I explained coming up behind them.

"Alright, alright, geez," Theon said backing away. "I won't touch."

We sit around on the sun-warmed stone stage, forming a rough circle. How do we begin? "Kitca has to repeat the pledge to join the club," Selyzar said.

"Do we even know if Kitca wants to be a Secret Warrior? Before we do anything else, I think we should ask her if she wants to join our group."

"I'll ask her," but before I can do so, Kitca is chattering away rapidly.

"Well, what did she say?" Theon asked impatiently.

"She said she wants to be a Secret Warrior and her mother's name is Chiita, not Chitter. She also said, she can understand everything you say through me," I followed up with some discomfort. Is there no way for me to detach myself from all this?

"She understands everyone?" Halren asked shocked.

Kitca responds and I report. "She says no. It's hard to explain. She doesn't exactly understand you, it's like she can pick up my comprehension of what you say."

"Oh." There is an awkward moment.

"Well, if there is no further pre-meeting discussion, we might as well get started," Halren suggested. "Repeat after me. This is a meeting of the Secret Warriors. Everything we say and do is held to secrecy." One by one we repeat the pledge of loyalty. When Kitca attempts to do the same, the boys turn to me for confirmation.

"She agrees."

"Kitca, you are now a member of the Secret Warriors," Halren confirmed. Another awkward moment follows. There seems to be a lot of these. Even though Kitca knows our purpose, we can't just start interrogating her. "Are there any questions you would like to ask us, Kitca?" Smart move, Halren. Let her ask questions first.

Her question solves all our problems. "She wants to know if you want to hear the story of her people."

"Yes, yes." The boys are as surprised by her question as I am. Why is she making it so easy for us, I wonder?

Then Kitca stands and slowly speaks giving me a chance to interpret her impressions. "Our ancestors were nearly wiped out during the great rumbling darkness. Food became scarce and even with their reduced numbers, there was little to go around." The rumbling darkness must refer to the Dark Devastation.

"Reproduction was halted and the fertile, faintly glowing life seeds the females produced, preserved in their shells of translucent stone, were stored in sacred places in the mountains to await better times instead of placed in reproductive pouches. The hard times lasted over many cycles of seasons leaving the people weakened and in time infertile. No more life seeds were produced."

"So star stones are chitter eggs!" Theon gasped.

"Shush!" Selyzar hissed not wanting Kitca to stop telling the story.

"Very few of the saved life seeds survived the mountains' turmoil, but some did. The preserved life seeds were the people's only hope of continuation until they were all used up. Chiita was once one of those life seeds."

"So where did you come from?" Halren asked when Kitca paused.

Kitca bows her head before answering. I translate. "Chiita stole the life seed that developed into me from Caleeza when she visited our valley."

In shocked silence we stare at Kitca, Caleeza's lost star stone. In panic I grasp for the star stone in my pouch. It's still there.

"Chiita isn't a bad person, she was the last of her kind. It was her only hope," Kitca said in her mother's defense.

"So you came to our valley looking for more star stones," Halren concluded.

"Yes," Kitca admitted.

"Are you planning on stealing them?" Selyzar asked.

"No," she denied. I can hear the difference in how the words sound. "We came to look for life seeds, not steal them."

"Is Chiita planning on stealing another life seed?" I dared to ask.

"No. Chiita is no longer fertile and I am still too young. There is also another reason Chiita and I came here."

"What's that?" Halren asked.

"We wanted to be part of a community. We didn't want to live out our lives alone."

CHAPTER 40

Lozar

The formality between captain and crew has relaxed greatly on what has become more a pleasure cruise among friends than an interplanetary government expedition. I like it. I haven't had a lot of friends.

Why have I never noticed before Glisa and Yanzic's feelings for one another? Have I really been that unaware, uncaring? Their servitude to the palace prevents them from uniting. No, it's their servitude to me that keeps them apart. I am the guilty one.

Surveying the coastline, we find areas where the ubiquitous high cliffs have collapsed into small rocky beaches that go nowhere. We pull up to the largest such rockslide we've seen thus far, anchoring the *Princess Thayla* to the rocky shore. The star Seaa is at its zenith providing abundant light. "You have anchor watch," I informed Anthya. She gives me a look of surprise, but doesn't object.

Yanzic, Glisa, Melinda and I disembark to explore the extent of the slide. Could we possibly find another entrance into the continent? But after a long, arduous hike, the rocky valley ends at the base of more formidable peaks of the Coastal Mountains.

"Well?" Anthya questioned upon our return.

"Not here," I informed her. "Perhaps we will find an opening further up the coast." Anthya looks doubtful. We continue on just to see what we can find and to give Xanthe time to give up her search for the colonists so we can go home.

The fresh fruit we brought back with us from the Zayla Valley quickly runs out, but fresh fish remains in abundant supply. The shoreline though doesn't change. "How strange! No beaches! No access into this huge island continent but one. I find it hard to believe these mountainous cliffs continue all the way around back to Lavender Beach."

"Unless you can prove otherwise," Anthya retorted.

"Maybe I will." I never back down from a challenge, but by Seaa set, we still haven't found an inlet or beach.

"According to the chart the High Council provided, we have traveled a third of the way around Lynnara already. Should we turn the *Princess Thayla* around and return to Lavender Beach?" I asked.

"Do you want to rejoin Xanthe's search for Thayla?"

"Not yet. Thayla is safe for now." I haven't explained to Anthya the Twakan bond between a brother and a sister. It is not the same between sisters.

"Then sail on. At this point we might as well go on," Anthya said.

Xanthe, Quaylyn, Kaydra, Arpen, and Rabiam have probably reached the interior by now, but I'm not worried. I accept Anthya's reasoning. The colonists would not have chosen to settle in the reportedly less hospitable interior.

The wind picks up as Seaa sets behind us, allowing the abundance of stars to fully express themselves for a spell before sunrise lightens the sky. Although there has been little to no floating debris around this side of the island, I call a halt. Taking advantage of the curvature of the landscape, we find a bit of calmer water sheltered from the wind and drop anchor.

Long after the others retired to their bunks, Anthya and I sit together in the wheelhouse talking. My wheel watch ends and hers begins as we continue to dig up our pasts, contemplate our futures and speculate on our current venture.

"What will you do if we don't find the colonists?" Anthya asked. "What will you tell your people?"

"The truth. They were not found. At some point Xanthe will have to give up her search and return to Twaka to be queen. That is her destiny, isn't it?"

"You don't sound very happy about that."

"I'm not. My one solace is Thayla made it out alive."

"You're certain of that?"

"I can sense her. I know she is alive."

"Then Xanthe must sense her too."

"No. It doesn't work between sisters. You will have to trust me on this." Anthya doesn't push back. "What will you do when you go back?" I asked seeking insight into her life. She sat silent a moment before answering.

"It's strange to admit," she said, "but for once I haven't thought beyond the here and now." A fleeting smile enhances her demure beauty, then she shuts the door again. "I will continue to serve on the High Council and undertake any missions assigned to me."

"Spoken like a true councilwoman."

"How about you? Where do you go from here? You're a prince, what will your people expect of you?"

"My duty will be to guard the queen." Several quiet moments pass. "Not much to go back to, is it?"

"Sounds like your destiny is as pre-set as mine." Why does it have to be this way?

"What if we do find the colonists?" Anthya asked after some quiet reflection.

"Ideally we will find the colonists before Xanthe does, but I guess there's little chance either of us will find them. Xanthe will always feel her reign is threatened as long as Thayla lives. It's best she believes Thayla is dead."

No one speaks for a while. Haunting images of the vast Zayla Valley and Cremyn Valley come to mind. Then I have to ask, "Is it just me or is there something alluring about this place? It's so isolated, so empty, so mysterious! Do you feel it?"

"I know what you mean, this is my second visit to this devastated land," Anthya said. "It beckons one with its challenging mystery." With a faraway look she continues. "I can understand why the colonists wanted to be here. I can also understand the colonists' motivation for uprooting their lives in search of total self-determination. I believe it is the ultimate freedom."

CHAPTER 41

Rojaire

Seaa has set and the sun is up before I wake. Traevus, Gyro and even Thayla sleep on. No one is guarding us. I struggle to achieve an upright position with my aching body without uttering a moan. Stretching carefully, I gaze out toward the distant water sparkling in sunlight. What a sight to behold! The wind has died down leaving a calm sea. It has been many cycles of seasons since I've seen the ocean. I hadn't realized until now how much I actually miss being by the seashore. Somehow we have to find a route to it, there are still obstacles in the way.

I scout around, moving slow at first. The mountain ledge we are on isn't very big and tightly wedged in. Before long Thayla is beside me.

"We may be able to get down that way," Thayla said pointing to a winding rocky pathway between two tightly packed peaks.

"Or we could always ask Gyro to show us the way down," I said half-jokingly.

"That might not be a bad idea," Thayla agreed with a rare smile. Traevus and Gyro are stirring awake.

"Anyone else sore?" Traevus asked groaning with every move. I'm glad no one witnessed me unfurling. "What's for breakfast?" he asked Thayla planting a kiss on her cheek. To my surprise, although she doesn't reciprocate, she doesn't push him away.

"Trail food until you catch us a fish," she said.

As we prepare to move, Traevus brings up another issue while sharing his food with Gyro. "Uh, what you said before about traveling with pets, you think maybe you could amend that?"

"The creature can go with us if it wants to. It really isn't up to me anyway. It's up to Gyro."

After taking some nourishment and working out some stiffness, with Gyro riding Traevus' shoulder, we start down the way Thayla pointed out earlier. There really isn't any other option. Everything else either climbs up or drops off into the abyss. For the longest, we lose sight of the sea as we stumble through the narrow passes, hoping for a way out. As the day progresses, we catch more vistas of the ocean looming ever closer.

Then suddenly the ground levels off into a high alpine meadow of wispy yellow grass and low blooming pink flowers, the first plant life we've seen in a long time. Continuing on across the meadow, we finally come to the edge of the cliff. Before us stretches a panoramic view of Lynnara's coastline and the Golden Sea. Far below us, sheer cliffs, characteristic of Lynnara's shoreline, drop straight down, a long way down, to golden water lapping against dark purple rock wall.

But an even more intriguing discovery beckons off to our left. An inlet of water makes its way through a long, narrow serpentine gorge cutting through the towering cliffs to a tiny inland sea with sandy shores. The entrance to the inlet would be invisible from the water, the way the narrow entrance hugs the cliff then curves away, but from up here it is mapped out perfectly.

"An opening to the sea," Traevus gasped.

"We just have to find a way to get down there," Thayla said.

"There has to be a way to reach the beach surrounding the inlet." We spread out to search. The meadow is broad and long overlooking the sea and for a ways, the narrow gorge. I follow the dwindling ledge overlooking the gorge, hugging the curvature of the cliff, hoping to discover an escape route before it gives out, but the shelf comes to an abrupt end. There is nowhere to go from here. The sheer cliff wall rises behind me and drops before me. If the cliffs weren't so dangerously high, I'd jump down and swim my way inland. But I decide against it for now. I want better odds of returning to Kaylya and Setas and Jack.

Turning back, I spot something coming into view from the west on the open water. With my heart beating fast, I run back to the cliff edge for a better look. I can hardly believe what I am seeing.

"A boat!" I shouted to the others. It can't be? I rub the sweat out of my eyes to be certain. "A boat!" I shouted again. Thayla and Traevus come running, quickly joining me at the cliff's edge.

"It's not Captain Setas' ferryboat," Traevus said. "I wonder who it is."

"The High Council must have built a boat to search for us. But what is it doing here? They should have put in at Lavender Beach."

"Lozar!" Thayla gasped.

"Who?"

"It's my brother, my brother, Lozar!"

"You can't possibly know that from this distance."

"Your brother? Doesn't your family want to kill you?" Traevus asked in alarm.

"Not Lozar." Then Thayla brings out a collapsible spyglass and extends it. She gazes out toward the boat. "Oh look, he's named his boat after me. How sweet!"

Hopefully that is a good sign. Passing the spyglass to me, Thayla reaches into her satchel again and brings out a small object. "You may want to cover your ears," she warned placing something into her own ears.

"What are you doing?"

"Letting Lozar know we are here."

"Are you sure you want to do that?"

"Yes, cover your ears." Heeding Thayla's warning, Traevus and I do so immediately, just as she puts the strange object to her lips and blows. The volume of sound emitted, far exceeds the object's profile.

The boat comes to a stop.

"Crystal shards that was loud!" Traevus marveled.

"What is that thing?" I asked uncovering my ears.

"It's a bahirl, a warrior's call to battle."

"Are we anticipating a battle?" I asked concerned.

"My brother hasn't come to fight me, but to protect me."

"I hope you're right."

"If they want to fight us, they will have to find a way to reach us first," Traevus pointed out. Good point.

I focus the spyglass on the individuals coming out on deck while Thayla twists movable parts of the bahirl around transforming it into a signaling device. Catching the sunlight on a reflective surface she discloses our location and the *Princess Thayla* comes closer to the cliff. "There are at least three Twakans on board that I can see, so they must be looking for Thayla." As the boat nears the cliff, I focus the spyglass on a woman standing next to the Twakan I assume is Thayla's brother, Prince Lozar. I recognize her at once. Councilor Anthya is the last person on Aaia I expected to see.

"And Councilor Anthya is with them," I informed the others. "That means the High Council is looking for us too, and Thayla is leading them right to us." A fifth person on deck looks familiar. I'm sure I've seen her before, however briefly, but I can't place her.

"So what do we do now?" Traevus asked.

"Can you communicate directions with that thing?" I asked Thayla.

"Yes," she said concentrating intently on her flashes of reflected sunlight. "I'm giving him instructions to find the opening to the inlet." We watch as the *Princess Thayla* creeps perilously close to the rock wall. Fortunately the sea is fairly calm and with some careful jockeying about, the *Princess Thayla* finds the entrance to the gorge and enters into its calm protected water. The boat's fit in the narrow curvy space is snug, but navigable.

"Now all we have to do is make our way down there," Thayla said.

"Has anyone seen Gyro lately?" Traevus asked. As though on cue, Gyro comes scampering down a rock formation of giant boulders behind us.

"Where have you been off to?" Traevus asked.

While Traevus inquires, Thayla and I investigate. Climbing up the stack of boulders, we eventually come to a long narrow cave with light visible at the other end of the tunnel. Stooping low we worm our way through the opening. Practically crawling on hands and knees, we squirm our way through the rocky passage. The opening at the other end draws closer.

"I hope this leads to something good," I said.

"Hey, wait for us," we heard Traevus call out followed by Gyro's soft whine.

Finally we step out onto a long gently sloping mountain side that leads down to the inland sea just as the *Princess Thayla* exits the gorge below us. With anxious anticipation and curiosity, we head down to greet them.

CHAPTER 42

Anthya

We wake to a fairly calm day with brilliant sunshine. "What a beautiful day!" Melinda declared coming up on deck. Lozar steps out of the cabin to join us. "Blaka," she greeted him.

"Blaka otta," Lozar said solemnly touching his heart and mind. "It's how a warrior recognizes another warrior. Try it."

"Blaka otta," Melinda said touching her heart and mind. Lozar nods his approval.

After a breakfast of trail food and tea we pull anchor and move on. It is a late start, but no one seems in a hurry. Once again Lozar has taken the wheel. I sip on a cup of Twakan tea, I'm actually developing a taste for it, and stare out the wheelhouse window. The landscape hasn't changed, if anything, the cliffs are even taller.

It isn't long before an incredibly loud horn of some sort shatters the tranquil quiet, the sound reverberating off the water.

"What was that?" I cried out.

"A signal only Thayla could have made."

Lozar immediately cuts the engine back letting the boat jog in place. The sea is calm, the water deep, and there is nothing out here to hit.

He steps out of the wheelhouse to look around. I follow Lozar out in time to see a flash of reflected sunlight high upon a cliff. Yanzic, Glisa and Melinda stand together at the starboard railing. The flashes continue in what looks like code. "It's Thayla," he said with high emotion. "She says there is an inlet, a narrow gorge that leads inland. To see the opening, we have to hug the cliff."

Taking the controls again, Lozar brings the *Princess Thayla* closer to the cliff. Even with directions, the entrance proves hard to find. With great skill Lozar maneuvers the boat in the gentle swell to within inches of the rock wall until the opening finally becomes visible, and squeezes the boat into calm still water with cliffs towering above us. The gorge is deep, but there is little clearance on either side, the walls so close, I can actually reach out and touch them. Gradually the passage widens a little as it curves around towering walls of stone. "Does this mean we have found the colonists?" Melinda asked excited.

"We can hope."

"There is an opening up ahead." Melinda pointed out. Soon the *Princess Thayla* glides out onto a small inland sea surrounded by steeply sloping mountain sides and a narrow dark purple sandy beach. Three of the colonists we have been searching for are hiking down the mountainside to meet us. My heart soars with joy to see them alive. Lozar was right all along. Princess Thayla is still alive and there is another opening into the continent.

Thayla, Rojaire and Traevus approach solemnly. No doubt they are as surprised to see us as we are to see them. The five of us disembark onto the dark purple shore to wait for them. As the colonist draw nearer Lozar and Thayla rush out to meet each other, exchanging warrior greetings. They seem to be on friendly terms. I notice Lozar bow slightly in deference to her, but she will have none of it, patting him playfully on the shoulder and giving him a gentle embrace, obviously glad to see him.

Then Rojaire and Traevus approach. "Greetings, Councilor Anthya. Welcome to Lynnara. How may I serve?" Rojaire greeted.

"Greetings, Rojaire and Traevus. It is I who owes you service."

Thayla and Lozar rejoin us and Thayla takes over the introductions. "Rojaire and Traevus, I would like for you to meet my brother Lozar," Thayla said proudly. Lozar intently studies the men he has heard so much about. "Thank you, Rojaire, for keeping my sister safe."

"You're welcome," Rojaire said, "But mostly she keeps us safe."

Lozar nods his approval, then turns his attention to Traevus. "And you're the one Anthya and Quaylyn found on a previous expedition."

"That's right. Welcome to Lynnara."

"And this is Glisa and Yanzic." Thayla introduces everyone like a friend introducing friends to friends, without the titles "Prince" and "Warrior."

What is that?" Lozar asked indicating the pointy little creature looking at him intently.

"We aren't sure what he is, but his name is Gyro," Traevus said. "Don't worry, he's friendly."

"He doesn't look very round to me," Melinda said.

Then I reach for Melinda and introduce her. "Melinda is from Earth." I catch Rojaire's flash of recognition. He met her as a young girl on Earth when he was reunited with Kaylya. Of course, that was many cycles of seasons ago.

"Greetings, Melinda. Welcome to Lynnara," Rojaire said.

"Thank you, Rojaire. I'm happy to be here. Is Ilene still alive?"

"Yes, of course," Rojaire said a bit confused.

"We thought possibly you were all dead," I explained.

Rojaire smiles warmly. "Ilene is very much alive. She will be thrilled to see you." Melinda breathes an audible sigh of relief. Then she boldly steps up to Thayla. "Blaka otta," she greeted Thayla touching her heart and forehead.

Thayla doesn't blink. "Blaka otta," she greeted Melinda touching her chest and head. "Welcome to Lynnara, Earth warrior."

"Why did you think we were all dead?" Rojaire asked.

"It's too much to drop on you all at once. Perhaps we could have some refreshments," I suggested.

"Of course. We have plenty to discuss," Lozar agreed. "Come aboard the *Princess Thayla* where we may share food and drink. We have Twakan tea and roasted fish."

"Did you say fish?" Traevus said with a wide grin. "I would be glad to partake of your offer."

Boarding the *Princess Thayla*, we gather on the roomy aft deck where two overturned storage bins, side by side, serve as a low table. The little pointy creature they call Gyro doesn't join us, but instead chooses to wait on shore, despite Traevus urging him to follow. Yanzic lays out what we have to offer in food and drink and everyone joins in. The colonists gorge on fish like they haven't had it in a long time, which Traevus quickly verifies to be true. "We just reached the sea today for the first time since the massive ground shake." Apparently, encountering us is not the only momentous event of the day.

"We come with a warning," Lozar said once we had eaten. "Xanthe is searching the continent looking for Thayla to kill her. Two of her warriors, Arpen and Rabiam, are with her".

"Let Xanthe come. I will fight her to the death," Thayla said taking the warning in stride as though she anticipated as much all along, but Rojaire and Traevus are shocked by the news.

"I will protect Thayla," Traevus vowed. Thayla looks at him as though she is about to retort, but remains silent.

"Also Councilor Quaylyn and the former Mentor to Twaka, Kaydra, are with her."

"Quaylyn and Kaydra are here too!" Traevus said excited over the news. "Where are they?"

"We left them in the Cremyn Valley, but they may be in the interior by now," Lozar said.

"Princess Xanthe is really serious," I added. "If she finds your colony, your people will be in great danger."

"Let her search all she wants," Rojaire said. "I respect your concern, Councilor, but she won't find us."

"How can you be so certain?"

"There's no access to the colony from the interior."

"That's good to know," Lozar said.

"How many are there of you?" I asked.

"We'll talk about that later, after we learn more about your mission," Rojaire said. "So again, why did you think we were all dead?"

"Alaia Island is gone, it has sunk into the ocean, and we found Captain Setas' ferryboat, a pile of rubble carried far inland by what we assume was a tsunami."

"Alaia Island is gone?" Traevus asked incredulously.

"You may be happy to know, Councilor, Captain Setas did not go down with Alaia Island and she didn't die in the tsunami. Captain Setas made it safely to the colony where she and Theon lived out their natural longevity," Rojaire said. "What exactly is your mission from the High Council?"

"We came in two ships, the *Princess Thayla* and the *Xanthe Queen*. Quaylyn, Kaydra, Melinda, and I were chosen by the High Council to assist Princess Xanthe and Prince Lozar in finding their sister, Princess Thayla."

Then I tell the story of our journey. I detail our voyage through the Pinnacles, our search for Alaia Island and our trek from Lavender Beach to the Cremyn Valley, describing the damage we observed and the growth of the young forests the colonists had planted. "Who built the shelter in the Cremyn Valley?"

"Ollen built that shelter," Traevus said. "He is with us too."

"Ollen? From the lost expedition?"

"Yes, and Caleeza is with us too."

"Caleeza is living in the colony?" Melinda asked her excitement growing. According to Melinda and the Oracle of Light, Caleeza lived with Melinda's family for a while on Earth, in Alaska. The High Council hasn't been able to verify this.

"I tried to convince Xanthe you are dead," Lozar said addressing Thayla, but she wouldn't return to the boats. They are still searching for you in the interior."

"The colony is not accessible from the interior," Rojaire repeated. "It used to be reachable by the underground passage, but that route has long been closed by seismic activity."

"There was no mention of a hidden valley in Kiril's report," I casually bring up to get a reaction.

"No, there wasn't."

"If the passage is closed, how did you get here?" I asked.

"By a route I hope never to repeat."

"I'm not here to arrest anyone or force you back to Mainland," I said. "In fact, I have a charter for your colony from the High Council."

"We don't need a charter from the High Council. We are a free nation," Rojaire said defiantly.

"A free nation. How many are you?" I found myself asking again.

"What will you do with the information? Take it to the High Council?"

"It was Lozar and Xanthe who initiated this search. The High Council is not after you."

"We intend keeping it that way," Rojaire said bitterly.

"I can hardly blame you for feeling the way you do," Anthya said. An uncomfortable silence follows.

Then Rojaire speaks up. "There are twenty-five of us, fifteen adults and ten children."

The number far exceeds my expectation. "Ten children?"

"Kaylya and I have two of our own."

The colonists have been pairing off and creating families, I suddenly realized. The silent rebel in me smiles inwardly imaging the High Council's reaction to that. They will never learn of it from me I vow to myself.

"What do we do now?" Thayla asked. It's the question we all have on our minds. After a detailed description of the Stairs from Thayla, Rojaire and Traevus, we all agree another route to the valley needs to be found.

"So are you joining us?" Traevus asked.

"Yes," Lozar said without hesitation. "If you will have us." Melinda and I stare at Lozar in shock, but pleased by his decision. "We will leave the *Princess Thayla* safely moored here and join you." Then he turns to Glisa and Yanzic. "I hereby relieve you of your duties now and forever. You are free to join the colony if you wish." Glisa and Yanzic's faces beam radiantly with joy.

"What about you, Councilor?" Rojaire asked.

"Melinda and I will also join you. By doing so I am no longer a councilor."

"I wonder where that cut leads to," Traevus said pointing out an irregularity in the mountain slope at the far end of the inlet."

CHAPTER 43

Quaylyn

When we are alone again, I lay out a plan with Kaydra. "We want to skirt wide the point of the Crescent Mountains."

"Why?"

"Because the ruins of the Temple of Tranquility are located right around the inside of the crescent point of the mountains. The ruins exude dangerous negative energy." I tell her the story of our expedition long ago with Councilor Zayla and Councilor Brakalar. Theon, Rojaire and Ilene, now colonists, although I doubt Theon is still alive, were also with us on the expedition. "Councilor Zayla died in the ruins of the Temple of Tranquility by Councilor Brakalar's hand. The temple ruins is not a place for Xanthe. If we can give the point a wide enough berth, she won't see it and won't be tempted to enter."

"Then what? Do we take her deep into the interior?"

"Hopefully, after seeing enough uninhabited and barren landscape, Xanthe will be ready to go home and claim her much desired throne long before we reach the Crystalline Landscape."

"Do you think we will find the colonists?"

"No."

"So you think they are all dead?"

"No, just hidden."

It isn't long before the princess is bored and ready to move on. To my surprise, I manage to dissuade Xanthe from attempting the underground passage to the interior. Or maybe it was seeing the destruction from the tsunami that convinced her. Regardless, we return to the Zayla valley.

From here it would be far easier to leave than go on. Apparently Kaydra has the same idea and decides to take a stance.

"Why don't you give up this search, now?" Kaydra asked. "You know we aren't going to find the colonists, they're gone."

"This has all been your fault from the start," Xanthe lashed out. "You let Thayla go off on this misconceived adventure."

"Princess Thayla made up her own mind to go with the colonists."

"You should have gone with her, to protect her."

"If I remember right, Princess Thayla was appointed to protect me."

"Don't get insolent with me, Mentor. You will never see Twaka again. Give her a blade," Xanthe ordered Arpen. Arpen hands Kaydra her blade and to my dismay, Kaydra accepts it.

I step up to intercede. "You're not going through with this?" The Twakan blade looks heavy and unyielding, dwarfing Kaydra's smaller frame. I remember Kaydra saying she often sparred with Princess Thayla. Has she kept up the training?

"Stay out of this, Councilor Quaylyn," Xanthe warned. "This is a fair fight."

"Yes, stay out of this, Councilor Quaylyn," Kaydra mimicked focused on her adversary. "This has been a long time coming."

"Listen to her, Councilor," Xanthe spat.

Arpen and Rabiam urge me to desist. I have to trust Kaydra knows what she is doing since she has been steeped in Twakan culture. Kaydra and Xanthe face off and reluctantly Arpen, Rabiam and I move out the way.

"You aren't fit to rule your people. I don't doubt there are many on Twaka who feel the same way I do. Taking you out will be doing them a favor," Kaydra taunted.

"You don't have the courage to strike me. You're through, a loser, a failure," Xanthe countered.

In a flash, Kaydra strikes first, narrowly missing Xanthe's shoulder, saved only by Xanthe's almost too late defensive move. With lightning speed, Xanthe strikes back, nipping Kaydra's forearm before she deflects the attack.

I want to stop the fight before serious injury occurs, but for the combatants it has become an issue of honor. Having been disposed as

Mentor to Twaka, Kaydra probably feels she has nothing to lose, but her life. What good is dying for a lost cause?

The battle rages on. Rabiam stands tensely by with blade drawn. What is his intent? Will he pick up the fight if Kaydra defeats Xanthe? There seems little chance of that as Xanthe continues to keep Kaydra on the defensive. However she also manages to make a mark here and there evidenced by the trickles of blood on both women.

Then suddenly Kaydra strikes a powerful blow that knocks Xanthe's blade out of her hand, sending it flying over the rocky ground. Immediately Kaydra rushes in preventing Xanthe from retrieving it. She tackles the princess to the ground, forcing the blade against her throat. I watch Rabiam and Arpen closely, but neither of them attempts to intervene.

"Go ahead, Mentor, eliminate me!" Xanthe panted. Both women are bleeding and breathing heavily.

"I choose concession for your life, my right as granted by Twakan law."

"This isn't Twaka," Xanthe argued. Kaydra moves the blade a fraction closer to Xanthe's throat, drawing a thin red line. "Name your price," Xanthe concedes.

"You will discontinue your search for Princess Thayla and return to Twaka immediately, never to set foot in Lynnara again."

Xanthe attempts to spit at Kaydra, deepening the red line on her throat, but misses her mark. "I will gladly leave this forsaken land."

Carefully Kaydra moves her blade and rises, releasing her hold on Xanthe. The silence is eerily strange as the rite of concession plays out. Not another word is spoken as Xanthe works her way up off the ground, and without retrieving her sword, marches off toward Lavender Beach. Arpen and Rabiam silently follow her. Kaydra and I watch them go.

Kaydra doesn't move. "Are you alright?" I asked rushing to her side as soon as Xanthe and her warriors are a safe distance away.

"Yes," she said. "At least now Thayla and the colonists are safe." She drops Arpen's blade and leans against me for support. I lead her to a shady spot among tall brush alongside the Zayla River and ease her down. Then I wash her wounds and bandage them with strips of cloth I tear from a shirt. She obviously needs to rest. Xanthe, Arpen and Rabiam are no longer in sight.

"I'm concerned they will leave without us," I said.

"Trust me, they will leave without us," Kaydra confirmed. "You can run after them if you want to. I'm just going to lie down right here and rest."

I watch as Kaydra stretches out on the cool grass by the river and goes to sleep. I don't leave her side.

CHAPTER 44

Rojaire

I don't know quite what to make of Lozar, but I have great respect for Thayla and Councilor Anthya who obviously trust him. We move the *Princess Thayla* to the far end of the inland sea and moor her securely. Gyro still refuses to come aboard and follows along on shore.

I can see Lozar is hesitant to leave his boat unattended, but chances of Xanthe finding it are nearly non-existent. The gorge entrance and inlet are only visible from above. Without Thayla's signal, Lozar would have simply passed it by.

The eight of us pack up all the provisions we can carry, for there is no food in these mountains, and head up the narrow rocky cut with Thayla and Lozar in the lead. The narrowness of the cut forces us to go single file. I follow behind Lozar, and Yanzic and Traevus take the rear with Anthya, Glisa and Melinda between us. Gyro rides on Traevus' shoulder as usual.

The going is steep. The passage is similar to the ones we hiked through to reach the cliff edge, little more than a water gutter when it rains. Oftentimes loose rock moves from under our feet cascading down to those that follow with "Heads up!" shouted frequently. One water drainage leads to another as we drop down to the depths only to climb ever higher. One mountain peak follows another with only a crack in between. Traevus sculpts parallel lines into the rock walls along the way marking our passage in case we have to back track. Then we have to do just that when a drainage track ends far below a steep mountain peak, leaving us boxed in with no place to go. We return to the last intersection where Traevus chisels a diagonal line across the parallels to indicate a dead end.

High up in the mountains our rocky path levels out into a broader saddle between three towering peaks. From here, an endless array of sky-reaching peaks stretch even higher before us, sowing doubts we will ever make it through. The air feels cooler even though the sun arches high in the sky. It is time to call a break. We cannot go on without rest.

After eating what little Traevus offers him, Gyro takes off on his own. "Where're you going?" Traevus calls after him, but Gyro keeps going.

"He'll be back," Thayla reassured him. "Maybe he will find a way out of here."

"Doesn't look like we are over the divide yet," Lozar said joining me. "Strange we haven't come across any water yet running through these gullies,"

"Let's hope we are out of these mountains before we have a downpour. There is a waterfall at the northern end of our valley, so water must gather somewhere."

"Do you think we will ever find your valley from here?"

"I have a family waiting for me. I will find a way through."

Just as we are thinking of moving again, Gyro comes back squealing. He seems to want us to follow him. I'm not sure how far or how long the others are willing to explore, but after a brief rest we let Gyro lead.

We know the general direction we need to go. The sun acts as our guide. The mountain peaks press ever tighter together with no valleys in between, squeezing us between rock walls. Then finally we break out of the crack in the rock and find ourselves on top of the world. Below us a rock scree leads down to a narrow stream of water in a tight gorge flowing south. The stacked peaks of the rest of the mountain range stretch out before us. And in the far, far distance a slit of an opening enclosed by mountains gleams in the sunlight. It is our valley.

"How are we ever going to get there?" Traevus asked gazing out toward home.

"We'll get there."

"Is that where we're going?" Anthya asked.

"It looks like a secret magical place," Melinda said.

We can't go on until we have a period of sleep. We cross the divide in search of a protected place to sleep and drop down into another rocky trough until we reach a junction large enough to accommodate us. Thayla and Lozar volunteer for the first watch.

Once rested, we are raring to go again. Seeing home in the distance gives us renewed hope. Traevus and I lead with Lozar and Anthya at the rear. We weave through what amounts to little more than a rocky trough between adjacent mountain peaks when suddenly the bottom gives out under Traevus' feet, and Traevus and Gyro disappear from sight. Like a layer of snow covering a crevasse in a glacier, the rocky gully we are traversing is nothing more than an accumulation of loose rocks, caught high in the mountain hiding the drop below.

"Get off the loose rocks," I shout back to the others as the opening over a deep crevice lengthens with more rocks crumbling down. I jump up on the rocky sides straddling the crevice. The mountain sides are too steep to do more than cling to rock.

"Traevus!" Thayla shouts already spread eagle, climbing down two rock walls to Traevus below. Traevus neither answers nor moves, only Gyro whimpers in response.

"Thayla!" Lozar shouts after her. Thayla doesn't respond, all her focus is on Traevus. Straddling the opening from above, I detach the rope secured to my pack and drop one end down to her. Thayla has already made her way down to where Traevus is stuck, suspended between two mountains.

"It becomes solid ground again where the gully trail starts to descend," Thayla shouts back. "You might want to move everyone down."

"Tie yourself in," Lozar shouts down as Thayla grabs the rope, but she ties the rope around Traevus, looping it twice, instead.

With Glisa, Anthya and Melinda safely on solid footing once again, Lozar, Yanzic and I straddle the crevice ready to pull. Then Thayla grabs the still whimpering Gyro and tosses the little creature up to me. I catch Gyro and toss him to the others. Melinda catches him and hugs him closely trying to console him.

"Ready," Thayla calls up. We pull, but Traevus doesn't budge.

"I'll have to cut off his pack before we can lift him." Thayla cuts the straps to the pack and we break Traevus free. His pack tumbles out of reach further down the narrow crevice. The loss of provisions will mean even stricter rationing of food. "Careful, he has a head injury," Thayla informed us.

Thayla guides Traevus' limp form from below as we raise him up. Finally we manage to all reach the safety of firm ground and lay Traevus down. Thayla pours precious water onto a torn piece of fabric from her tunic and gently dabs his wound while we feel for broken bones. Traevus begins to move under Thayla's gentle caress, groaning lightly.

"Traevus, can you hear me?" Thayla coaxed.

"Thayla?" Traevus whispered softly.

"What do you think you were doing, risking your life for this man?" Lozar demanded now that the crisis seems to be over.

"Traevus is my heart mate," Thayla said. Her statement stuns us all.

"I am? ...your heart mate," Traevus said obviously comprehending Thayla's words, which is encouraging. We can find no other visible injuries other than the bump on his head.

"Then we have lots to talk about," Lozar said.

CHAPTER 45

Kaylya

Rojaire will be pleased over what we have achieved as a community while he was gone. We are finally putting the roof on the new schoolhouse and everyone is here to help, even the children. With two rooms, two lessons or events can occur at once. And each room has a separate entrance from outside. The younger group and older group of children have already chosen their classrooms.

The building project has helped occupy my mind while Rojaire has been away, but as more time passes I fear we will never see the explorers again. I can imagine a thousand things happening to them, there's probably another thousand I can't. I'm fine as long as I'm busy with the children and the building project, but when all is quiet and the children are asleep, I painfully long for Rojaire's return. Rojaire has been gone so long, Jack and Setas have quit asking when their father is coming home. According to Caleeza, Chitter is certain they have perished on the Stairs despite the fact that she and Kitca made it out alive.

Work has been difficult without the skills and labor of Traevus, Rojaire and Thayla, but the long held community policy, everyone learns all they can about every task, has paid off. A pile of split wood shingles are ready for the roof. Meanwhile, Drak and Ollen continue to split wood shingles refusing to stop until certain we have enough to cover the roof and more.

"Can we go to school tomorrow?" Jack asked helping me carry the wood shingles to Edty.

"Well maybe, we will have to wait and see," I said. "The building isn't finished yet."

"You will be going to school soon enough," Edty said carrying the shingles up the ladder to Kiril, Ilene and Wessid tacking them in place with the crude nails Zaloka and Tassyn forged with Inventor Sulyan's help.

Suddenly one roofer after another stops work and stands up looking out toward the north. "What is it?" I called up.

"There are people coming, heading this way," Kiril informed us. All work grinds to a stop.

"People? What kind of people?" I asked. The arrival of people is a major concern. We don't get a lot of visitors.

How many?" Ollen asked. "More than three?"

"I count seven or eight moving through the trees. It looks like some of them are Twakan," Wessid said.

"Who's coming?" Aurora and Halren asked.

"We don't know," I told them. "Everyone stay close."

"Should we gather all the children and hide them in the schoolhouse, Chitter and Kitca too?" Zaloka asked.

"What good would that do? We can't hide them forever."

"They have Thayla," Ilene called down.

"As a prisoner?" I asked. I feel my heart pounding, fearing for our safety. If they can take Thayla, they can take any of us.

"I can't tell. I don't see any weapons out."

"Is that Councilor Anthya?" Wessid asked.

"It is," Kiril confirmed. "Oh no, how did they find us?"

As the group approaches, the roofers climb down. Parents gather their children close and together we stand strong, forming a solid wall of weaponless adults defending our children and homes. What will happen to us now?

"Ilene!" a young woman cried out, immediately breaking from the group after entering the schoolhouse clearing and running up to her joyfully. I recognize her.

"Melinda?" Ilene asked her jaw dropping in shock. "Melinda!" she cried engulfing her in a fierce embrace. "Oh, Melinda, it's so good to see you. But how?" she stammered, tears running down her cheeks.

And then I see him! Overcome with joy, I blindly dash into Rojaire's crushing embrace. "Dad!" two children scream, dashing up behind me. Rojaire grasps us all together into his arms.

CHAPTER 46

Anthya

The rest of the colonists watch us quietly taking in our presence. I realize they probably perceive a troop of Twakans and a councilor of the Crystal Table as a threat. But after Melinda's joyful reunion with Ilene and Kaylya's tearful reunion with Rojaire, they begin to relax a little.

"Anthya, I want you to meet my son Jack and my daughter Setas," Rojaire said as proud as a father can be. "And you know my heart mate, Kaylya."

"Greetings Kaylya, Jack and Setas. It is wonderful, Kaylya, finding you alive and well. I can see, Rojaire, why you were so determined to get home."

"You named Jack after Jack Faulkner," Melinda said with delight.

"That's right," Kaylya said. "And of course Setas is named for Captain Setas."

I stand back while the colonists warmly greet Rojaire, Traevus and Thayla, embracing them back into the fold. Their great joy over the return of their own proves emotional to watch. So many familiar faces, and the children nearly outnumber the adults. The children are beautiful and wildly curious over the presence of people they have never seen before. Two strange looking feathered creatures, perhaps a parent and child, are also part of the group. I shouldn't be so surprised by life forms I've never seen before after seeing kurpers and callelas and meeting Gyro.

Thayla brings Lozar out into the forefront. "This is my brother, Lozar," she announced. There is an audible murmur of surprise.

"You mean he's a prince?" a young girl asked.

Lozar graciously bows to the colonists. "It is a pleasure to finally meet you. I thank you for your friendship with my sister. She thinks highly of all of you."

"And this is Glisa and Yanzic," Thayla said introducing them.

"I am pleased to meet you," Glisa said. Yanzic nodded in agreement. There are so many introductions to be made.

Ilene moves through the group introducing Melinda to people who know her only from the stories they have been told, except for Kaylya and Caleeza. Melinda does not shy away. "Caleeza!" she cried as they embrace. It's like she has come home to a place she has never been. It is I who is out of place.

Kiril steps out diplomatically with his family, "Greetings, Councilor Anthya. How may I serve?"

"Greetings, Kiril. I am honored to be in your presence. I wish to assure you we have come in peace. This is a joyful occasion, not an invasion. We mean you no harm."

"If Rojaire, Thayla and Traevus thought you were a threat, you wouldn't be here. Let me introduce to you my son Theon and my daughter Aurora," Kiril said. "Ilene named our daughter. Homesick for Alaska, I guess. Of course, Theon was named after Ilene's father."

But Kiril isn't done. "And this here is my little brother Halren," he said proudly reaching for the tall boy standing by Wessid and Zaloka, Kiril's chosen mother and chosen father by the High Council.

"Your brother? Greetings Wessid, Zaloka, Halren, Aurora and Theon. "You have quite the family, Kiril!"

"I am indeed fortunate," Kiril said.

I see Tassyn, Edty, Inventor Sulyan and Drak. I know them all and greet each one. Then I find two more members of the lost expedition. "Greetings, Ollen and Caleeza. So the stories I've been told are true. You are here."

"Greetings, Councilor Anthya. It was never our intent to deceive the High Council," Ollen said for both of them. "We ask for forgiveness."

"You are forgiven by me. It lightens my heart to find you here. I only wish Quaylyn and Kaydra could be here too. They have also been looking for you. I wish they could know you have been found. And these are your children?"

"Yes, Alaia, Selyzar, Cremyn and Sarus," Caleeza said naming them off. Three of them are named for members of the expedition they were part of, the other one named after Alaia Island. I don't have the heart to tell her at this joyful moment, Alaia Island has sunk into the ocean. There will be time for all that soon enough.

"And over here is Chitter and her daughter Kitca," Caleeza said indicating the brownish orange downy pair with intelligent round eyes in almost humanlike faces.

"Greetings, Chitter and Kitca. How may I serve?"

The one called Chitter wears an ancient looking medallion and twitters what I assume is a greeting. "She welcomes you here," Caleeza translated. At least I think it was a translation. But how could that be?

"And what are we building here?" Rojaire asked spreading his arms in amazement.

"It's our new school," Setas informed him. "Do you want to see it, Dad?"

"I certainly do. I like the choice of location."

"That was Halren and Selyzar's idea. The schoolhouse is almost done. We were working on the roof when you arrived," Kaylya said.

"Come and see it, Dad," Jack urged pulling him toward the open entrances at the front of the schoolhouse, with Kaylya still holding on to Rojaire's hand. The crowd follows.

The schoolhouse and its surroundings are beautiful. The largest tree I've ever seen dominates the schoolyard. Across a babbling brook, stand more of the giant trees. The walls of the schoolhouse are constructed of purple mortar and stones framed in with rose-colored timbers. Split timbers cover the roof beams overlaid with overlapping split wood shingles to shed the rain. An interior wall, visible through the open entrances, dissects the building into two rooms, adding to the sturdiness of the structure. I can hardly wait to see the rest of the community.

"Has anyone seen Gyro?" Traevus asked.

"Over in that tree," I said pointing to the schoolyard giant.

"I guess he doesn't like crowds," Traevus murmured going off to search for him.

"This calls for a celebration," Kiril announced. "I officially call this a holiday. But our guests are tired and famished. We must provide them with food and a chance to rest while we prepare a feast to really celebrate."

Then Traevus returns with Gyro. "And this is Gyro." Children and adults alike gawk at the strange little bluish gray creature.

"Can I hold him?" Aurora asked.

"Eventually, but he's a little shy right now." Traevus places Gyro on the ground so the children can get a better look at him. It takes a little while, but eventually Gyro decides he likes the attention after all and struts from child to child as they giggle over his amazingly strange tail and triangular features.

After a tour of the new schoolhouse, the colonists lead us to the community fire ring located in the village circle. We pass by several sturdy stone, mortar and wood cottages set in the trees connected by pebble pathways. More cottages are visible through the trees surrounding the clearing. I'm certainly impressed with what the colonists have achieved.

The children hang around fascinated by the presence of people they have never seen before. I try to imagine what it is like to grow up isolated from the world and see strangers for the first time. The colonists who disappeared after Kiril's call for food and drink quickly reappear with laden trays, far more food than we can possibly eat. Then they settle around us waiting for our stories.

Lozar coaxes the children closer with sweet treats and patiently answers their questions as they become more trusting. I didn't know he had a soft spot for children.

"Are you a warrior like Thayla?" Jack wanted to know.

"Of course he is," Theon said before Lozar could answer.

"Thayla has taught me everything I know," Lozar said giving Thayla a brotherly wink. "She is incredible, isn't she?"

"Yes," Setas agreed.

Melinda pulls the box containing the flute from her pack and hands it to Ilene. "I thought you might like to have this." Recognizing the case, Ilene's eyes tear up immediately. Her hands tremble with suppressed tears as she opens the case and caresses the instrument. "So often I've wished I could have brought it with me. It reminds me of home in Alaska's Susitna Valley. Thank you," Ilene said her voice quavering.

"So that's what it looks like!" Inventor Sulyan exclaimed.

Everyone wants to see the flute from Earth, especially the children who crowd around her to reach out and touch it. To everyone's delight, Ilene quickly assembles the flute, raises it to her lips and blows out a little tune to hear its sweet sound.

Then Rojaire stands up to deliver the report everyone has been waiting for.

"It is so great to be back," Rojaire started. Everyone applauds and cheers. "As you may have guessed, we found a route to the sea and much more. "And you were right, Chitter, the Stairs are a nightmare." Chitter chitters in agreement.

The colonists listen intently as he tells them about the inlet, spotting Lozar's boat, and Thayla guiding them in. He tells them about Princess Xanthe and her crew, including Quaylyn and Kaydra, still searching the continent for Thayla. "Lozar, Glisa and Yanzic are here to protect Thayla. Xanthe is searching for Thayla to kill her," Rojaire explained. "She sees Thayla as a threat to her throne."

"She won't find us here," Drak shouted out.

"Probably not, but we must always be on our guard," Rojaire reminded them.

"What about the High Council?" Ollen asked. "Are they after us too?"

"Good question," Rojaire said. "I yield the floor to Councilor Anthya."

Reluctantly I stand to speak. "The High Council neglected to look for you until Twaka, represented by Prince Lozar and Princess Xanthe, threatened Aaia with inter-planetary treaty violation if we failed to help launch a search for Princess Thayla." Everyone turns to glance at Lozar and Thayla sitting together so pleased to be reunited, amazed that inter-planetary intrigue could reach their isolated world.

"The Councilors have softened considerably on the issue of your colony," I continued. "The Runes of the Crystal Table decreed the High Councilor issue a charter legitimizing the colonization of Lynnara." There are mixed reactions from the colonists to this announcement. There are a few whoops and cheers, but I detect a hard-earned, deep-rooted sense of freedom among them that places very little worth on a charter from the High Council. Nevertheless, I pull the tube containing the printed charter from my pack.

"Rojaire claims you don't need a charter, you are already a free nation," I said presenting it to Kiril. Kiril looks over the charter while the colonists roar in agreement. Obviously this statement agrees with them more.

"I feel you should know that the seismic event that closed the underground access to the valley also took down Alaia Island." There were audible gasps. Some stole a glance at Alaia, named after the ill-fated island. "And Captain Setas' ferryboat, moored at Lavender Beach, was destroyed when a tsunami swept it far inland. When we made the discovery, we feared not only Captain Setas, but all of you perished in the event. Rojaire has since assured me Captain Setas joined the colony and arrived safely in the valley."

"You will have a chance to visit her grave site," Kiril said. There is a moment of silence while the villagers soak in all the news. Then Rojaire changes the subject.

"When are we going to see this play I'm hearing about?" he asked dispelling the solemn mood.

"After our guests of honor get some rest and before the big feast," Kaylya announced having already discussed it with Ilene and Caleeza.

CHAPTER 47

Rojaire

"Are you going to leave us again?" Jack asked as I settle him in for a period of rest. "I wish you wouldn't."

"I'm not planning on going anywhere for a very long time. By then you may be old enough to go with me."

"I'm already old enough."

"Almost," I said kissing his forehead. On a cot across the room Setas is already sleeping soundly. It has been an exciting day for them...for all of us.

"I hope you like our play," Jack said as I start to leave.

"I'm sure I will. Get some rest now."

I walk out to find Kaylya waiting for me in the front room, a decanter in her hand. "Drak just dropped off a welcome home gift," she said smiling. Setting the decanter on the table, she comes to me radiantly beautiful in the setting sunlight streaming in through the window.

"I'm so proud of you," I said basking in the comforting joy of holding her in my arms again. Building a schoolhouse is a big accomplishment."

"Team work, remember? I didn't accomplish it alone. Everyone participated. Where are the new arrivals staying?"

"The Twakans are staying in the schoolhouse. There's nowhere else to shelter them. Thayla offered her shelter to Councilor Anthya. And Melinda moved in with Ilene and Kiril."

"So Lozar and Yanzic have one classroom and Thayla and Glisa have the other one."

"Not quite. Glisa and Yanzic are a couple and share a classroom. And Thayla moved in with Traevus."

"Oh, really? So Thayla and Traevus have finally made a commitment to one another?"

"I guess learning someone is searching for you to kill you changes a person's perspective or maybe it was Traevus' brush with death in the mountain crevice that sealed the deal."

"What does Lozar think about that?"

"He and Traevus discussed things, I don't know what they agreed to. I don't think Lozar has much ground to object on. Have you seen how he looks at Councilor Anthya? Who by the way, claims she is no longer a councilor."

"Interesting. And what about you? You found a route to the sea and a boat."

"Well I didn't do it alone. Team work, remember? Everyone participated."

"How long do you think Anthya and the Twakans will be here?"

"I don't know. They don't seem to be in a rush to go. But when they leave, we no longer have a boat."

"Do you really think we are safe from the High Council with Anthya here?"

"We're safe for now."

"Our village will be forever changed," Kaylya said softly with a kiss.

"It'll be alright," I whispered kissing her lips, her neck, her throat...."

When we rise again from our bed, Seaa is high in the sky. Of course the children are up before us, foraging the storage bins for food. The play is scheduled at Seaa's zenith, after preparations for the feast celebration.

"Now remember, Rojaire, you are one of the honored guests at this feast. You are not expected to work. Let the rest of us do the preparations," Kaylya said as I start for the door.

"I'll just look around."

"Can we go with you?" Setas asked. "We don't have any lessons. Kiril called a holiday."

"Certainly. Let's go see who's up to what?"

"Now, you children stay out the way," Kaylya said. "You probably won't have them in tow very long," she whispered in my ear. "They will abandon you as soon as they encounter some the others." She doesn't realize how much I've missed them. It feels great to be home.

Jack, Setas and I start to head for the village circle when we hear what sounds like hammering. Following the pathway across the bridge to the newly built schoolhouse, we find Kiril, Wessid and Lozar tacking wooden split shingles on the roof. Halren, Selyzar, Aurora and Theon are helping, carrying up materials to the roofers.

"Greetings, need any help?" I asked.

"No, we are almost done here," Kiril said. "Besides you aren't supposed to work today. You are an honored guest."

"So is Lozar, especially Lozar," I pointed out.

"We couldn't stop him," Kiril admitted.

"Where are Glisa and Yanzic? They can't be inside with all that banging going on."

"They went to help Ilene and Melinda with food preparation. I'm told Yanzic is quite the chef."

"I'm starting to feel unneeded around here."

"Let us finish here and you can help set up benches for the play."

"We can help too," Jack volunteered.

Soon Drak and Edty show up and join the others on the roof. With so many working, the job will quickly come to an end. Then Councilor Anthya and Inventor Sulyan arrive on the scene.

"Mighty fine schoolhouse, don't you agree, Councilor?"

"I certainly do, Sulyan, and please call me Anthya."

"Why, of course, Anthya."

"Well, we're finished here," Wessid announced standing up. The hammering quickly stops and the men climb down off the roof. Filled with holiday spirit, we all head for the village circle. Anthya and Lozar walk together.

When we reach the village circle, Ollen and Tassyn are already at the fire ring taking turns at turning the roasting spit over the open fire. Eight benches with a capacity of two or three seats to a bench form an octagon around the fire ring. Beyond the benches, three tables stand ready to receive food. Alaia, Caponya, and Little Sarus shriek with delight when Jack and Setas join them at the playground.

At the edge of the clearing Ilene and Caleeza are stuffing wood in the firebox of the village ovens. Six loaves of bread wait to go in. Edty rushes over to help them.

"What are you roasting?" Lozar asked.

"Kurpers," Ollen said basting the meat. "We figured you Twakans would appreciate some meat."

"We sure would," Lozar agreed.

"Tassyn and I went out hunting earlier, speared three of them. So we're roasting two over the open fire and I'm making a pot of stew with the other one. Three kurpers should feed thirty people since not everyone partakes of meat."

"It looks good. We've had enough of fish," There was an audible moan from the others who haven't seen a fish in a long time.

"What I would give for fish?" Tassyn said.

"I was bringing back dried fish, but my pack was lost in a gorge," Traevus said arriving on the scene with Thayla and Gyro. Immediately the children rush over to see Gyro. Traevus tries to tell the story, but leaves out most of the details.

"How would you know what happened, you were unconscious most of the time?" Thayla said.

"While we have a crowd, we should carry the benches from the fire ring to the pavilion for the performance," Kiril said.

"There are enough of us here we can carry most of the benches in one trip," I pointed out. "Come on children. Let's take a little hike to the pavilion."

Ilene, Caleeza, Ollen and Tassyn join us, leaving only Edty to mind the spit. When we arrive at the pavilion with the benches, the children become very protective, refusing to let the adults up onto the low natural stone stage. "You can't touch anything," Setas said. Ilene and Caleeza agree with the children.

I'm surprised by all the work that went into setting up props. "How long have you been working on this play?" I asked walking around amazed.

"I got the idea to do a play with the younger children shortly after you left, to serve as a distraction for Setas and Jack," Ilene explained. "Then Caleeza and Chitter joined in to help. Edty did all the props."

On the way back, Kiril and I take Councilor Anthya to see Captain Setas and Theon's graves. The short pathway through the trees to the grave site veers off from the trail to the pavilion. Blue-violet headstones with their names etched into the stone, mark the graves. Solemnly we stand together in reflection. Captain Setas and Theon's lives were legendary.

"Two legends buried right here. They must never be forgotten," Anthya said finally.

"They won't be," I assured her. Kiril repeatedly orates their stories to the community."

"It is my duty," Kiril said.

It isn't long before the enticing aromas of baking bread and roasting meat fills the village circle. Gradually the many food preparers arrive with more and more dishes, placing them on the tables. Seaa's zenith is fast approaching. After delivering their contributions to the food tables, Ilene, Caleeza and Chitter turn their attention to gathering up the actors.

CHAPTER 48

Aurora

We are finally going to see the play Kitca was connived into taking part in. Everyone is excited, chattering away. Mother and the actors are hidden behind a curtain offstage and Caleeza is directing us to be seated. The boys and I are seated at the end of the first row stage right. Seaa's light, lights up the stage. A half dozen hand printed programs are circulating around. Zaloka hands Halren a copy and we read it together.

The Four Little Girls
By Ilene

Little Girl 1	Setas
Little Girl 2	Alaia
Little Girl 3	Caponya
Little Girl 4	Kitca
Bear Beast 1	Jack
Bear Beast 2	Little Sarus
Brave Warrior	Chitter
Narrator	Caleeza
Flutist	Ilene

Props and Sound Effects   Edty

"Maybe we should do a play sometime," Halren said. "Looks like it could be fun."

"Looks like a lot of work to me," Theon said.

"Nearly everyone in my family is in this play," Selyzar pointed out.

The flute music begins and everyone becomes quiet. Then Caleeza walks out on stage left and the play begins. Alaia, Setas, Caponya and Kitca are cute delivering their lines. The bear beasts run around the stage like crazies. When they huff and puff, and Edty intensifies the effect with a bag of air, the audience laughs uproariously. The dropping wall on the shelter of sticks is a clever idea. When Chitter chases the bear beasts off with wooden swords, chittering fiercely, the audience cheers her on, bringing the play to its climactic ending.

Then everyone listed on the program gathers in a line on stage and takes a bow to a standing ovation. Rojaire and Kaylya rush up on stage and hug Jack and Setas praising them heartily. Ollen and Caleeza are just as proud of Alaia, Caponya and Little Sarus. The little ones are getting a lot of kudos. Perhaps Halren is right. Maybe we should do a play sometime.

When Kitca, now a member of the Secret Warriors, joins us, we take turns congratulating her. The five of us have agreed to keep the true nature of star stones secret for now.

The feast is incredible, just like the day. Not only has Rojaire, Traevus and Thayla returned, they brought five more people with them. Melinda is actually staying with us. We're even sharing a room!

Turns out, Mother and Melinda are good friends. Melinda was just a girl when Droclum killed her father and took her prisoner. She was rescued by Rahlys, Guardian of the Oracle of Light. Melinda actually knows the man Jack is named after. She says he is together with Grandmother Elaine on Earth.

Melinda and Glisa became good friends during the voyage from Mainland. They have been learning to speak each other's language. Maybe I should learn Twakan. After all, one day I may be going out into the world. Not only is there a route to the sea, but there's a boat too.

Melinda says Glisa and Yanzic are a couple and they were hoping to find us so they could join the colony. The Twakans are staying in the schoolhouse. So we won't be going to school at the schoolhouse for a while. That's a relief.

Thayla has moved in with Traevus, letting Councilor Anthya have her little cottage. We all knew Traevus and Thayla would be together one day.

"A toast," Drak shouted, lifting a mug of his brew. "To the greatest people in the galaxy...that's all of us!" All of us roar in agreement.

Then Inventor Sulyan pulls out a pack and carries it a short distance away. Everyone, except the uninformed newcomers, rise and move back putting more space between the inventor and themselves. "What's wrong?" Melinda asked.

"You'll see," I said.

Taking that as a warning, Melinda steps back. Soon colorful explosions arch across the sky. Mother says the fireworks remind her of the Aurora Borealis. Maybe one day I will see if she is right.

Books by Cil Gregoire

Oracle of Light series

Crystalline Aura
Book One of the Oracle of Light

Anthya's World
Book Two of the Oracle of Light

Elemental Forces
Book Three of the Oracle of Light

Interstellar Ruse
Book Four of the Oracle of Light